Tʜᴇ
BROTHERHOOD

Alan Williams

SAPERE
BOOKS

THE
BROTHERHOOD

Published by Sapere Books.

20 Windermere Drive, Leeds, England, LS17 7UZ,
United Kingdom

saperebooks.com

ISBN: 978-1-80055-153-4

PREFACE

It was in the small hours of the morning that Jack Paine, a truck driver from Reading, made his statement to the Berkshire police. *I was driving out of London on the M4 Motorway, just before the turning to White Waltham, doing about 45 m.p.h., when the car passed me. It was going at a terrific speed. I couldn't even see what make it was, except that it was a big saloon. It had been raining and I got a lot of muck thrown up on my windscreen. By the time my view was clear again the car was about a quarter of a mile ahead. I saw the White Waltham flyover coming up in its headlamps and then the whole thing — the flyover, I mean — seemed to jerk over to the left, and the central pillar just exploded in a great flash and went out. Then the noise came. I could hear it even above my diesel. It was more like three noises, first a crack like a gun going off, then a sort of thud, then a terrible clanking, and that was all. I never saw his brake lights come on and there wasn't any other traffic on the road. He just seemed to drive smack into the flyover.*

Paine pulled up a few yards short of the accident, but stayed only long enough to see that the engine-block had been forced back through the boot. What was left looked like a ball of crumpled carbon-paper. In the silence the noise seemed to linger like smoke after an explosion. There was a faint ticking and dripping in the darkness, then a twang! as a crushed spring released itself through torn leather.

It was already growing light by the time the fire brigade, with the help of oxyacetylene equipment, was able to remove the wreckage — most of it on the back of a lorry, the rest under a blanket in an ambulance. It was more than hours later before any identification could be made.

PART 1: WHEN BAD MEN COMBINE

CHAPTER 1

The day had begun badly for Magnus Owen. When the taxi dropped him at 11.20 — twenty minutes late — outside the sombre building in High Holborn, his eyes still burned and his feet did not seem to be touching the pavement. An hour earlier, in his Battersea flat in Albert Bridge Road, it had taken two Vitamin C tablets, a tumbler of saline solution poured from a jar of Hungarian pickles, and a bath in pine-needle extract to steady him enough to shave — always a tricky operation on account of the long welted scar along the angle of his jaw. Then half a pint of fresh black coffee, and he was just about ready to face the taxi ride to work.

This had been more or less tolerable until an unsettling incident just below the Strand. His taxi had pulled up alongside a parked sports car, just as a long-legged girl in a white mini skirt was climbing ungracefully out of the bucket seat, her thighs aiming directly up at the dark predatory Welsh face pressed against the glass above her. The image had lingered in Magnus' mind with cruel clarity for the rest of the way to the office.

It was a chill, wet morning, but as he got out of the taxi he pulled off what he called his 'rapist's mac' — a sheath of crackly black plastic with shoulder straps and air-vents under the armpits, redolent of Pigalle pimps and Gestapo informers. Not a garment to be seen worn about the precincts of *The Paper*. His presentable coat, along with his car — a battered Citroën DS — had gone astray somewhere during the night. Wrapping the offensive thing inside a roll of morning newspapers, he started up the steps, swinging his left leg out in a noticeable limp.

The entrance hall was like an old-fashioned bank: a row of brass grilles fenced in the small ads and agony column clerks; while ahead, guarding the Gothic portico leading to the lift and mezzanine, sat the commissionaire between two engraved plaques. The first of these, tarnished to the point of illegibility, bore the inscription: The Written Word Is A Mighty Weapon Never To Be Used In Malice, Fear Or Favour, But Always To One End — The Truth. Sir William Finlay son. Founder. 1896. The other one, shining like gold, proclaimed simply: Virtue Industry Order. James Broom.

The commissionaire, a retired R.S.M. with a Kitchener moustache, called Bostock, managed to invest the words with a certain fatuous authority. Eyes front, bolt upright, he now watched Magnus Owen limp towards him across the marble floor. No one who entered or left *The Paper*'s offices managed to escape Bostock's eye. The man had never been known to miss a day's work, six days a week, except for two weeks' annual holiday when his place was taken by another superannuated martinet who might have been his twin. Magnus had sometimes wondered if the man were real, if his organs functioned, if he ever slipped out for a pee. But not only was Bostock real; he was — in his limited field — powerful. There had been the celebrated occasion when a bright young Member of Parliament and T.V. personality, claiming an appointment with the editorial powers above, had been kept hanging about in the hall for ten minutes while Bostock made three separate phone calls before allowing him to go up. It had never been clear whether he had simply been doing his duty, or whether it was because the M.P. had been wearing a suede jacket over a maroon waistcoat.

Bostock gave Magnus a nod that missed nothing: dark tie, worsted suit, polished black shoes. Magnus passed muster. But the five steps to the lift were giving him trouble this morning. His leg ached more than usual and he was out of breath — a condition that reminded him that there were worse things in the world than a king-size hangover. Like having only one good lung and three steel pins in your knee.

He stared at a printed notice on the wall of the lift: 'Anybody found shouting or spitting will be instantly dismissed.'

It had been there ever since Magnus had joined *The Paper*, four years ago; yet this morning the threat seemed oddly uncomfortable — almost personal. A warning that from now on he must tread more carefully — not only in his work, but also in his private life. There had been that man yesterday at the flat. A thin fellow in a mackintosh: said he was from the Gas Board and there had been complaints about a leak in the block. He hadn't found one, though — not in Magnus's flat, anyway — and he'd gone even before Magnus could finish shaving. But he'd been poking about in the kitchen, long enough to find the drink cupboard, the vodka in the fridge, see the double bed as he went out.

The lift stopped at the third floor, under the gilt letters: EDITORIAL. A carpeted corridor led round a block of cells with frosted glass doors where the leader writers worked — anonymous men who communicated with the proprietor and Editor-in-Chief, Sir James Broom, through a system of private telephones and sealed memoranda. At the end of the corridor was the Newsroom. There were walls of bookcases containing bound volumes of Hansard, *The Times* and *The Paper*, leather-topped desks bearing antique typewriters that looked like cash registers, and made much the same noise. At the back was the door leading to the News Editor's office: a cosy little place with a gas fire, two armchairs and a rolltop desk surmounted by a pipe rack. It might have been a schoolmaster's study, except for a hatch in the wall that opened on to the fury of the sub-editors' room, full of glaring neon and clacking teleprinters.

The News Editor, Mr Hugh Rissell, was a lean saturnine figure who arrived every morning at ten o'clock, commuting from Esher, and would spend half an hour in front of the gas fire, studying the agency messages that were passed to him through the hatch in the wall, before ascending one floor to attend the Editorial Conference.

This morning he was still upstairs when Magnus Owen entered the Newsroom.

At that same moment, some six odd miles away, Thomas Pike was in the Press box of No. 2 Court at South-West Magistrates' Court, Knightsbridge. The first name on the charge sheet that morning was Nesbitt. But at 10.30, when the court opened, the man had not been there to answer the charge. An hour later the magistrate had a quick conference with the Chief Clerk, then called to a blond young man in a sports jacket who was standing against the far wall with a buff file under his arm.

'This is your case, Sergeant Skliros?'

The young man came to attention. 'It is, your Worship.'

The magistrate spoke now to a solicitor sitting in the well of the court: 'I don't think we can spend any more time on this, Mr Jameson. If your client isn't here by now, we had better postpone the hearing until tomorrow.' As he spoke, a uniformed policeman appeared through a side door, went up to the blond detective sergeant and handed him a sheet of paper. The sergeant glanced at it, then took a couple of steps forward. The whole court was very quiet, watching him. He spoke in a flat neutral voice that belonged to no definable class or region: 'Your Worship, I have just been informed that Mr Nesbitt received fatal injuries during the night in a motor accident near Slough.'

Thomas Pike was already on his feet, hurrying out of the Press box, past a row of dull-eyed traffic wardens, through the door into the entrance foyer, where there was a public telephone. The name of Nesbitt still meant nothing on its own, but the presence of a distinguished solicitor promised some importance.

At the end of the foyer he caught sight of the young detective sergeant, just leaving by the main entrance. Pike padded up to him, bobbing his head in a deferential nod.

'Sergeant Skliros? I'm Pike of South Star News Agency.'

Skliros stopped. He looked very clean next to Pike, his short blond hair shining silver under the glass ceiling. 'Yes, Mr Pike?'

'I believe you're the officer dealing with this Nesbitt case?'

For a moment the young man smiled. It was no more than a creasing of the cheeks, for the eyes did not smile; they were a hard bright grey, too old for the rest of his face, and crinkled at the edges as though straining to look at something far away.

'So you want to know about the late Mr Nesbitt, do you?' He glanced up and down the foyer, and saw they were alone. 'You'd better come over here, Mr Pike.'

The smile was still on his prim little mouth, as he took the buff file from under his arm and opened it.

Magnus Owen grunted to his colleagues, slumped into his chair and began to open his mail: a heap of P.R. handouts, an abusive letter typed in red calling him 'a typically arrogant little crypto-fascist', and yet another communication from his wife's solicitors. This he screwed up and bowled inaccurately at a wastepaper basket, then leant forward, preparing to nurse the incipient headache.

It was six months now since she'd left him — a fast little rebel-deb who'd come running to him in search of further kicks. Because he was different and clever: History First from Cambridge, author of a minor political scandal and a best-selling book, now a famous journalist. She'd found him exciting; he had been wounded in battle and his body bore the scars to prove it. He was a new experience; but the novelty did not last. She soon found that marriage cramped her style, and her next experience had been more amenable: a successful fashion photographer with an exquisite profile and a Lotus Elan.

Magnus didn't want her anymore; but he didn't want the divorce either. The Welsh worm of Puritanism was at work, nurtured by that middle-class Chapel upbringing which he had rejected superficially, but would never be able to root out altogether. It had taught him guilt, but little compassion.

He picked up the heap of newspapers which he had not had the strength to read at breakfast, and carried them through to an oak-panelled door marked 'Principals' — *The Paper*'s euphemism for the lavatory. It was a solemn place, highly conducive to contemplation. The only graffiti ever to sully its walls had been the absent-minded jottings of a reporter trying to solve *The Times* crossword. Magnus sat down and began to read.

This morning *The Paper* was running a second leader entitled 'A Scornful Abdication of Responsibility', attacking the B.B.C. over a recent television play about a bank manager who was bathed every night by his mother.

Magnus groaned and closed his eyes; his headache was worse and the black tumours were churning. At such moments he wondered why he worked for *The Paper*. Secretly he despised it for its pious rectitude, its smug high-minded moralising and intellectual conformity. It was true that in the old days it had had a reputation for eccentricity. There had been one editor at the turn of the century who had grown his fingernail unusually long, slit it up the middle and used it as a quill. But those times were past. In the late fifties *The Paper*'s fortunes had begun to decline and rumours were abroad that the Finlayson Trust was threatening to dissolve itself and sell out. Finally, after a series of secret negotiations, *The Paper* passed into the hands of James Broom, a millionaire of obscure antecedents.

There was soon a new layout, which included a woman's page, higher salaries to attract bright young men, and the introduction of by-lines. But otherwise *The Paper* remained its virtuous old self; the leader columns continued to rage against the decline of moral standards, while the political staff sat high on their Olympian fences, reluctant to commit themselves to any decisive line for fear of being thought partisan.

But perhaps the oddest feature of *The Paper* under its new regime lay in the character of its new proprietor and Editor-in-Chief. Throughout the whole controversy concerning the takeover, Broom — soon to become Sir James Broom — remained the sole personality in the whole drama never to enter the limelight, never to speak in public, never to be interviewed. Only one photograph of him ever seemed to be published, showing a shadowy middle-aged face that might have been any businessman's passport photograph. Who's Who awarded him with only a few lines, listing his address as Finlayson House, the offices of *The Paper*. He had no clubs, no recreations. He was said to be of Central European extraction, to have made a fortune first in South America, then in Australia, before moving on to the more influential heights of British public life.

But although the details of his career were spare to the point of mystery, his influence within the corridors of the establishment was considerable; and while some people still dismissed him as a social upstart who had bought *The Paper* merely as a ticket to the House of Lords, he was known to have the confidence of several prominent politicians of both parties, as well as access to the world of big business and the communications industry.

During the four years that Magnus had worked for *The Paper* he had only met Broom once. It had been a formal interview, lasting less than five minutes, and would have been quite unexceptional but for one curious incident which had stuck in his mind ever since. He had gone up to the Editor-in-Chief's office on the fifth floor, to be told by a woman secretary to wait in an ante-room until Sir James Broom was ready to see him. The room had been empty except for a round-shouldered man on a stepladder dusting some books. He had asked Magnus what he wanted, and without saying anything had climbed down and disappeared through an inner door. A few minutes later the secretary came in and told Magnus that Sir James would now see him. He passed into a panelled room, lit by a single lamp on a long bare desk. Behind this sat the proprietor of *The Paper*. He was the same man Magnus had just seen next door dusting the books.

Sir James Broom asked him a number of routine questions, and hoped he was happy on *The Paper*. Magnus received almost no impression of him at all except that he appeared to have no eyebrows — just smudges of pale fur that gave his eyes a naked, startled expression.

Yet it was the wry impersonality of the man that made Magnus wary of him. He belonged to the remote world of power and the manipulation of power. It was a world that made Magnus, by comparison, feel almost a bohemian.

But while he had come to despise *The Paper*, he also needed it. It was not just for the money, or even the fame. It was something more personal, something of which he had grown aware only gradually over the years he had worked for the organisation. His job on *The Paper* had become a weapon in a private vendetta.

He was leaning forward now, his eyes still closed, his face almost touching his knees. The memory was as clear as it had been in those first blurred hours in the Nicosia military hospital. Splintering sunlight along Murder Mile. Ducking through the bead curtain into a bar which was out of bounds to all troops, after a sluggish patrol through the Walled City. All three of them National Servicemen — a boy called Bruce who had wanted to get back to camp but hadn't dared spoil the fun, and a big Jew called Josh Stone who played the saxophone and could put back eight pints in a row — all drinking beer at the bar when there had been a flash and a roaring darkness, and Magnus had been crawling on his hands and knees, hearing Bruce screaming somewhere through the dust; then seeing Stone sitting against a pillar with his intestine swelling out under his shirt like a blue bubble; and he had drawn his revolver and emptied it into three Cypriots at a corner table — one of them, an old man, already wounded. He had killed all three, reloaded, killed the barman, then passed out. Both his companions died and the terrorist escaped.

He had lain in hospital for five months, before being discharged with one serviceable lung and a gammy leg.

Meanwhile, at home, there had been a public ballyhoo. The British Government was already shying off the Cyprus fiasco, and the Greek Press seized on the incident as an example of British atrocities against Cypriot civilians. Certain London papers lifted the story, and without naming names, warned of growing evidence that British troops were taking the law into their own hands on the island; while a group of M.P.s pressed successfully for a Court of Inquiry, and at least one, using his Parliamentary Privilege, cited the case of Second Lieutenant Magnus Owen.

Most of the drama had unfolded while Magnus was too ill to care. The findings of the enquiry had been typically ambiguous, exonerating him of the most serious charges. He remembered the words: '...In self-defence, during a difficult and confused situation.' Although there had never been any serious question of a court martial, the stigma remained. Talk of atrocities in Kenya, Algeria, Cyprus was now common diet for the liberal and left-wing press, and the name of Magnus Owen became one of the by-words.

He had left hospital in time to take up his scholarship at King's. But the rarefied leisure of Cambridge life totally unhinged him; at the end of his first year he had a breakdown. He passed his second year more calmly, working out his obsessions on his book based on the Cyprus experience. Since its central target was neither EOKA nor the British authorities, but the sloppy wishful ignorance of liberal intellectuals back in Britain, the book met a mixed reception.

Those same journals which had previously castigated the anonymous Second Lieutenant Owen, now reopened the wounds with relish. The reviewers recalled the author's identity, and after conceding that he had a certain nasty talent, dismissed him as a precocious beast who had strayed out of the right-wing undergrowth. Because Magnus was still young and impressionable, the role ascribed to him stuck. His sense of guilt and grievance hardened into a hatred of all those who had attacked him, so that by the time he joined *The Paper* his attitudes were clear. He knew his enemies and he wanted his revenge. *The Paper* offered him the chance.

He concentrated largely on the cultural scene, many of whose champions had been his contemporaries at Cambridge, where he had come to revile them as avant-garde adventurers. While the job brought him a measure of fame, it won him no friends.

When he got back to the Newsroom, Hugh Rissell was waiting in the mouth of his den, beckoning with his pipe. Inside he greeted him with a sheet of telex. His face sloped down to his pipe, which he smoked in the middle of his face, making his words hard to follow. 'Ivor Nesbitt's dead. It just came in.'

Magnus took the telex message and read: *NESBITT FLASH 11.40. IVOR NESBITT WEST END THEATRE IMPRESARIO AGED 57 DIED RPT DIED EARLY THIS MORNING (FRI) STOP IN MYSTERY CAR CRASH ON M4 MOTORWAY ONLY HOURS BEFORE HE WAS BAILED TO APPEAR AT SOUTH-WEST MAGISTRATES COURT THIS MORNING (FRI) STOP ON CHARGE OF IMPORTUNING STOP THE CHARGE AROSE OUT OF AN INCIDENT YESTERDAY (THUR) EVENING STOP THERE WAS DRAMA IN COURT WHEN MR NESBITT FAILED TO APPEAR AFTER HIS NAME HAD BEEN CALLED TWICE STOP DRAMA GREW WHEN DET. SGT. PETER SKLIROS …*

Magnus looked up. Rissell was watching him carefully: 'Well, what do you think?'

'The charge, or the crash?'

Rissell sucked hard, the corners of his mouth turning down in a grin. 'The two would seem to go together, wouldn't they?'

Magnus glanced back at the telex. There were no details of the accident. 'It was raining last night — he could have skidded,' he said, frowning into the fire. 'But what's that got to do with the charge? Hasn't the new Act changed all that?'

Rissell removed the pipe from his mouth, and stood examining his toes. 'Only between consenting adults — in private. Sexual Offences Act, 1956, Section 37, making it illegal for one man to procure another for an act of indecency.' He jabbed his pipe at the sheet in Magnus's hand. 'And in this case it looks as though the charge was made by a policeman. This chap Skliros.'

Magnus nodded. In plain clothes, no doubt. The old story-smart young sleuths hanging round the clubs and pubs waiting for the old pooves to come out.

Rissell had lowered his head further, watching Magnus through his eyelashes. 'He was rather a social sort of chap, wasn't he? Very conscious of his position?'

Magnus shrugged. 'I didn't know him that well,' he muttered. 'He was quite happy to be seen at Glyndebourne or Goodwood one day and at some protest rally in Trafalgar Square the next. But that doesn't mean to say he committed suicide, does it? Anybody can have a car smash.'

Rissell chuckled through his nostrils. 'That'll be up to the police and the coroner. You just do the obit.' He leant out and touched Magnus's arm. 'But don't be too soft on him. Remember that you cannot libel the dead.'

By four o'clock Magnus had written six hundred words on the life and times of Ivor Nesbitt, patron of the modern arts, creator of the Theatre of Evil, famed party-giver, friend of nobility and pop world, habitué of the gossip columns. Magnus was collecting up the top copy and three carbons, when the telephone rang on his desk.

A man's voice said: 'Mr Owen? Albert Mansions? North Thames Gas Board here. I believe you were making an enquiry about a gas leak in your block? No, I'm sorry, we've no report of one here.'

'But a man came round yesterday,' Magnus said. 'He said he was from the Board.'

'Are you sure?'

'Of course I'm sure. He came about half-past ten in the morning.' He sat gripping the receiver, feeling the first twinge of anxiety. The man at the other end said, 'I can't understand that, Mr Owen. If we'd sent anybody, there'd have been a note of it here. I can check on it again, if you like, but I think there must have been a mistake.'

'Thanks,' said Magnus. 'It doesn't matter.' He hung up.

So they were sending people round to spy on him. Yet what the hell did they hope to find? Some slatternly girl between his sheets at half-past ten in the morning? Unwashed whisky glasses, pornography on the bookshelf? There hadn't been much to compromise him, but at least it pointed to one thing: they were getting serious. They wanted to involve him, and for some wild reason he wanted to get involved.

He reached inside his jacket and drew out the gilt-edged invitation he had received five days ago, addressed to *The Paper*. It was for this evening: 8.30 p.m. An Evening of Amateur Boxing. Dinner, black tie. In the bottom left-hand corner the words, R.S.V.P. Ten Guineas: The Treasurer, Regent's Park

Sporting Club, had been crossed out, and underneath added, in bold handwriting: 'Be my guest — DO try to come. John.'

Magnus looked at it again, frowning. He disliked solicited charity — even if someone else was paying for it — and he particularly disliked boxing. But he knew he would have to go. If his hunch were right, and someone was interested enough to send a man round to his flat to check on his private life, then he was equally interested to know what they wanted of him.

That brought him again to the person of his host that evening. John Austen Cane. Oxford scholar, Fellow of All Souls, one of the first British mountaineers to conquer the Eiger; passionate idealist during the thirties, flirting with many faiths from the far Right to the Communists; then a brilliant war record, finishing as colonel of Military Intelligence in Nazi-occupied Poland. With the war over, he had retired to a poultry farm in Kent where his old political fervour gave way to a moral crusade, expressed in his prolific books and pamphlets such as *Men of the Hour*, *Britain on the Brink*, *Sodom and Tomorrow*.

An avid zealot, fluent and fanatical — hardly a man to have much in common with a dissolute journalist like Magnus Owen. Yet there was a bond between the two men which Magnus had found hard to break.

It had begun more than seven years ago, while he lay in a London hospital recovering from his wounds and the Court of Inquiry was sitting to decide on his case. His own evidence had been given in a deposition from his bed, and had been partly supported by his commanding officer. But among all the voices raised against him, only one witness — unknown to him, and uninvited — had volunteered an unqualified plea in his defence. That witness had been Colonel John Austen Cane. From then on Magnus had felt in his debt.

He also began to come under his cloying influence. In his first year at Cambridge, Cane visited him regularly, insinuating himself as a kind of unofficial tutor; and although Magnus liked him — even felt a genuine affinity with him — he found the man's friendship just a little too keen and overbearing. He also disliked the unspoken obligation to feel grateful.

But Cane had been tactful enough to realise this too, for gradually, during Magnus's second year, their meetings became scarcer, then ceased altogether. For the next five years Magnus had heard nothing more from him. Then just over a month ago, without warning, the invitations had started.

The first had been a handwritten card from Cane, addressed to him at *The Paper* and asking him to a cocktail party next day in Chester Row. He had gone, intrigued; but it had been a grisly evening — brown sherry and biscuits, and almost no one he knew. Cane had been charming, but too busy to exchange more than formal greetings, and Magnus had found himself cornered by a brisk woman with bat-winged spectacles who'd forced him to listen to her views on cleaning up television and banning war toys. Unable to get drunk, he had fled before the end, without even thanking Cane.

But a couple of weeks later his phone at *The Paper* had rung again and Cane was asking him to lunch in Charlotte Street. It had been an excellent meal, and although wine had hardly flowed (Cane drank none himself), the compliments had been lavish. Cane seemed to have read everything Magnus had written, and they found their views coincided nicely. Perhaps too nicely. For by the end of this second meeting Magnus had a good idea that his host's attentions were not entirely innocent. In the old days at Cambridge he had always suspected that Cane — perhaps without realising it — was identifying him with a younger incarnation of himself. Both were university scholars, had both been in the Army and both seen violent death. Cane had also had polio as a child and been lame. He used to tell Magnus how at school he had been teased to the point of madness because of his limp, but that he had refused to be broken by it, had taken up sport, swimming, rock-climbing, and had finally become one of the great mountaineers of his day.

Magnus had been embarrassed by their friendship, but never troubled. This time, however, he had the uncomfortable feeling that somehow he was being 'got at'.

He looked again at the gilt-edged invitation, in aid of the Regent's Park Sporting Club, and decided he would like to know more about Colonel Cane's evening of amateur boxing.

CHAPTER 2

Outside the hotel, commissionaires with umbrellas hurried about in the rain; overcoats were given up, dinner jackets brushed down. Inside, a pair of young men in dark flannel suits collected the gilt-edged invitations, bowing each guest up the stairway to the reception room.

Magnus noticed that his own card was checked quickly, but with some interest; Cane's autograph in the bottom corner clearly impressed the young man.

He passed on up the stairs, recognising no one. They were all men, and without exception at least ten years his senior. Professional men, immaculate in their uniforms of double-breasted midnight blue, complexions clear, figures firm — hardly a trace of blood-pressure or sagging belly in sight. They also seemed to have no smell — not a whiff of tobacco or aftershave — but instead, an antiseptic purity hung about them, almost as though they were not wholly of flesh and blood. Magnus checked himself; he was allowing his imagination to get the better of him. There was nothing unusual or sinister about any of them. Just a herd of middle-aged, middle-class men out on a stag evening to raise money for a sports charity.

Yet he was not at ease. Back at the flat while he dressed he had braced himself with a couple of stiff vodkas, and he was now feeling slightly light-headed, with a febrile excitement that was not entirely due to the alcohol.

He entered a long room with tables laid with soft drinks and bottled beer. His heart sank. He could have done with another vodka, but made do with a light ale which he could scarcely hold from spilling. He put the glass down and steadied himself against the table, noticing that no one seemed to be smoking. He saw one man tugging at a pipe, but it was unlit. He was in for a gay evening, he thought, as he felt someone pluck at his sleeve.

'Mr Owen? Magnus Owen? Splendid!' He was a small round man, pink and bright-eyed. 'I'm Mervin Pym — must have missed you in the crush! Colonel Cane and the others are over here.'

There were three of them, standing against the far wall slightly apart from the rest of the crowd. One of them broke off in midsentence as Magnus approached. 'Ah, there you are, Magnus! Glad you could make it.'

Magnus shook hands, feeling an irrational stab of stage fright. John Cane smiled warmly — a straight dark man with heavy eyebrows and hair that showed scarcely a streak of grey. He turned and introduced his companions. The one on his left was a public figure Magnus recognised from newspaper photographs: Sir Lionel Hilder, World War I air-ace, now head of a pyramid of engineering companies and a millionaire many times over. He was a big pouchy man in his seventies with a slight stiffening to one side of his mouth, giving him a fixed sneer. Beside him stood Mr Henry Deepe — a quiet grey man with a cold handshake and eyes the colour of celluloid.

'And Mr Pym you have already met?' Cane said. He glanced down at the glass in Magnus's hand, still smiling. 'I see you've already got something to drink?'

Magnus felt himself flush, and knew that Cane had noticed it. There was a trace of mischief now in his dark smile: 'Like another?'

'Thanks, I'm fine!' Magnus tried to smile back, feeling furious as he did so. What the hell had he let himself in for?

None of the other three were drinking; and he suddenly had the impression that the whole performance had been laid on as a test. Like the man in the mackintosh yesterday who had been sent round to pry through his flat. Yet it was ridiculous that a man as upright as Cane should have had anything to do with such an incident. Magnus was again allowing his imagination to get the better of him; he sipped his beer and acknowledged a few gruff compliments from Sir Lionel Hilder on his work for *The Paper*.

Presently Cane looked at his watch. 'Well, gentlemen, we might think about going in to dinner.' He started first, with Sir Lionel Hilder a step behind — almost, it seemed to Magnus, like a commanding officer with his aide-de-camp. The crowd at once drew back with nods and smiles, accepting the odd greeting as Cane passed; then fell in behind and filed through into a private banqueting room. Cane's table was in the corner, laid for five. There was no menu, no wine glasses; just a jug of iced water which a waiter poured into tumblers as they sat down.

Magnus decided there was nothing to do but grit his teeth and bear it. From the start Pym and Hilder did most of the talking. Mervin Pym was a schoolmaster — a name that triggered a memory for Magnus, somehow connected with an incident a couple of years ago — something faintly unpleasant, he remembered.

During the soup Pym expounded his views on modern education. The public schools were hotbeds of homosexuality, but the so-called progressive system was even worse: lipstick and pop music from the age of puberty, breeding a race of mindless morons. Sir Lionel Hilder then took up a broader theme of national decline: the rule of the Long-Haired Lilac

Brigade, the smarty-pants who had permeated every level of society.

Magnus sat chewing in silence, dismayed to realise that many of their views were merely a dull reflection of his own pieces in *The Paper* — a catechism of clichés that could be heard at any City gathering or businessman's club. Yet he could not help feeling that this was all on the surface. There was something disconcertingly false about the four men round him; it was as though each of them held to his face a mask of dreary anonymity.

Henry Deepe, he now gathered, was something to do with the Home Office. The man said almost nothing throughout the meal, yet several times Magnus caught those pale celluloid eyes watching him across the table, sizing him up.

It was a weird assembly, he decided. Cane, who hardly spoke either, was clearly the dominant personality; and as the meal progressed, Magnus began to feel that the whole conversation had been stage-managed, like a television discussion, with Cane as its compére. The only role in doubt seemed to be his own. He would just have to wait his cue, and when it came, take it as best he could.

Lamb cutlets were served, and the conversation moved from fraudulent psychiatrists to immoral writers, and how the Soviet Union had the right idea — according to Sir Lionel Hilder — when they either jailed their delinquent intellectuals or sent them packing to a lunatic asylum.

Suddenly Cane leant out and gripped Magnus's arm.

'Magnus, we've all read your work. And it's clear you're a man of pretty strong views. I'd say, even prejudices. No, don't worry! I'm not criticising. We all have our prejudices — we'd be hypocrites to deny it.'

Magnus gulped at some iced water. 'Yes,' he said carefully, 'I have my prejudices.' His words fell into a leaden silence. 'I'm prejudiced against this new narcissistic elite of pop idols and model girls and grotty young actors.'

He had a bad moment when he thought he had overdone it; but the others seemed to be enjoying it, hanging on every word. Cane patted his arm with encouragement, as he launched into his thesis on the decline of modern British drama. He had just started on what he hoped, even in this company, would sound a reasonably balanced attack on the current Theatre of Evil, when Sir Lionel Hilder interrupted with a series of knuckle thumps on the table.

'He's finished! We've done with him. There's justice for that sort — putting on his filthy plays — smut night after night…!'

Cane held up his hand: 'Let's first listen to what Magnus has to say, Lionel.'

Hilder's laugh barked across the crowded room: 'But we won't have much more of it! That charlatan Ivor Nesbitt — trying to wriggle up the social ladder with his money and airs and graces. Well, he got what was coming to him!'

Cane said quietly: 'We must not speak too hard of the dead, Lionel. I have no brief to make for Mr Ivor Nesbitt, nor any of his kind, for that matter. But he leaves a wife, remember. And it was a terrible way for a man to go, whatever his sins.'

The capillaries round Sir Lionel's nose were standing out like tiny worms. 'The man had been drinking. A damn drunk and a pansy to boot! Picked up sniffing round that gambling club of his…!'

'Lionel, I beg of you!' Cane's face was dark with rage. 'I said we would not talk hard of the dead. I find it in the worst possible taste…'

But Magnus was hardly listening. He remembered there had been no mention of the circumstances of the arrest — let alone of a gambling club — in any of the evening papers or in the telex message. He was certain of it. His face was hot and his heart pounded, while the waiters served coffee and cheese. Cane had soothed the conversation, but in the last minutes of the meal he seemed to have lost his zest, becoming withdrawn and preoccupied. Finally he drained his coffee and stood up, rapping for silence.

'Gentlemen, I suggest we now move on to the main attraction of the evening.' His voice sounded flat, one hand fidgeting with his coffee cup. 'And on behalf of the hotel I would ask you to remain quiet during rounds, and reserve your applause for the end of each bout.'

Cane led the procession into a high-ceilinged room with chandeliers hanging down in darkness. The only light shone low above a roped-off platform between two blocks of chairs.

The guests took their places as though by prearrangement. Cane and his party sat in the front row, just below the ropes: Cane in the centre, with Magnus on his left, next to Mr Henry Deepe. It seemed almost an act of protocol, as though the civil servant were surrendering his place beside Cane to the evening's guest of honour.

A man in a cummerbund climbed under the ropes with a microphone. 'Gentlemen, welcome to an evening of amateur boxing between some six up-and-coming youngsters!' He swung on his heel to face one side of the hall and then the other. 'First is a lightweight contest between Don Mocham of Finchley' — as a dark nimble youth in mauve trunks sprang into the ring — 'and Ted Seaton of Camberwell!'

A muscular young man with ginger hair shorn to the scalp at the back and sides climbed in, bowed into the darkness and sat down.

'First round, seconds out!'

The two men came out of their corners, the skipping of shoes and thud of gloves amplified by the silence. By the end of the first round a fleck of blood had appeared on Mocham's lip and one eye began to close up. Magnus caught a glimpse of Pym, sitting forward in his chair, lips parted, as the panting and grunting of the two fighters grew louder — almost obscene in the crowded stillness, like sounds of breathless lovemaking.

Before the end of the second round Mocham was helped to his corner like a drunkard, and Ted Seaton was the winner. Both Cane and Hilder clapped hard, and Magnus followed dutifully. The next fight was between a great brute called Judd, and a tall pale youth who looked more like a theology student than a boxer. He came into the ring with a mournful face under a blond crew cut, his studious appearance belied only by a green snake wrapped round his left biceps in mortal combat with a lion, over the tattooed words *Virtus Vinci*. Magnus had just time to read them, as the young man — who was introduced as Tom Meredith of Cardiff — paused above them, looked down between the ropes and gave Cane a deliberate bow.

Judd came out of his corner, his hairy arms burrowing away at Meredith who held him off with a steady and careful defence. The fight lasted three rounds, and Meredith won on points.

Magnus fidgeted in confusion. He was again wondering what the hell he was doing here, when Cane turned to him and said: 'That Welsh boy Meredith, he's a good clean fighter!'

Magnus nodded dumbly. 'You know him?'

Cane hesitated a fraction of a second. 'I've met him — yes.' His tone was perfectly affable, but there was an inflection in it that suggested that the question had been mildly impertinent — like asking a C.O. how well he knew one of his men. Magnus said no more, aware of a suppressed yawn at his left where Mr Henry Deepe was enduring the evening with polite fortitude.

The referee was in the ring again, announcing the last fight of the evening. Magnus glanced at Cane, but his profile was immutable. A Scots boy with curly black hair had gone to his corner, and a slim fair man now swung under the ropes, as the referee cried: 'And Peter Skliros, of Fulham!'

The fight began so fast that Magnus scarcely had time to ponder the coincidence. Skliros went in with a calm and deadly skill, even to Magnus's untrained eye. He moved like a dancer, his eyes unblinking. His opponent did not stand a chance. Skliros moved round him, striking blows that seemed to land with no sound at all. What might be described, Magnus thought, as another 'clean fighter'.

The Scots boy had lurched back against the ropes. For perhaps five seconds he sagged there, while Skliros went up to him with his grey eyes fixed on the boy's face, hitting with both fists like pistons to the head and body. The referee stepped in and broke them. The Scots boy's head drooped forward and he slid down to the floor — his buttocks, in their shiny blue trunks, jutting comically into the air, before he rolled over and the referee counted him out.

Magnus had a glimpse of his face as he was carried away by the seconds — puffed and bloody, with eyes closed and mucus trailing from the nose. He felt a little sick. The others were standing up and Hilder was saying loudly: 'What was the matter with that chap? He didn't put up any fight at all!'

'But the other one?' Magnus said vaguely, 'What was his name?'

Cane and Hilder had their backs to him and it was Henry Deepe who answered: 'Skliros. I thought he was rather good.'

'Do you know anything about him?' Magnus asked casually, as they moved towards the door.

Deepe shook his head. 'I'm afraid I'm not the world's expert on boxing, Mr Owen.'

Of course not, thought Magnus — *except that you remembered his name*. 'Skliros,' he said aloud: 'Unusual name.'

'Yes, it is rather unusual.' Henry Deepe paused just beyond the door. 'Excuse me, Mr Owen.' He gave a dim smile and slipped away to the head of the stairs.

Magnus was left standing by the door. He was bemused by the evening, yet he had gone so far and must see it through. Cane was his host, and at this moment Cane was taking leave of a pudgy balding man whose dinner jacket looked as though it did not quite fit. There was nothing the least remarkable about him, except that Cane was addressing him, fast and fluently, in some foreign language. They shook hands vigorously, and the little man gave a stiff bow and made off for the stairs.

Magnus's curiosity was growing. It had been none of the major European languages, he was sure of that. Czech? Finnish perhaps? He was standing just behind Cane, uncertain of the next move, when his host suddenly cried, 'Ah, welcome the conquering heroes!'

Magnus turned and saw two young men in lounge suits coming down the landing towards them, their hair still wet from the showers. One was Tom Meredith of Cardiff, the other Peter Skliros of Fulham. Cane greeted them with outstretched arms: 'What on earth happened, Peter? That Scots boy went down like a skittle! They might have found someone who would have at least given you a bloody nose!'

Skliros grinned, dimpling his strict little features. 'They haven't found him yet. By the way, Ted Seaton asked if you'd excuse him. He had to get back to work.'

'Yes, of course! Give him my congratulations.' He turned to Meredith: 'I thought you gave us a beautiful fight, Tom. I'm only sorry you didn't get a worthier opponent.'

'Ah, he's a bloody punchy — tried to do me with his nut, he did!' He spoke with a harsh South Wales accent that jarred oddly with his grave features.

Skliros grinned: 'Tom can deal with that sort — can't you, Tom?' And Meredith leered back: 'Bloody sure I can!'

As Magnus listened he found himself at the edge of the group, next to Skliros. 'Excuse me — Detective Sergeant Skliros?'

The neat young face whipped round, only a few inches from his own. 'What's that?'

'I wondered if it was just a coincidence. I work for *The Paper*?'

'Yes?' His eyes were a bright icy grey.

Magnus said: 'I've just finished writing Ivor Nesbitt's obituary. Your name was mentioned in the original story — about you being in court this morning.'

'That's right. So what?'

Magnus looked at him glumly. 'I'm sorry. I shouldn't have brought it up.'

'Why not?'

'Well' — he found himself avoiding Skliros's eyes as he went on — 'with that sort of case I don't suppose you'd want your name in it, would you?'

'No?' The grey eyes showed no expression; then suddenly he laughed, friendly, man-to-man. 'You mean because he was a Hampton Flasher?' He shook his head. 'I'm not sensitive — not about that sort of thing, at any rate.'

'What happened?'

'With that old bird last night?' Skliros grinned. 'Usual caper. I let him chat me up, and when he started getting fresh I pulled him in.'

'This happen in the street?'

The grin hardened. 'That's right.'

'Not in the club?'

Skliros stood there, his hands hanging at his sides with a curious menacing stillness. 'Who said anything about a club?' He spoke very quietly.

Magnus shrugged. 'I just wondered. Because Nesbitt was quite a lad for the night life.'

'Oh yes? You knew him?'

'Not well. I interviewed him a couple of times.'

'I see.' His voice took on that toneless precision he would have been drilled to use in court, the charge room, the cells, perhaps even at home. 'Well, I'm glad to have met you Mr —'

'Owen. By the way, when's the inquest?'

'Early next week, I expect. Doesn't *The Paper* keep you informed of these things?'

'It will in due course,' Magnus said evenly. 'I just wondered if there were any complications that might delay it.'

'Why should there be?'

'I'm asking you, sergeant.'

The grey eyes held his, deadpan. 'Don't keep throwing my rank at me, Mr Owen. I'm not on duty now.'

'I thought a policeman was always on duty.'

Skliros sighed. 'As you please, Mr Owen. Nice to have met you.' He turned to Cane. 'I think I'd better be getting along, John. Goodnight and thanks for everything.'

Magnus watched the policeman walk away, followed by the gangling figure of Meredith.

Sir Lionel Hilder now moved up to Cane and murmured, 'I'm going up to the billiard room, John. If you want, my chauffeur can run you home.' As he spoke he glanced at Magnus: 'Well, young man, glad to have you with us!' He gave his stiff smile and a bone-crushing handshake, and for a moment an uneasy thought crossed Magnus's mind — the legendary sign of the Masons, the touch of the palm, the unspoken greeting of the secret society.

At the same time Cane's hand closed round his free arm. 'Do you want to stay, Magnus, or would you prefer a little chat before turning in? You didn't bring a car? Good!' He was already leading him towards the stairs. 'I'm just off Piccadilly. It's on your way, isn't it?'

Magnus nodded, but said nothing. So Cane knew he lived in Battersea, although so far he had communicated with him only at *The Paper*. Magnus's address was listed in the directory, but then why should Cane bother to look it up, unless he wanted specifically to get in touch with him? Or to send a little man round looking for a gas leak, perhaps?

At the foot of the stairs the two young men in dark flannel still waited like sentinels. As Cane passed each raised his hand in a stiff half-salute, which was not acknowledged. Outside stood an old-fashioned black Rolls-Royce — registration LH 1 — its door held open by a chauffeur in a peak cap and grey uniform buttoned to the chin like a Cossack trooper. A glass partition separated him from the rear.

For some time they rode in silence, each sitting back in his soft leather corner, insulated from the roar of traffic outside. As at the end of the dinner, Cane seemed strangely preoccupied, and for the first few minutes Magnus did not disturb him; but soon the silence began to unnerve him. He badly needed a drink; he also badly needed the answers to a number of questions, but knew that excessive curiosity could ruin everything.

'I enjoyed the evening, John. That last fight was really something!' He tried to keep his tone as jocular as possible. 'What was that chap's name — Skliros?'

'Ah, Skliros! Yes, he's a really tough customer.'

'He's in the C.I.D., isn't he?' He sat watching carefully for Cane's reaction; but the man's face was turned to the window and all he could see was the line of his jaw against the shifting lights outside. He did not even nod.

Magnus paused for a second, then went on: 'It's rather a coincidence, but I was on a story this afternoon and he came into it.'

'Oh yes?' Cane still did not move; his tone was quiet, abstracted. 'How was that?'

'He was involved in a case today at South-West Magistrates' Court. That fellow Ivor Nesbitt who was killed last night.'

Cane had turned slowly and sat stroking his jaw, then muttered: 'Yes, a beastly business. Even his end had to be messy and sensational.'

They were now moving in heavy traffic down Shaftesbury Avenue, full of theatre crowds and slack-faced mobs spilling out of Soho side streets. Cane watched them for a moment, then groaned quietly. 'Just look at it! The great West End of London, centre of what was once one of the finest cities in the world!'

The car had pulled up at a traffic light, and just then a group of youths with hair down to their shoulders, and girls with naked thighs and beads round their necks, passed Cane's window, peering inside and giggling. One of the girls stepped in front of the Rolls, ran her finger along the top of the radiator grill and sucked it with a grin. Magnus noticed that she was exasperatingly pretty; but her gesture aroused far greater emotion in Cane.

'Oh my God!' he cried, 'how do we tolerate it? Once they just used to make me angry, Magnus, but now they make me frightened. If that is the future of our nation, then we will perish just as surely as Rome!'

Magnus could think of no suitable comment to this. Cane, meanwhile, relapsed into gloomy silence, until they pulled up a few minutes later in the forecourt of Albany, off Piccadilly. The chauffeur opened the door, standing to attention as Cane led the way past the porter's lodge and along the stone passage called the Rope Walk, with its staircases marked in alphabetical order.

Cane's chambers were on the top floor. A Steinway grand piano filled one corner; there were old armchairs, walls of bookcases, an oil painting of a glacier under the midnight sun. A sombre masculine room, lit by two lamps over the mantelpiece below a framed photograph of Edward Whymper, leader of the first ill-fated conquest of the Matterhorn in 1865.

Cane rubbed his hands and smiled: 'What about a nightcap? A little Scotch?'

Magnus hesitated: 'If that's all right?'

Cane grinned conspiratorially. 'Come on, we're alone now. No need to keep up appearances. Relax, sit down.' He moved over to a cupboard in the corner. 'Soda or water?'

'Soda please.' He sat down and looked up into the grim face of Whymper, while Cane brought over an unopened bottle of Ballantyne's, a syphon and one tumbler. 'You're not having one?' Magnus asked.

'No. But just help yourself.' He sat down on the chair opposite, and in the silence Magnus opened the bottle, poured a dribble into the tumbler, and added a long squirt of soda. When he looked up, Cane was watching him with his dark smile.

'Go on, for God's sake man!' he laughed: 'Don't pretend you don't like the stuff — I know quite well you do! Anyway, you look as though you could do with one.' Magnus poured another inch of Scotch, with no soda.

'You look tired,' Cane said. 'You're all eaten up inside my boy.' Magnus took a long pull at his drink trying to fight down his embarrassment. 'And I'm here to help you,' Cane went on. 'We all are.'

'All?'

'My friends, Magnus. I invited you this evening because I wanted them to meet you, to hear you talk.'

'I didn't do much talking.'

'Oh, you did well. We were impressed. I was proud of you, Magnus. But now I want to know what you thought of us?'

Magnus took another drink and sat back. 'All right, John, let's have it! What's it all about? Old Boys' reunion for Alcoholics Anonymous? A breakaway branch of Moral Rearmament? Some newfangled Masons' Lodge with a touch of the Scouts? You tell me.'

Cane watched him for a moment, then smacked the arms of his chair and laughed: 'No, nothing so elaborate! We're not even a society — in the sense that we have no official membership. Let's just call it a loose association of ordinary people from different backgrounds and professions bound together by the same views and striving towards the same ends. Nothing political — nothing to do with Right-wing, Left-wing — they're just tags. We're after something above politics — something that'll cut across dogmas and economic barriers. Something truly great my boy!'

Magnus sat very still, beginning to wonder if Cane were slightly mad, or merely a crank. 'What is this great thing, John?'

But Cane held up his hand: 'Not so fast! Before we go any further I must warn you of one thing, Magnus. This evening you were good. Too good. Oh, I know I said we were impressed. We were. You spoke very well, and you fooled the others completely. But not me. I can smell a phoney a mile off. Phoneys, impostors — smelling them out was my job during the war. You knew that, of course?'

In the pause that followed the whole room seemed to grow smaller, darker, everything focusing on Cane's black sunken stare. Magnus heard a ringing start in his ears.

'So you think I'm a phoney?'

'I didn't quite say that. I'm saying you weren't being entirely honest with us. I'm not talking about your views. They're clear enough from your work. It's the little personal things — like pretending you don't drink. You were lying there, Magnus.'

Magnus had a sudden desire to swallow his drink and bolt for the door. He had been called a phoney and an impostor. But what of the phoney gas man yesterday at his flat? If he'd had just a couple more drinks inside him he might have brought the matter up and saved himself a lot of trouble. But Cane had invited him up here for some purpose, Magnus wanted to find out what it was.

Across the room Cane sat watching him, unblinking. Like Skliros, Magnus thought: *Going in for the kill against the ropes, sure and deadly.* He waited for Cane to go on. 'If you drink, that's your own problem. And I happen to know you drink too much. You drink because you're unhappy, lonely, frightened of yourself.'

Magnus flushed and poured himself another whisky without asking, and Cane went on, without comment: 'You drink because of your wife.'

'To hell with my wife.'

'Tell me about her. What went wrong?'

'Everything. Everything except bed, and that was usually only after a good lunch.' He stared into his drink, as Cane went on, gently: 'But the final thing? There's always a final thing, isn't there?'

'Perhaps. We'd been to some club, I think. She's a very good dancer — she was enjoying herself. And I can't dance. I'd had too much to drink, I suppose, and lost my temper and tried to drag her out. She wouldn't go and then there was a row with some of her friends, and I was asked to leave. It was all pretty trivial.'

'I don't think so. And then?'

'I called her a whore, and she called me a cripple. It was that kind of scene.' He put down his whisky and spread his fingers along the arms of his chair. 'But I don't see where this is getting us, John. You didn't invite me all the way up here just to ask me about my wife?'

'I want to find out more about you. I want to help you.' When Magnus said nothing, he went on: 'What happened after the row? You didn't just leave her?'

'We tried to make it up, but it didn't work. Just another washed-up marriage. Happens every day.'

'Put it behind you, Magnus. You've got too much ahead of you to allow yourself to be dragged down by a woman. Not that I don't sympathise, mind! I've been through the whole beastly business myself. But with one difference. I didn't try to escape by drinking. I didn't hide myself away and hate myself and hate the world round me.'

'No?' Magnus tried to hide his rage in another gulp of whisky. *You sanctimonious soul-bugger!* he thought. 'So what happened to you, John? Your marriage wasn't too good either?'

'No.'

'What happened?'

'Happened?' Cane gave a quick sigh. 'It was in 1942. I was in North Africa and hadn't had any leave for more than five months. Then one day I was told there was a plane leaving for England in three hours' time. I had a ten-day pass, so I just hopped on. When we arrived — somewhere in Hampshire, I think it was — I had the chance to telephone home, but I didn't. I knew my wife was in London, but I still had my own key — I kept it as a sort of talisman against the bombs — I wanted to give her a surprise. I did.'

He was no longer looking at Magnus, his eyes turned down, almost inwards; and when he continued, his voice was low and strained:

'She was already up, in her dressing gown, when I got to the bedroom. But the man was still in bed, with the sheets pulled up round his chin like a scene in a French farce. Which was not altogether inappropriate, since the blighter actually was French.'

Magnus would have laughed had it not been for the expression on Cane's face. 'A Free French liaison officer, I think he was. I remember I felt extraordinarily calm at the time. I drew my service revolver and sat down on a chair facing them. My wife did a lot of talking — tried to plead and reason with me, and give me a lot of underhand rot about war creating special moral circumstances, and so on. I don't think the Frenchman said much. Nor did I. I stayed there for nearly two hours, making up my mind whose brains to blow out. In the end I just stood up, put my gun away, and left without a word. I walked for a long time through the blackout, and then got deliberately and horribly drunk in the R.A.C. Club. I woke up with the worst and last hangover I've ever had, but also with a strange sense of inner cleanliness and peace. I had purged my anger and could start life afresh.'

Magnus winced and reached for his drink. Cane went on: 'You, Magnus, have yet to find that peace. You are still in pain, and you need help. I'm here to give you that help. But before I can do anything, I must first have your confidence and your honesty. Above all your honesty — in all things, at all times!'

Once again Magnus's irritation at this ridiculous, vainglorious man was overcome by his curiosity. He realised that this was the challenge. He took a deep breath.

'Very well, John. I'm not happy. My wife ran out on me, I drink too much, I have no clear purpose in life. And you say you want to help me, on condition that I'm honest with you. All right — if I'm to be honest with you, I want the same in return.' He tried to look Cane in the eye. 'What the hell's this all about? What did Sir Lionel mean when he said to me, "Glad to have you with us"? Was this evening some kind of initiation ceremony?'

'In a way. And we are glad to have you with us — providing you want to come. We need people like you, Magnus. You don't swim with the rest of the fish. You're not one of these soft-headed liberals or sickly humanists. You've got more guts.'

'Guts?' Magnus muttered.

Cane sat forward, his eyes bright under their black brows. 'Let me just tell you a little story to illustrate what I mean by guts. It happened some years ago when I was on a winter holiday in Zermatt. At the time a party of four climbers were attempting a particularly difficult ascent of the Matterhorn.

'The weather had been bad and on the third night I couldn't sleep for thinking of them. In the end I got up and went for a walk. It was very late and the town was deserted. Then suddenly I saw a solitary figure coming down the main street. He was staggering against the wall, and kept stumbling and picking himself up. I could hear him gibbering, and at first I thought he was a drunk. When he got closer I saw that his hands and feet were wrapped in bundles of felt, like a tramp. Just as he reached me he fell down and lay moaning in the snow. I was about to help him, when a Swiss-German voice called out of the shadows: "Don't touch him!" It was a local policeman.

'I should have known, of course. He was one of the four climbers, and I'd been on the point of breaking the sacred code of all mountaineers — that even after a climber has got to the summit and come safely down, he mustn't accept even a gesture of help until he has crossed the threshold of his hostel.

'I didn't know it then, but the poor wretch was the only survivor of the expedition. His three companions had dropped to their death on the Hörnli Glacier, and he had finished the climb alone. I and the policeman followed him back to the door of his hostel, where he collapsed and was taken to hospital. Next day he had both hands and one foot amputated.'

He paused, as though allowing Magnus time to contemplate that lone hero, hunched in some hospital bed, maimed and half-mad. Then, as though to answer Magnus's thoughts, he said: 'The pointless sacrifice of a young healthy body, you think? Perhaps. But in that sacrifice there was also proof of something noble and rare — the victory of human endurance over the most terrible forces of Nature. A victory of guts, Magnus. Guts and grandeur!'

Magnus nodded into his empty glass, while Cane went on with gentle urgency:

'That's what we all need today — people with the guts to fight the forces round us. We're sick and we need help. We need help desperately. But there is very little time. Too little to leave it to the politicians and so-called leaders of our society. For that society is rotted through, Magnus. Yet we are not threatened like ancient Rome. There are no barbarians hammering at our gates — for the barbarians are already inside!

'I tell you, I don't exaggerate when I say that we have around us a deliberate conspiracy of cunning, wicked men who are eating into our society like a cancer. These modish free-thinkers, these vermin from the cultural swamp who glorify everything from sexual depravity to highway robbery, spreading crime, doubt, disorder, artistic anarchy. Yet what do the leaders of our society do — our teachers and churchmen and statesmen? They have become passive allies of these vermin, preferring to get in there and giggle, rather than be giggled at!'

Magnus nodded dismally, finding himself in terrible agreement with much of what Cane was saying.

'The cancer, Magnus, must be cut out! The cells must be destroyed, one by one, or else they will destroy us.'

He stood up, and his eyes had a staring look that Magnus found slightly alarming. He was reminded suddenly of the master at school who had taken him through Holy

Communion: a stern bachelor and ex-Army chaplain who talked of purity and virtue and the evils of masturbation.

'You're still young!' Cane cried, 'but you've seen the danger too. Let us fight it together!' He came striding across the room, and Magnus stumbled out of his chair to meet him. Cane put both hands on his shoulders, and they faced each other, in an odd moment of intimacy.

'In these times of peril, Magnus, it is as well to remember Burke's dictum, "When bad men combine, good men must associate; else they will fall one by one, an unpitied sacrifice in a contemptible struggle".'

Magnus took a step back, glad to feel those hands slip from his shoulders. The man was not only a crank — he was raving mad. Yet there was a logic to the madness, and behind the logic there was an organisation. An organisation — if Magnus guessed right — which included a multi-millionaire, civil servant, schoolmaster, and at least one member of the Police Force. He said slowly: 'You quoted Burke just now. The bad men combine and the good men associate. Fine. But then what? What are you really trying to do, John?'

Cane's gaze had shifted to a point beyond Magnus' head. 'We are trying to achieve purity, Magnus. Purity and decency in our world. But there are so few of us — a dedicated minority — and we have our backs to the wall. If we fail — slacken for one moment, forget our duties in deference to some feeble principle of tolerance — then I tell you, my boy, history will not be kind to us.'

He paused and looked at his watch. 'Good gracious, it's past twelve! I had no idea —' His voice had become brisk, matter-of-fact, as though he'd switched personalities in mid-sentence. Magnus felt like one who has laboured through a difficult seduction scene, then at the moment of fulfilment is shown with great courtesy to the door. The evening had answered only a few questions, while giving rise to many more.

Outside on the landing Cane pressed into his hand a visiting card with the single inscription, John Austen Cane M.A. (Oxon.) followed by two all-figure telephone numbers. 'We'll be in touch again, Magnus. And if you ever feel you need me — want to ask my advice, discuss some problem — don't hesitate to call up. One of those numbers will always find me.' In the dim stair-lighting his face had a drained hollow look — the face of a man who does not sleep well. 'God bless, Magnus! Careful how you go.'

But by the time Magnus reached the lights of Piccadilly, he was already overtaken by a wholesome sense of the absurd. Cane's voice still rang in his ears, a call of doom in the wilderness while all around, London roared and sparkled — a Rome with its defences down, deaf to all the warnings.

He quickened his steps, looking up and down for a taxi. He had still to fetch his car from where he had abandoned it last night; and he badly needed another drink — several drinks, for that matter, before he set out on what he knew must now be done.

Close to the Ritz he passed the Icelandic Tourist Office, its windows full of photographs of glaciers and northern lights. They reminded him of something that he couldn't place; they worried him all the way down Piccadilly while he still looked about for a taxi.

It was only when he got to Hyde Park Corner that he remembered: a painting on Cane's wall opposite the grim face of Edward Whymper. An oil painting of a glacier under the midnight sun. Cane might be a lunatic, but he was also a romantic — which perhaps made it worse.

CHAPTER 3

The third club Magnus visited that night within the 'manor' of
South-West Central Police Station was off a narrow mews,
behind a mock-Georgian portico and leaded windows with
wrought-iron bars. A pair of electric coach lamps shone down
above a spyhole and brass plaque with the words, Congreve
Club. Members Only. He pushed the bell.

The door was opened by a broad young man in a single-
breasted dinner jacket. A whiff of expensive aftershave drifted
after him into the night air. 'Can I help you, sir?' The light,
shining into Magnus' eyes, glinted on the edges of the man's
hair — a reddish-gold, short back and sides.

Magnus said loudly: 'Evenin' sport! This the Congreve Club?'
The accent was spontaneous — Australian Outback, blaring
from his mouth almost before he was fully aware of it.

'You're not a member, are you?' The man's voice was still on
its best behaviour.

'I'm not, sport! I just got into the old town and a mate o'
mine staying at the Dorchester said you had a dinkum little
place here.'

'There's a forty-eight-hour waiting list for membership.' He
stood there blocking the entrance — his left hand, with strong,
square fingers and nails cut to the quick, leaning against the
door jamb. The same nasty left that Magnus had seen earlier
that evening beating the slim dark boy called Don Mocham
from Finchley.

Magnus had a moment of panic. He knew that Seaton need
only to have glanced down between the ropes to have
remembered him. But either the light above the ring had been

wrong, or Seaton had not looked down. He showed no sign of recognition.

Magnus gave him a friendly leer. 'I know it's late, sport, but I'm looking for some action. It's London, y'know — the swinging city!'

Seaton sneered: 'You bet.' He was rapidly dropping the tone of the gentleman's gentleman; soon it would be pure South London. 'You an American?'

Magnus laughed: 'Shake the snakes! Do I look like a flamin' Yank?'

'I don't care what you look like.' There was no pretence in the voice now: soft and surly with boredom. He began to inch the door shut, when Magnus shouted: 'I'm from down-under, mate! Australia!'

Seaton paused. 'An Aussie, eh?' His voice relaxed a little. 'I once knew a few Aussies. They were good blokes.'

'We're all bloody marvellous blokes,' Magnus said; and suddenly Seaton grinned. 'Come in a mo. I might be able to give you a temporary membership.' He stepped round him and closed the door. 'I'd like to go to Australia,' he added; 'sounds like a good place. Better than this dump!'

'Yeah? You don't like the old country?'

'Britain's finished. Just take a look round yer! Can't tell the boys from the girls — whole place run by a lot o' creepy pansies!' He turned, and in the light his face had a grey texture like porridge, the eyes dull brown with something calf-like, yet brutish about them. 'Got your passport?' he added.

'Not right on me.'

'We can't accept cheques without identification.'

'I won't be cashing any cheques, sport.'

'No?' He sounded wary again: 'But you've come to play?'

Magnus glanced round with another leer: 'Well, that's the object of the little place, isn't it?'

There was a smirk now in Seaton's voice: 'Sure! You won't find much else here.'

'How's that?

'Not if you're after birds, I mean.' The smirk became a grin: 'Unless you prefer ginger.'

'Ginger?'

'Beer, dear.' He was still grinning, and Magnus thought: *rhyming slang — it seemed to go with these boys like their short back and sides.* He gave a bogus laugh.

'You ever meet an Aussie who was queer?'

Seaton laughed back: 'I live and learn. But I guess you're all right. Come on in.'

Magnus followed him through a red curtain to a desk where he paid two guineas temporary membership fee, and signed the proposal form with the name Kelly.

The gaming room beyond was dim as a grotto, full of young men with knife-edge trousers and sunlamp complexions, shooting their cuffs over the green baize. The only women present seemed to be a blonde girl with a Nell Gwynn bodice behind the bar, and a blue-haired woman with a face like chewed toffee who was playing chemmy from a stack of £50 chips.

Magnus made his way cautiously towards the bar. Across the room he saw Seaton brushing down one of the chemmy tables while the packs were changed. On a closer look the girl behind the bar had a tired complexion and her blonde hair was growing out dark at the roots. 'It's all right, drinks are on the house,' she said, as she handed him his whisky, her eyes straying for a moment down the scar on his jaw. 'Haven't seen you before.' She had a sharp expressive voice that made him think she might be an out-of-work actress. He nodded. 'The bouncer made me a member for the evening.'

'Really! That was nice of him.'

'Yes?' He let the Australian drop: 'Why do you say that?'

She shrugged and got out a cigarette. 'Not my type.'

'Has he worked here long?'

'Only a few weeks.'

A man with orange hair and a white smoking jacket tripped against the bar and shouted: 'Give us a drink, darling!' She poured him a brandy and said, 'Hello Gary, how's it going?'

'Bloody! Down a couple o' ponies and the bugger won't give me any more credit.'

'You ought to stop.'

He gave her a slack grin. 'Darling, I'm going to stop. Tonight I'm feeling lecherous and sadistic.'

'Sorry. You'll have to find someone else.' She turned back to Magnus, who had finished his drink and was leaning closer to her across the bar.

'Do you happen to know someone who comes here called Peter Skliros?' he said quietly. 'Young chap with fair hair?'

She thought for a moment, then shook her head. 'Not by name, anyway.'

'He might have been here last night. With someone called Ivor Nesbitt.'

She stood eyeing him carefully. 'You mean the Ivor Nesbitt — who's been killed in a car smash? Yes, he was here last night. It must have been just before he was arrested.' She turned and shook her head. 'God, it's a bloody shame they go on hounding these people! Why can't they leave them alone?'

Along the bar the man with the orange hair was swaying back and forth, calling peevishly, 'Come on, love, what about a touch of lily-lash?'

'Drop dead,' she said, without looking at him. Magnus waited while she served another client, then leant across to her and said, 'Was he with anyone last night?'

'Why do you want to know?'

'I'm interested.'

'Are you from the police?'

'No.'

She moved away and poured some more drinks. The orange-haired man began to kick his suede chukka-boot against the bar. When she came back she said, 'I only saw him for a few minutes last night.'

'Was he with anybody?'

She picked up his empty glass. 'You want another?'

'Please. And try to think. Was he with a slim young man with blond hair?' A white sleeve slid along the bar beside him, and a voice said: 'I've had a shitty evening.' Magnus did not look at him. The girl had moved away again.

'Look, I said I'd had a shitty evening.'

'Glad to hear it.'

The young man grinned lazily. 'That's nice of you. Real sweet!' He looked up at the girl as she brought back Magnus' drink. 'Darling, this friend of yours says he's glad that I've had a shitty evening. Isn't that sweet of him?'

'Oh be quiet, Gary.'

Magnus said: 'A slim young man with fair hair, rather good-looking...?' He vaguely heard the young man say, 'Who is this bastard, Sandra?'

'Oh do belt up, Gary. You've had too much to drink.'

She turned to Magnus: 'Yes, I think there may have been someone. Was he wearing dark glasses?'

'He might have been.'

She nodded. 'I haven't seen him before, but I remember him because he was only drinking ginger ale. Mr Nesbitt was on Scotch. When he left, this young chap disappeared just after him.'

'After him? Into the street?'

'I suppose so. I didn't see him again. Either of them.'

Magnus gasped and stepped back, blinded with pain. For several seconds he stumbled about, unable to see anything; then a hand gripped his elbow. 'All right, break it up! What happened, Sandra?'

Magnus blinked and drew back. The first thing he saw was Seaton standing between them, solid, crouched for action. The girl gaped at them both. 'Gary here —' she began.

Seaton turned to Magnus. 'What happened, Mr Kelly?'

Magnus wiped the liquid from his eyes, recognising it now as brandy. Then he looked at the young man along the bar; he was grinning at him and his brandy glass was empty. Magnus took a step forward, and felt Seaton's fingers round his elbow.

'We don't want any trouble here, Mr Kelly. Why don't you finish your drink and call it an evening?'

Magnus stiffened, aware that all eyes were on him, then drained his whisky and turned. As he did so he heard the young man call: 'Bye, bye, scarface!'

He stopped, but Seaton nudged him gently. 'Let's go, Mr Kelly.' Magnus knew it was hopeless. As they reached the outside door, Seaton patted his shoulder. 'Sorry about that, Mr Kelly. But we don't want trouble do we?' Seaton opened the door.

'Good night, Mr Kelly.' For a moment his eyes held Magnus', dull and watchful in the doorway; and this time Magnus knew that he would be remembered.

The next moment he found himself alone in the street.

The Paper's library was a tall airless room, divided up into a catacomb of filing cabinets. A morgue for millions of forgotten words, presided over by an untidy man called Poole who had a wall eye and a photographic memory. He read everything that passed through his hands, and the mass of knowledge he had accumulated over the years, although largely uncoordinated, was daunting. He could tell how many horses fell in any Grand National, recite whole speeches by Sir Stafford Cripps, name every variety of poisonous snake. Magnus often wondered why he had never tried his talents professionally; but Poole's only excursion into public life had been in the 'thirties when he'd been a Communist with a pitch at Speakers' Corner.

Today Magnus brought him a list of ten names. Poole was away nearly a quarter of an hour before returning with a pile of envelopes. 'Blimey, that's a load! What's the story this time?' His good eye fixed on the top envelope, where Magnus read excitedly: MOCHAM, Donald — See Crosshead DUZINSKA.

'There are four on that chap Hilder,' Poole said, 'and two Edward Seatons. What's it all about?'

'Just background. Rissell trying to keep me busy.'

'Ah!' His eye glared knowingly. 'That detective, Skliros, I did him just yesterday.'

Magnus nodded. The four bulky packets on Sir Lionel Hilder contained biographical material and business details which he knew already. The cuttings on Skliros was also disappointing: all fresh from yesterday, concerning only the Nesbitt case, with nothing new. Of the two Seatons, one was a lawyer, the other had murdered his wife in 1939; and the only Tom Meredith had come to grief in a balloon accident in France. There was no Henry Deepe.

But there was a fat envelope marked, PYM, Harold — Tregunter School. Assault. Report to Minister of Education.

He started on this one first, realising now where he had heard the name before.

Until a couple of years ago Pym had been headmaster of a coeducational school in the Midlands. Scandal broke when a girl and boy, both sixth formers, were caught coming in late after a dance and each given six strokes of the cane on their bare buttocks by Pym, in the presence of the staff and ten prefects — five boys and five girls. The repercussions had been swift. Both pupils were withdrawn, and charges of indecent assault brought by their parents against Pym. He was fined by the local magistrates, but remained unrepentant, and finally had to be removed from his post by the Ministry of Education.

Magnus moved on to Don Mocham's file, which was accompanied by a much heavier one marked DUZINSKA. Once again the story was familiar. He read:

Iron Curtain Cabaret Star On Shoplifting Charge.

Ydviga Duzinska, the attractive young Polish cabaret star from Warsaw who opened on Tuesday in a two-week season at the Swift Club, was arrested yesterday afternoon in a Hatton Garden jewellers. She has been charged with stealing a diamond ring valued at £350. Police were called to the shop after an assistant, Mr Donald Mocham, noticed that the ring was missing. Miss Duzinska was on a sightseeing tour of the West End and was accompanied by an official of the East-West Cultural Association, Mr Jan Steiner, who arranged her visit to Britain. She will appear at Bow Street Magistrates' Court this morning.

There were many photographs of her, mostly taken on arrival at London Airport; bare knees above Courrèges boots and a wide face laughing under a haystack of blonde hair.

The facts seemed clear enough. She had gone into a jeweller's shop with Mr Jan Steiner, a naturalised Pole, and had spent about ten minutes looking at a selection of rings and brooches, but had not bought anything. As they left, the assistant, Mr Don Mocham, had caught up with them and asked her to open her handbag. Inside had been found a diamond ring — one of those she had just handled in the shop. This was later to explain why her fingerprints were found on it. She was unable to explain what it had been doing in her handbag, except to insist that someone had put it there.

The magistrate had decided to treat the case as a lamentable lapse, provoked by the temptations of Western life — an opinion she had loudly disputed, before he had been able to fine her £50 and ordered her to be deported within seven days.

Magnus turned to some criticisms of her act at the Swift Club. *The Times* had greeted her as a 'gust of fresh air to blow away the sagging cobwebs of our own satire industry ... A clear measure of the new cultural freedom sweeping Eastern Europe.' He noted that apart from the Communist *Morning Star*, the only begrudging review had appeared in *The Paper*, which had called her act 'facile, malicious, and often in doubtful taste'.

He packed the cuttings away in their envelopes and stood up. Poole gave him a boss-eyed grin: 'You found what you wanted Mr Owen?'

'Thank you, Mr Poole.'

The inquest on Ivor Nesbitt lasted less than ten minutes. The coroner recorded a verdict of death through misadventure.

CHAPTER 4

It was seventeen days since Magnus had last seen or heard from John Cane, on that night in Albany.

He was sitting in the Newsroom of *The Paper*, starting on his fifth mug of tea after a day of almost complete idleness, when Hugh Rissell called him into his study.

'Magnus, not busy? Good.' He stood rummaging on his desk among the spiked proofs and dead pipes, finally pulling out a big shiny brochure. Magnus read across the front: First International Cardiff Festival of Live Art.

Rissell stood chewing his pipe. 'You know all about it?'

Magnus nodded gloomily: 'Wales' answer to the Edinburgh Festival. Or another gang-bang for the psychedelic avant-garde. Are we going to give them publicity?'

'It'll probably be a routine story, but there might be an angle.' He consulted a note on his desk. 'As it's rather short notice, I'm afraid we could only get you into one of the cheap hotels. The Bute. Cardiff's going to be very full next week.'

'And with some lovely people,' Magnus muttered, turning a page of the brochure and wincing. 'Speak-In on Censorship, Poetry of Protest, our old friend Bernie Berliner and his Paintings of Hate. Holy Moses!'

'You don't care for Mr Berliner, then?'

'He's the one man I've met who makes anti-Semitism live.'

Rissell looked up, with his saturnine grin: 'You should have fun in Wales. By the way, I'd better warn you that you've been recommended for this assignment by Sir James Broom himself.' His eyes strayed towards the ceiling, as though the name invoked the Holy Ghost. 'I hear he's very impressed by your work. I don't know what kind of treatment we'll be giving this Festival, but I can rely on you to be objective. And it'll be encouraging to know that Sir James has his eye on you.'

Marvellous! Magnus thought sourly. Praise from the almighty Sir James was the final accolade. But what had it brought him? A trip out of town to watch the London literati and their pop-culture cronies in another weary effort to spread their gospel to the provincial wastelands of Britain.

Still, he would be able to make a little on expenses. And then there was always the chance, he thought, as he left Rissell's room, that something unexpected might happen down in Cardiff.

It was a cold blue morning when Magnus Owen hauled himself from the taxi outside Paddington Station, carrying an overnight bag and portable typewriter, and wearing his rapist's mac as a concession to Live Art. His face was still raw from a too hasty shave and he badly needed more coffee.

The Pullman coach was three-quarter full, with waiters busy preparing breakfast. A moment before the whistle blew, a girl came down the car, followed by a porter carrying one small piece of white luggage. She gave him a tip without looking at him, then stood slowly unfastening an oyster-white raincoat that was tightly belted over high hips, making sure that everyone in her path of vision had time to appreciate her.

Magnus did not waste this time. He noticed she had beautiful ankles, and that her bronze-red hair was either genuine or so well dyed that it scarcely mattered. Her skirt was short enough to be tantalising, without being ridiculous.

He sat eyeing her with cantankerous envy. He recognised the type too well. Flaunting figure, masculine get-up, casually expensive luggage. She belonged to his wife's caste — glossy magazines and dirty weekends in stately homes. But the next moment she confounded him by taking out a copy of *Encounter*.

He began to wonder how far she was going. Cardiff, and its Festival of Live Arts, crossed his mind, although she looked rather too well-groomed for that. Certainly not one of the PVC-LSD set, he decided.

Soon after they started she ordered a British Rail breakfast of kippers, poached eggs, toast and honey, and a pot of tea which he noticed she drank without milk or sugar. He kept catching himself looking at her, and once she caught him, returning his stare with an indifference that made him flinch. A bold dramatic face with not a line wasted. Wide eyes, straight nose, a mouth that was just a fraction too large — half beautiful, half vulgar. Her complexion was brown eggshell without obvious make-up; and he saw she wore no ring — no jewellery of any kind.

Half an hour before Cardiff she ordered a drink that looked to Magnus like vodka-on-the-rocks, which she disposed of in two gulps. He took his cue and ordered a double brandy that lasted him into Cardiff Central, where he watched excitedly as the girl stood up and began refastening her raincoat.

He was right behind her as they stepped out into the brittle sunshine, noticing that she trailed a thin delicious perfume.

They walked almost abreast along the platform, down the tunnel to the exit. Outside, she walked to the head of a queue waiting for taxis and raised her hand. Magnus hurried forward, and was pushed back by a man in a pork-pie hat who yelled, 'Can't you see there's a bloody queue!'

He had been mistaken. The girl had been signalling to a private car — a black Humber from which a young man in a dark suit had emerged and was now opening the rear door for her. Then something clicked in his mind: a pair of young men in dark flannel saluting Cane — Sir Lionel Hilder's chauffeur coming to attention outside Albany. But the association was ridiculous, he thought, as he watched the car drive away, wondering again who she was. Something to do with the Festival perhaps? An actress or ballerina? He found the puzzle pleasantly invigorating, as he set off on foot towards the Bute Hotel.

It was only a few minutes away, under a railway bridge that had been smartened up with red and green bunting. The building itself looked cheap and grim. Bute Commercial Hotel — weekly terms arranged. Hardly up to the standards of *The Paper*, he thought irritably, as an old wrinkled man shuffled from behind the desk and took his luggage.

Magnus followed him up three floors to a chilly room with a window overlooking the railway sidings. The old man stood in the doorway, eyeing him up and down for a moment, then said, in a wheezy Welsh voice: 'You're here for the Festival, I suppose?' It sounded like an accusation.

'The town's overflowing to capacity,' he went on, 'and I can tell you now, there are some pretty peculiar people about at the moment.'

'Oh yes?'

'Foreigners. Very weird, they are. Beatniks!' He spoke the word in a hushed whisper, as though it conveyed immeasurable evil. 'Here in the hotel.' He paused, as though to satisfy himself that Magnus was respectable, then added: 'I'm at the desk till eight in the evening, sir, if there's anything you want.'

When he was gone, Magnus sat down on the bed, not bothering to unpack, and spent a few moments leafing again through the Festival brochure. After the inaugural ceremony that afternoon in the Castle grounds, the Lord Mayor and civic dignitaries would visit the art exhibition in the Temple of Peace. But Magnus guessed that the highlight of the Festival — and very likely the high-jinks too — would come tomorrow evening in the Reardon Smith Lecture Room during the Speak-In on Censorship. One of the speakers was to be Garth Scammell, the self-styled People's Poet of Protest; and the first forty minutes were being televised 'live' by the B.B.C.

Magnus decided it was time for a drink, then lunch. Downstairs he found the old porter back behind his desk, staring at the wall. Magnus nodded at him, but the old man seemed to have forgotten him. He reached the front door, just as two people were coming in — a pale girl in jeans, with long black hair, followed by a blue-chinned man in a leather jacket and wrap-around dark glasses.

As Magnus passed them he heard the man mutter, 'Well for Chrissake, the doc's not here, so just shut up and settle for coffee!' It was a vaguely familiar voice, harsh and pitched like an actor's. Magnus wondered whether these were the old porter's beatniks. He noticed that the girl had been rather pretty, in a morbid way.

He walked back under the railway tracks and started up St. Mary's Street, which was crowded and full of bunting, wondering what on earth he could find in this Festival that would be of any interest to *The Paper*.

The Temple of Peace, part of Cardiff's noble Civic Centre, stands behind a façade of square grey pillars. The paintings hung on screens that divided up the bleak interior like a maze. There were splurges of swirling colour, eye-wrenching op art, angular nudes. But Magnus' favourite was one by the Painter of Hate, Bernie Berliner; it was called simply 'Famine' and depicted a pair of scrawny buttocks with a cobweb growing across them.

Nearby, under another of Berliner's works — a vast confusion of screaming children and howling faces under U.S. helmets, entitled 'Vietnam — Guernica Revisited' — was the refreshment table, lined with bottles of non-vintage champagne and plates of rather nasty-looking canapés.

The exhibition was filling fast, with a conspicuously divided crowd. There was the local set — baggy trousers and Plaid Cymru badges, baying at each other in shrill Welsh voices and grabbing for drinks. And there were the foreigners — flowered shirts and Neanderthaloid hair, with girls in boots and bells.

Flashbulbs flared, corks began popping. Under Bernie Berliner's 'Vietnam', a well-known actor was telling jokes to T.V. personality, Peter Platt — an ageing hipster in a knitted shirt that matched the mushrooms under his eyes. Platt was due to chair the Speak-In on Censorship tomorrow evening; and although Magnus deplored him, he had to concede that to have arranged forty 'live' minutes of unscripted television with a man like Garth Scammell was something of a feat. It was also, from the point of view of the B.B.C., something of a risk.

He collected a glass of tepid champagne, made just tolerable by the fact that he had already drunk half a bottle of wine and several brandies over lunch. He began to move among the screens of paintings. Bernie Berliner's work was enjoying some success when the Lord Mayor and Corporation officials made their entrance. There was a pumping of hands, more flashbulbs going off, and Magnus hurried off to refill his glass. He thought there might be some interesting reactions here.

The Mayor, a chunky man with a miner's build, stopped for a few words with Peter Platt, then led the round of inspection, followed by a woman who was evidently his wife, and an overdressed lady with a hat the size of a sou'wester. The Mayor had very good manners; he gave each work his attention, nodding, occasionally smiling, pausing at 'Vietnam' which he treated with grave respect. But as his party were about to take a left turn, away from the rest of Berliner's Paintings of Hate, the artist himself stepped out, as though to cut off any retreat.

He stood in front of them, a squat white-faced man with ginger crew cut and drooping moustache, smoking a hooked pipe which he removed long enough to shake hands with the Mayor's wife. The others now turned back to Berliner's paintings.

The crowd closed in. There was a murmuring and tittering all round as the party reached 'Famine'. The Mayor's wife moved close to it, peering short-sightedly, then someone laughed, and the next moment the stout lady in the sou'wester hat came sailing through the crowd like an icebreaker, her shoes snapping on the floor, past the ranks of champagne drinkers as though she were running the gauntlet. She was followed by the Mayor, who looked confused and flushed, with his wife at his heels, eyes on the floor. The two councillors who came behind looked very angry.

Bernie Berliner had not moved. He watched them, pipe between teeth, his face creased into a grin like a basking toad.

Peter Platt was at the door, waiting to see them off. The Mayor was determined to put the best face on it, especially with the photographers on all sides.

Magnus caught up with the party outside, just as they were getting into the Corporation's Austin Princess. He introduced himself, and the Mayor wrung his hand with a calloused grip. 'Ah yes, *The Paper*! Glad to meet you, sir!'

'I'd be interested to know what you thought of the exhibition, Mr Mayor.'

'Well now.' He drew himself up to his full five foot five, assuming all his civic dignity. 'I'm not exactly an art critic, you know. Don't pretend to be. And some of the stuff they've got in there is rather advanced, shall we say? Advanced for me, that is!' He smiled, and his wife smiled from inside the car, while her companions sat watching Magnus with faces like stone.

'You don't have any comment to make?'

'Comment? N-no! As mayor I can't rightly make comments. Not on matters of art, I don't think. It would hardly be appropriate, would it?'

'You weren't at all shocked?' Magnus asked brutally.

'No-o! Never shocked. I've seen enough in my time. A bit extravagant, you might say. Not quite the sort of thing to take the family to. But then art exhibitions are not really family entertainment, are they? We have to keep up with the times. And I hope this Festival helps to keep Cardiff on the map. All right, sir?'

'Thank you, sir.' They shook hands again, and the car drove off. Magnus returned up the steps, feeling that round one had gone to the Mayor. Without scandal or controversy Platt and Berliner could hardly be said to be giving — or getting — their money's worth.

Back inside, the party had grown hot and noisy. Magnus decided it was time to try and get drunk. He saw Platt and Berliner surrounded by a retinue of hip-swinging acolytes. Farther along he recognised the pale girl with the long black hair he had passed in the hotel that morning. She was still with her badly-shaven escort in his leather jacket, but he was no longer wearing his wrap-around dark glasses, and Magnus now remembered who he was. It was Garth Scammell, the People's Poet himself, with whom he was sharing that scruffy little hotel across the railway tracks. No great coincidence, of course; they were both in town for the Festival, and the Bute had been one of the last places with any rooms. Rissell had said so.

Magnus got another drink and moved towards them. Platt and Berliner had now joined the group, with a big tousle-haired man in a T-shirt whom Magnus recognised as 'Chuck' Ortiz, founder of America's 'Culture of Destruction', known as COD. Berliner was saying: 'I sure shocked the pants off that fat-arsed bitch!' Garth Scammell shook his head and began slowly snapping his fingers. 'Bernie man, you're too hung-up on this concave-convex distillation of the absolute. If you're gonna move 'em, you gotta get in there and fight 'em. Kick 'em in the teeth, throw lion-shit under the horses' hooves during the Royal Parade — hit tradition! In a few years' time, your paintings'll be tradition too. Me, Bernie, I believe in giving 'em action!'

'Sure, Garth. You give 'em shit and I give 'em reality.'

Magnus interrupted: 'I talked to the Lord Mayor outside, Bernie. He said your work was rather advanced. With time he might become one of your fans.'

Berliner sneered: 'I don't have to carpetbag to your kind of publicity, Owen. Now piss-off.'

Platt smiled suavely and poured a round of champagne. 'Hullo, Magnus. Don't tell me *The Paper*'s actually getting interested in art?'

'All the news that's fit to print,' Magnus murmured; then went rigid.

Across the hall he had caught a glimpse of a balding pudgy-faced man in a lumpy blue suit. A nonentity, standing alone in the crowd: and Magnus remembered how he had looked last time, awkward and out-of-place among that sea of dinner jackets, and that Cane had wrung him by the hand and addressed him in a foreign tongue.

Magnus doubted coincidences. Platt had refilled his glass and moved on to other guests. Nearby, a grisled Irish novelist was pouring himself a drink from a half-bottle of hard liquor. Magnus made friends with him, and they drank garrulously in the corner until the bottle was finished.

The hall was breaking up into ragged groups. Everyone was either laughing or shouting; one man had fallen over; glasses began to get broken. Then Magnus saw him again. This time he was over by the door, saying goodbye to Peter Platt. Magnus murmured his thanks to the Irishman and began to grope his way between the screens, arriving to find that Platt's guest had already left. He grinned. 'Hullo, Peter, who's your friend?'

Platt looked at him distantly. 'What friend?'

'The little balding chap you were just talking to. A foreigner, isn't he?'

Platt began to frown. 'You know him?'

'If I knew him I wouldn't be asking you who he was.'

Platt shrugged. 'He's on the Festival Committee. He's called Steiner. A Pole, I think.'

Magnus suddenly felt very sober. 'Not Jan Steiner, by any chance? Of the East-West Cultural Association?'

Platt looked at him with his large debauched eyes. 'What are you getting at, Owen?'

'Facts. Is this Steiner who's on your Festival Committee the same Steiner who belongs to the East-West Cultural Association?'

'He is.'

'What's he doing here?'

'There are some East European jazz groups over for the Festival. Steiner's Association helped to arrange it. Now what's all this about?'

Magnus grinned slyly over his glass. 'Like a drink, Peter?'

'I'm sorry, Owen, I'm busy.' He was already looking around for a fresh audience.

Magnus said softly: 'Ever heard of Yadviga Duzinska?' Platt turned, frowning again. 'A Polish cabaret star,' Magnus went on. 'She was in London last year — till she got deported for shoplifting.'

Platt took a step forward. 'What the hell are you driving at, Owen?'

'Only that Duzinska was invited over here by the East-West Cultural Association, and your friend Steiner was with her when she was arrested.'

Perhaps it was the heat of the party, or the champagne, but Platt's upper lip had grown moist. 'You're not bloody well suggesting — !'

'Not suggesting anything, Peter! Except that what happened to the Duzinska girl was bad luck. Hope it doesn't happen again.' Someone knocked into him from behind and his glass splashed over his wrist. He stumbled and began to turn, and a hand steadied him by the elbow. He straightened up and muttered something. Platt was already walking away.

The hand still held him, as he looked round and squinted at a tall girl in a plain black cocktail dress. 'Sorry about that,' she said, 'but you don't want to go on talking to these people.' She began to lead him out through the door. He stopped and put his glass on the floor, then looked up at her and laughed. 'Don't tell me! You travel light, you drink vodka before lunch and you read *Encounter*, which means you must be intelligent too.'

She laughed with him, taking his arm. 'Come on, you've had enough to drink.'

'Not so fast!' He steadied himself on the steps outside. 'I'm a great believer in the age of chivalry, but I'm well past the age where girls pick me up when I'm drunk.'

'I was rescuing you.'

'You thought I needed rescuing?'

'I thought you were going to make a fool of yourself.'

He stood on the steps and shook his head. 'Ah, the age of chivalry! You were eavesdropping, I suppose?'

'I couldn't very well help it. You were talking rather loudly, you know.' She was smiling, a wild beautiful smile, and he leant out and touched her cheek.

'My God, it's real!' he muttered, then he looked up at her hair. 'Pure Renaissance. Where do they make girls like you? You're not English?'

'I've got a British passport. But I wasn't born here.' She had slipped her arm through his and was leading him down the steps. The sun had gone and there were rain clouds blowing up over the park.

'What are you doing in Cardiff?' he asked, remembering the black Humber and the young dark-suited chauffeur.

'I'm just here, like everyone else.' Her voice had only a trace of accent.

'Where did you say you were born?'

'Poland. Don't look so surprised! We're the largest foreign colony in Great Britain.'

He walked along, feeling a little giddy. They might be the largest foreign colony, and there were at least two of them now in Cardiff connected with the Festival. Even when drunk, his training had taught him that two coincidences were too many.

'You belong to the East-West Cultural Association?' he said at last, and saw her face stiffen.

'You know, you're very indiscreet for a journalist, Mr Owen.'

He stopped. 'How the hell did you—?'

'It's all right, I read *The Paper* too. You're quite well known, you know.' Her smile broke out again, dazzling him. But he did not smile back.

'How did you know who I was?'

'I recognised you. You've got a very distinctive face, you know.' The smile was now mischievous, taunting.

He began to get angry. 'How do you know what I look like? *The Paper* doesn't print my photograph.'

She paused only a fraction of a second. 'I read your book. Your photograph came out with the reviews. It was very good — the book, I mean.'

Magnus walked slowly beside her, nodding. 'So you saw my photograph in a review four years ago, and now you follow me all the way from London to Wales, just to tell me how much you like my book?'

She let go of his arm. 'I think we ought to have a little talk together.' They had reached the Park Hotel, and without waiting for him to agree, she turned and swung through the revolving doors, disappearing across a dark lobby. She sat down at a low table, stretched out a pair of legs that made him swallow hard, and got out a packet of cigarettes. 'Like one?'

'I don't smoke.' He sat down stiffly opposite her and looked at his watch. 'In five minutes we can have a drink.'

She lit her cigarette and sat watching him a moment through the smoke. 'You drink too much.'

He put his head back and laughed bleakly at the ceiling. 'And I'm going out of my mind too! Who the hell are you, anyway? Who sent you here? Who's the young chauffeur who met you this morning at the station?'

'You're very observant. What else do you know about me?'

'I don't know a damn thing about you. Not even your name.'

'Maya.'

'Maya what?'

'You wouldn't be able to pronounce it if I told you.'

'What about your telephone number?'

But she did not answer. A waiter appeared beside them. 'It's just time for a vodka-on-the-rocks,' Magnus said, looking at his watch. 'One vodka with ice,' he told the waiter, 'and one double brandy.' She watched him with a faint smile, but there was no gaiety in her voice: 'You accuse me of following you here from London. What made you say that?'

'It was a joke.'

'A silly joke.'

'It was the best I could do. But the more I think about it, perhaps it wasn't such a joke. You still haven't told me what you're doing here.'

She sat forward in her chair, holding a cigarette in both hands, her elbows on her knees which jutted above the table. But Magnus was watching only her face: it had a quiet authority, it was suddenly very unfeminine and very sobering.

'Mr Owen, you talk too much. You were talking too much this afternoon. Why did you shout your mouth off to Peter Platt?'

He stared at her blankly. 'I didn't shout at him, I was asking him questions.'

She nodded. 'Questions about Jan Steiner.'

He sat bolt upright in his chair. 'Steiner! What do you know about him?'

'What do you know about him, Mr Owen?'

'I saw him once — at a hotel in London.'

'So why are you so interested?'

'Me interested?' he shouted. 'I'm not the one — I was just asking Platt some questions—?' He groped helplessly for his words, feeling the conversation escaping on to a surrealist level. He had a moment's respite as the drinks arrived.

'It may be a coincidence,' he said at last, 'but do you know a girl called Yadviga Duzinska?'

'Not personally. I knew what happened to her.'

'What happened?'

'You know perfectly well. You were telling Platt all about it. Why were you doing that?'

He leant forward and gripped his brandy. 'All right, Maya. So you work for the East-West Cultural Association, and you want to protect your friend Jan Steiner from embarrassing questions.'

Her face went rigid, the skin drawn taut across her wide cheeks, her eyes hard and humourless. 'You are a fool, Mr Owen! A damned fool!'

He nodded and drank. 'So you picked me up back at the exhibition just to tell me that? Or are you trying to warn me off?'

'Why don't you stop drinking and just listen to me, Magnus!' It was the first time she had called him by his first name, and he was confused. 'All right, I'm listening.'

She swallowed her vodka, put the glass carefully back on the table and said: 'Magnus, I got you out of that place there because you were shooting your mouth off. You're supposed to be here covering this Festival for *The Paper*. Instead of that you start getting drunk and asking stupid questions from people like Platt. Why don't you just keep quiet — keep your eyes open and your mouth shut? That's what you're here for, isn't it?'

For a few seconds he just stared at her, helpless, almost mesmerised. Even Hugh Rissell would scarcely dare address one of his staff in this way.

He leant back at last and dropped his arms into his lap. 'Maya, I don't know what all this is about, but I'll only say right now that I don't believe one thing you've told me so far. I don't believe you recognised my photograph from book reviews published four years ago. I don't believe you just happened to be on that train from Paddington this morning — just happened to be at that exhibition — happened to be standing right behind me when I was asking about Jan Steiner. In fact, I think you're a lovely fascinating liar.'

She sat quite still, elbows on her knees, watching him; then suddenly the image became blurred, her face falling out of focus.

'Well?' he cried at last.

'Well what?'

He reached wearily for his brandy. 'Fun and games, Maya. You asked me why I was interested in Steiner. Now I'm asking you why you're so interested?'

She paused to light another cigarette. 'I don't know him well. I've met him a few times in London, at Polish clubs and parties.'

'What does he do?'

'I think he's a full-time official with the Association. He's been here since 1948.'

'You knew that he was with that girl Duzinska when she was arrested?'

She did not move, but there was a tension in her face as though she were biting against a raw nerve. 'Yes, I did hear something.' She glanced up to catch the waiter's eye. 'The bill,' she said, opening her bag and handing him a pound note. 'I'll do this,' she added to Magnus. 'After all, I invited you.'

He nodded: 'You're in charge, aren't you? After all, you did follow me here all the way from London.'

She gave a thin smile, telling the waiter to keep the change, then stood up, and he followed her round the table desperate to gain some initiative. 'I'm sending a story to *The Paper* at seven o'clock,' he called after her. 'I'll be through by seven-thirty. If you're free, let's have dinner together.'

She led him out of the lounge and halfway across the lobby before she replied, without turning. 'Yes, I'd love that.'

He caught up with her. For a moment he wanted to take her face in his hands and kiss that long mouth and feel her heavy hair through his fingers. He tried to sound casual as he said: 'Where are you staying?'

She moved on to the revolving doors. 'It's easier if I pick you up, I think. I've got a car.'

'The lad with the Humber?'

She laughed: 'You're really worried about him, aren't you? It's all right, I'll be alone.'

He gave her his most predatory smile and said, 'I'm at a place called the Bute, behind the station. But I suppose you knew that already?'

'I didn't, as a matter of fact. But you're in nice company there.'

'Company?' He frowned. 'Ah, you mean Garth Scammell? I saw him there this morning.'

'Berliner's there too, and that American, Ortiz. You've got the whole scene there. You ought to enjoy yourself.'

He looked at her carefully. Why would she know that Scammell and Berliner and his friends were staying at the Bute Hotel? And after all the sparring, he still had no real idea why she had approached him, picked him up drunk in the afternoon and whisked him off to a hotel bar where she called him a fool in the first few minutes, then gone on to question him about his interest in the mysterious Jan Steiner. He knew there was something wrong; that it had all happened too fast, too easily. 'Where shall we meet?'

'The Royal. I have to be down in that direction — and anyway, it's nearer you.'

'I'll be there. Downstairs bar at seven-thirty.' He paused. 'In case I get held up, is there anywhere I can contact you?'

'I don't think so. Just try not to get drunk, that's all.'

He leered at her. 'You begin to sound like one of those moral reformers. It doesn't suit you.' As he said it, he again saw that quick look of pain in her face. 'Can I get a taxi for you?' he added. 'It's raining outside.'

'I'll stay — I've got some phone calls to make.'

'Till seven-thirty then, Maya.'

'Goodbye, Magnus.'

He turned, and knew that she was watching him as he pushed his way through the revolving doers, out into the rain.

Back inside the Bute Hotel he was met by the old porter who came sidling out from behind his desk. 'Mr Owen — message from London on the telephone!' He handed him a sheet of paper scrawled with the number of *The Paper*. 'They said it was urgent, Mr Owen.'

Magnus looked at his watch; it was not quite five o'clock. From his experience of *The Paper* he knew there was rarely much urgency, even from outside London, until well after six. He asked the old man to connect him, and went through into a stuffy booth under the stairs. *The Paper* came on the line and he asked to be put through to the Newsroom. Rissell was not there. He told them who he was, and that he thought it was urgent; after another delay a secretary came on the line:

'Will you hang on for just a moment, Mr Owen? Mr Rissell will be right with you.'

It was a full two minutes before he heard Rissell's voice. 'Hullo — Magnus? How are you doing?'

'Fine. What's all the urgency?'

For a moment Rissell was silent. 'Hullo!' Magnus called.

'I'm still here.' The voice sounded distracted, as though talking to someone at the other end. 'Have you got a story yet?'

'I'd hardly call it a story — it's more for the parish-pump gazette.'

'What do you mean?' Even over the crackling line Rissell's voice was sharp with irritation.

Magnus replied as politely as possible. 'Picasso and Sartre and Bertrand Russell haven't shown up yet. All that's happened is that a few of the local bigwigs got a bit upset by some of Bernie Berliner's paintings in the exhibition.'

'What was the exhibition like?'

'Applecrap and poppycock. But what's all the fuss?'

'We've got a newspaper to bring out, that's what's the fuss!'

Magnus gripped the receiver and said, 'You'll have something by seven-thirty.' He was about to hang up, when Rissell broke in, almost shouting: 'You'll put your best into this, won't you, Magnus? As I said, Sir James Broom wants to give this festival quite a splash. And make sure you don't miss the censorship teach-in tomorrow evening.'

'Speak-in,' Magnus corrected him, thinking furiously, *I know my own damn job!* But he was becoming puzzled by the urgency in Rissell's voice. 'Anything special about tomorrow evening?' he added.

'That's what you're down there to find out. Just keep your eyes open.'

Drunk though he was, he paused and began to think hard. Those were the same words that Maya had used less than half an hour earlier in the Park Hotel; and as he stood propped against the wall, a thought crossed his mind that made him jerk upright, his hands sweating round the receiver. Maya and Hugh Rissell. Both telling him how to do his job. First the girl had picked him up, then she told him he'd made a fool of himself in front of Peter Platt and the rest; and now here was Rissell demanding an urgent story so that he could splash Platt's Festival of Live Art under the eyes of *The Paper*'s frowsty readers. Somehow it didn't make sense. Or did it?

But Rissell had already hung up. Magnus made his way up the three flights to his room, where he sat for some time racking his brains for something to write about. What was the most delicate way of describing Bernie Berliner's work? Was 'emetic' too strong? — or would 'non-emetic' be more appropriate?

At a quarter to seven he was in the Royal Hotel, booking his call back to *The Paper*. By seven-twenty-five he'd finished dictating copy and had spoken again to Rissell, who had sounded satisfied — and had even told him to enjoy himself.

He was now doing just what Rissell suggested, over a champagne cocktail in anticipation of the Polish girl called Maya.

An hour later, on his fifth cocktail, he was not enjoying himself at all. He had begun to check every ten minutes at the desk to see if there were any messages, and had now begun to ring the Bute Hotel in case she might have tried to contact him there. His first call had been received by the old Welsh porter, who sounded thrilled by his anguish; but the third was taken by a sour voice which had told him there was nothing, then hung up. He assumed this must be the night porter.

He returned to his seat, with a confusion of rage, disappointment and faint anxiety. He could not believe that she would heedlessly stand him up. The whole afternoon had been improbable, contrived and crazy, so why should he expect a logical follow-through? Yet he was worried. His pride, and perhaps instinct, would not allow that she had found something better to do for the evening, or had been too busy or too lazy to contact him.

He ordered another drink and sandwiches, then walked with dignity to the reception desk and asked again if there were any messages. They gave him the same answer. Outside, where someone had been freshly sick on the pavement, a man was singing, 'Bread of Heaven! Feed me till I want no more!'

He headed back towards the railway tracks. He passed the station; and after the dismal revelry of the town centre, it was dark and quiet. The door of the Bute Hotel was unlocked. A light burned over the desk, which was empty. Even the night porter had gone off duty. Whatever Garth Scammell and his friends got up to, they either did it elsewhere or left it till well after closing time.

Magnus went to check for the last time if there were any messages. There was nothing. He reached for his key, and noticed that almost all the keys were hanging on their rack. He took his own and started for the stairs. It was dark and he did not know where the stair light was. Besides the one above the desk the only light came from the half-open door of a small lounge down the passage.

He had taken a couple of steps before he realised that he was frightened. He stood quite still, listening to the silence. Someone was breathing, softly and very close.

He took a few steps forward and looked into the lounge.

The man sat in a wooden chair, his pale hair resting on the wall behind him, eyes closed. The light came from a lamp outside the uncurtained window and fell almost directly on his long face, giving it an unnatural ghost-like serenity, as he sat with his big hands lying palm upwards on his knees.

Magnus moved as fast as the darkness allowed, groping for the light switch, finding the stairs, feeling the width of the walls with his hands, each step with his toe, reaching the first landing without a sound behind him. Now the second flight — three in all — and the hotel was as quiet as ever. He wondered vaguely how many guests there were. The question was not idle; he did not want to be alone in this hotel tonight.

He had met the man downstairs once, after a middle-weight fight against a punch-drunk called Judd. He'd met him in the presence of a plain-clothes police officer, and afterwards John Austen Cane had called him a 'conquering hero'. Tom Meredith, from Cardiff, on whose biceps a lion grappled subcutaneously with a snake, above the words *Virtus Vincit*.

His room was exactly as before. There was no reason why it should not have been — unless someone had wanted to make off with his Olivetti. But after he had locked the door behind him, he took the precaution of wedging the chair under the handle. The window was open a few inches at the top; but it looked out on to a yard, and it would be difficult for anyone during the night to pull it open from outside.

He undressed and got into bed, but did not sleep well. For a long time he lay awake listening to groans of plumbing and the grinding of trains.

It was well after midnight when he finally dozed off; but only for a few moments. He was awake again, starting up in a sweat, lunging out for the table lamp and dashing it to the floor. He thought there was someone standing by the bed.

He leant down, retrieved the lamp, switched it on, climbed out of bed and drank some water from the basin. He was muzzy with sleep and had almost forgotten about the man downstairs.

It was some hours later when he woke again. This time he knew that he was not dreaming. It was still dark, and for a few seconds he lay half sitting against the pillow, listening. There were footsteps in the passage and they were coming towards him.

They came slowly, with hardly a sound except the creak of floorboards. Somebody coming in late, he thought — somebody who didn't want to upset the other guests. Hardly likely to be Scammell and Berliner and their gang.

They reached his door. He closed his eyes, waiting for the next step. Another board creaked, very slightly — this time, it seemed to him, a little beyond his door — and there was a pause. He opened his eyes and heard a key click.

In the silence it sounded very close. Then, for what seemed a long time, there was nothing. The next sound was a door closing, quite softly; a key turning again in the lock.

This time the footsteps retreated faster, with more noise. They passed his door; he heard them start down the stairs, then silence.

He put the chair back under his door and left the light on, before lying back.

He woke late. The lamp was still on beside his bed and there was sun behind the window. For the first few minutes, while he got up and ran the hot water tap for a shave, the events of the previous night were obscured by his headache. He was more concerned with the water which spluttered and coughed into the basin. It gave him an uncomfortable shave, and he wasted a few minutes cauterising the cuts along the edges of his scar.

It was only after he had finished dressing that he removed the chair from under the door handle, locking the room again behind him before going downstairs. On the second landing he could hear cheerful Welsh voices from below. They came from the little lounge where he had seen Meredith the night before.

It was full of sunlight, and a woman was down polishing the floor, while the old Welsh porter stood with his hands on his hips, watching her. He saw Magnus and winked: 'Up late, aren't you, Mr Owen? Had a bit of a night?'

Magnus walked up to the desk, with the old man behind him, and noticed that all the keys seemed to be on their hooks. He gave the porter his own key and half-a-crown.

'Now between you and me,' he said, leaning across the desk, 'could you do me a little favour?'

'Favour?' The old Welshman was sniffing scandal like a dog at a bone.

'It's about the beatniks,' Magnus said, and nodded down at the half-crown that the old man was already sliding under his hand. 'Which rooms have they got?'

'Got?' The old eyes were wet with cunning, as he glanced back at the key rack. 'They didn't come back last night. Not one!'

'Are they still booked in?'

'They're still booked in — but they haven't paid yet, you see! Their luggage is up there, but it's not much, mind! And if they've flown, it'll be the police for them, don't you worry. We're only a small hotel —'

Magnus said: 'Which rooms have they got?'

For a moment the old man's lips fluttered inaudibly. 'Next to yours,' he said at last: 'Numbers 18 and 19, and one of them's in there with a girl.'

'How many other guests have you got?'

'Guests? We've got a few guests — they come and go, like.'

'You've got one called Meredith?'

'Eh?' The old eyes wandered down to a second half-a-crown Magnus was pushing across the desk.

'A tall young man with blond hair. Tom Meredith. You know him?'

'Ah-h!' He cocked his head and gave a sucking noise: 'You're not from the police, are you?'

'No it's a personal matter. Anything wrong about this man Meredith?'

The old face thought for a moment, then said, 'Not that I know of. What's he been up to? Trouble?'

'How long has he been staying here?'

He shook his head: 'Not staying, he works here. He's a new lad — the night porter.'

'How long's he had the job?'

'Not long — only temporary. I don't see too much of him. He keeps himself to himself.'

'He's on early at nights?'

'That's it,' the old man said, nodding vigorously. 'I'm the main porter, you see — days only.'

'What time does this man Meredith go off?'

'Around eight in the morning, I suppose.' He scratched his head and gave a little snuffling noise. 'Now then, what's it all about, eh, sir?'

Magnus winked and slid a third half-a-crown across the desk. 'A little secret — just between you and me. Okay?'

The Welshman mumbled and sat down, studying the three coins in his hand, while Magnus walked out into the spring sunshine.

He lunched at the B.B.C. Club with a young man called Winters who was in control of televising the Speak-In that evening. Magnus had hoped it would be a private session, but almost at once they were joined by a tall thin man called Iorwerth Ab Probyn, a Crowned Bard and member of the Festival Committee, with a skin like rice paper. The meal was not an easy one. Magnus tried to interrogate Winters about the Speak-In, but Probyn held the conversation tenaciously, lecturing them both on the dangers that the Festival was bringing to Wales.

'The decent people of this country will not tolerate a Godless smearing of our ancient national traditions!' he cried, chewing his stringy meat, while Magnus and Winters listened, politely sipping beer.

The monologue passed from the tedious to the absurd. 'These fancy clever young men can come down here to Wales, casting about them their gifts from the Greeks, full of dirt and doubt. But mark my words! — before long they'll find themselves out on a limb, and when they do, God will come along and chop it off!'

They were interrupted by two men with bow ties and untidy grey hair who came across to greet Ab Probyn in gushing Welsh. He introduced Magnus and Winters, translating what was said into English, then translating what they said back into Welsh, although everyone knew that everyone else there spoke English perfectly well.

Afterwards Magnus and Winters took refuge in the bar.

'Phew! What a mad mob!' Winters ordered double whiskies. 'I've heard them now for a whole week, old boy. And I can tell you, if you don't speak Welsh — and it doesn't matter a fig if you're English — you're just a bloody traitor.'

'It's a fine old Celtic tongue,' Magnus muttered. 'Your health! To the Speak-In tonight.'

'You've said it!' Winters shook his head. 'To tell you the truth, I may have bitten off a little more there than I can chew. You know that several of the local Festival Committee members are threatening to break off diplomatic relations? Well, I grant you that some of that stuff at the exhibition yesterday was a bit ripe for the untrained palate, but I've taken on a forty-minute live programme tonight. It was going to be an hour, until I managed to get it cut down.'

'Why was that?'

'Well, I consider that Peter Platt pulled rather a fast one on me there. You see, I was the one who put up the idea of televising this debate in the first place, and I got it okayed — providing I could iron out the arrangements with Platt and ensure we didn't get a lot of jungle warfare on the screen. Platt agreed to chair the discussion, and the three main speakers were a fairly safe bunch. Then, just when everything was arranged, Platt comes breezing up to me and says he's got hold of that poet, Garth Scammell, as third speaker — after Mary Dunnock.'

'Oh not her!' Magnus cried: 'I thought she was dead.'

'Far from it, old boy. She's still the mainstay of the lending libraries — turns out at least two books a year — and lately she's got all enthusiastic about the Young Conservatives.'

'Platt will love her. So will the audience.'

'It's not her I'm worried about. It's Garth Scammell.'

Magnus nodded: 'You ought to have fun with him! I once heard him give a poetry reading in front of the Dirty Hampstead Set. They just loved his four-letter words!'

Winters groaned and gave the barman his empty glass.

'Don't worry!' Magnus laughed. 'If he gets naughty, you can always throw every switch in the building.'

'It's not so easy with an open debate, old boy.' He sipped his second Scotch as though it were medicine. 'All I pray is that Platt's opening piece, and the other two speeches, get spun out long enough to last the whole forty minutes. You'll be there, I suppose?'

'Oh, I wouldn't miss Scammell for anything!'

Magnus liked Winters, yet he could not help wishing that Garth Scammell would misbehave that evening. He had to find something to write about, after all. They finished their drinks, and again Magnus wished him luck — feeling that he might need it.

By seven-fifteen that evening the Reardon Smith lecture room was already crowded. Above the bank of seats, the ceiling had been fitted with a battery of arc lamps which was already filling the hall with a waxy heat.

Magnus had been given a place a few rows above the stage, beside a distinguished literary critic, a wry-faced man with a long chin and leather patches on his elbows. One glance up the slope of knees and faces above him, confirmed what he expected. The announcement of Garth Scammell's appearance had brought out his unwashed disciples in strength, now gathered along the rows of seats like crows on a telegraph wire. Behind him sat a big trousered girl with a badge on her sweater saying Warning! Your Local Police are Armed and Dangerous!

On the far side of the hall, among the sound-booms and camera equipment, Magnus saw Winters in shirtsleeves, whispering with the technicians.

Two minutes to go. The hall was now packed out, noisy and stifling. Magnus loosened his collar and looked down the seats in front of him. In the centre row he saw Garth Scammell, between the pale girl with the long hair and Chuck Ortiz, the 'Great Destroyer'; and a few seats beyond sat Mary Dunnock, the popular novelist.

Then suddenly he started up in his seat: the whole hall seemed to grow quiet around him. She must have slipped in through the side door, taking her seat at the end of the second row below him, still wearing her oyster-white raincoat, belted and buttoned to the chin; and for a moment he wondered how she could stand the heat. Her long hair was tucked under the collar, her head held stiffly, arms folded in her lap — an attitude that was at the same time calm and tense. She was also wearing enormous dark glasses …

He was on the point of going down to speak to her, but restrained himself. She had stood him up once, and the last thing he must now do was go running after her. When the Speak-In was over it should be easy enough to contrive an apparently casual encounter — if only to get an explanation for her behaviour the night before.

There was a burst of applause, as Peter Platt stepped on to the stage and took his place at a table in front of a microphone. The Speak-In on Censorship, at the first Cardiff International Festival of Live Art, had begun.

Platt's opening speech lasted just over eight minutes. It was an angry predictable tirade against the iniquities of censorship, ending with the cry: 'And I put it to you, to everyone who values freedom, that while there remains a scrap of censorship in this country, it can mean only one thing — that our society has something to be ashamed of, has something to hide!'

When the applause was over, he held up both hands and called: 'But we must agree to disagree. And I have no doubt that our next speaker will find a great deal to disagree with what I have just said. I give you one of our great lady novelists, the incomparable Mary Dunnock!'

To a chorus of stamping and hooting, Miss Dunnock mounted the stage with dignity. She was clad in an ankle-length sequined gown sparkling under the arc lamps, her hair piled in silvery coils above the profile of a Bourbon prince.

No, she was not in favour of censorship — certainly not political censorship — but some of the things one read today … it all had to be sex — sex the whole time, from page one to the end! (She was greeted with prolonged cheering.) If you didn't write a book that was full of sex you were told it wouldn't sell. (Cries of 'Hear! Hear!') Miss Dunnock flushed and stiffened, her self-confidence growing with the challenge of her audience. She was all in favour of sex in books — she had written about plenty of sex in her time!

'Sex with King Edward!' someone shouted, with a cackle of laughter that was taken up round the hall, like dogs barking.

Mary Dunnock allowed them their fun; then began appealing for a return to romantic love in literature — a call that aroused much hilarity. But she was not to be put off. She was sick to death of authors who seemed to think the only true relationship between a man and a woman consisted of a string of nasty biological details between dirty sheets.

Platt interrupted her graciously: 'Yes, but what would you do about these authors who choose to describe nasty biological details? Would you censor them?'

'I don't want to censor anybody,' she said, 'but I do think there has to be a limit.' A great groan went up as she went on: 'A happy medium, something between liberty and licence.' The groans swelled to a howl until Platt had to appeal for order. Miss Dunnock was taking it well: she looked angry but resolute. 'In some cases I think people should be protected!'

Platt rounded on her triumphantly: 'What sort of people, Miss Dunnock?'

'Children — impressionable young people. And don't tell me!' she cried, with sudden vehemence, 'that all this violence and sadism on the telly doesn't have an effect. You've only got to look at the crime statistics. Look at all these horrid murders you read about. These crimes against children…!'

Miss Mary Dunnock was allowed by Platt to run on for another fifteen minutes. When she finally stepped down, more than half of Winter's television time had passed, without disaster.

Magnus was getting bored. He wanted it over, wanted a drink, wanted to talk to Maya. He looked down at her, at the back of her head, rigid, detached from the rest of the audience — while Platt began announcing Dirk Pohlmann, well known for his documentary films. He was voluble: he found the theatre a dead medium, the cinema castrated by commercial demand, literature catered only for the paperback trade. His language was diffuse, and after five minutes his audience began to grow restive.

Magnus glanced down again and saw Maya move at last, taking something from her raincoat pocket; but it was only a cigarette. He sat back and looked at his watch. Winter's television time was moving mercifully to a close. By the time Pohlmann stepped down, there was less than eight minutes left.

Platt now called on Garth Scammell. The applause was thunderous. The audience wanted drama, and Garth Scammell was going to give it to them. He bounded up beside Platt, tensed behind his dark glasses as though for a fight, compact and sure-footed as a cat.

'Life is death! Life is all death, from wet foetus to bloated corpse! They tell us life is beautiful. They say, man, life is a gift of God and the birth of a child is the most beautiful thing on earth! And a man is just out of military academy, all fresh and hairy-arsed, and he fondles the latest air-cooled automatic M.16 — firing twenty rounds a second — and he says, man, this is a beautiful baby!'

Magnus yawned, and looked down, and she was still there. He looked up at the side of the hall and the cameras were still on. His watch said less than five minutes to go.

'We have death on stage, screen and radio! Bang! Bang! A man is dead, screaming in the mud with his bowels blasted out, screaming for mummy while his turds are squeezed out, steaming in the mud…!'

Along the row behind Magnus a bald man with a black beard let out a maniac laugh. Scammell raised his voice, shouting:

'So if we can have Death the Great Redeemer, why not sex? Real sex! Sex with its bowels blasted out, screaming in the mud! The great bang, the great Ram — Ram! Bang! Ram!' He beat one fist into the other, his black leather figure pirouetting under the arc lamps — 'Why not two people copulating on the stage?'

He paused dramatically, grinning up at the cameras, and the big girl behind Magnus shouted: 'That's right, give us the great Ram, Garth!'

There was a cheering and stamping of feet, with less than three minutes to go now. Scammell yelled: 'Death, blood — they're O.K., they're decent — but just show a girl screaming in childbirth, writhing under the rusted knitting needle, and you get every little Sunday car polisher up and down the country dashing off letters to the press, his M.P....'

The girl behind Magnus leant over and whispered loudly, 'Give us a purp, darling!' Magnus looked up again at the cameras. It must be almost over now. *My God*, he thought, *Winters must be holding his breath*, as Scammell went on: 'That's why we've got censorship! To protect the little man, the Sunday car washer, the man who doesn't want to know. The man who hates the truth about war, dying, sex. And why does he hate the truth? Because he's frightened of it!'

At that moment Magnus glanced sideways and saw a face in the curtained doorway just below him. He heard Scammell shouting: 'Censorship is Hitlerism!' And even under the heat of the arc lamps, he felt a chill up his spine. The man in the doorway was the pudgy balding figure of Jan Steiner; he stood only a few feet away from Maya, looking at his watch.

'Every time you watch a lousy television commercial!' Scammell cried, 'you're helping Hitlerism! Every time you give your wife a bad orgasm, you're helping Hitlerism!'

Steiner was gone. Magnus looked up and saw the technicians bustling about the cameras. Only a few seconds to go now, and Scammell was putting everything into them: 'The only way to break the circuit of fear and inhibition is to confront these little people with the truth — confront them with sex in all its awful detail!'

There was a sudden electric silence, followed by a gasp from all over the hall.

Later Magnus marvelled at how it had been done. She had slipped out of her seat and vaulted on to the stage before either Platt or Scammell could realise what was happening. The cameras must have covered all three. The next moment she had unfastened her raincoat and let it drop round her ankles.

She was naked — a nakedness made more shockingly exciting by her dark glasses and high-heeled shoes.

She stood facing the cameras for perhaps three seconds, her nipples poised like bullseyes against perfect breasts, the triangle of pelvic hair wine-red between the faint strip of a bikini mark. Then she turned, her long back and high buttocks shining like marble under the lamps, and bent down to pick up her raincoat. There was another gasp from the audience before she leaped off the stage, up the aisle and through the curtained door where Steiner had been lurking a moment earlier.

Then pandemonium broke loose. Platt was vainly appealing for quiet, and Scammell just stood there, trying to decide what would be the most suitable reaction. He was not used to having his fire drawn in this way.

Magnus allowed the shock to immobilise him for only a few seconds; then he did what no one else in the hall seemed to have thought of. He pursued Maya. He was delayed for perhaps ten seconds, striking his way ruthlessly over the legs beside him, then darted down the aisle and through the curtained door.

A few people noticed him, and he heard them applauding as he swung his bad leg down the two flights of stairs to the outside door, which was ajar. He crashed it open and ran out into the dusk. Under the trees, about a hundred feet away, a car door slammed and an engine started up with a howl. It looked like a sports car, but he could not see who was driving, or whether there were two people in it or one. The next moment it snarled away under the trees and was gone.

He slowed painfully to a halt. Behind him a small group had gathered by the side door. One cried: 'What happened? Where's she gone?'

Magnus returned, pushing his way between them without replying, hearing a man shout behind him, 'Who's that fellow?' as he leapt up the stairs, back into the hall.

Everyone seemed to be on their feet shouting. The batteries of lamps had been doused, but the microphones were still on and Platt was calling into them: 'All right! A very amusing diversion, and I'm sure the viewers appreciated it — but now please, let us get on with the Speak-In…!'

Magnus climbed round to the far side where the cameras had been stationed. A couple of technicians were dismantling the equipment. 'Where's Winters?' he asked. One of them pointed to the main stairs.

He found Winters outside the front entrance, lighting a cigarette. He was with his chief technician and a couple of journalists. 'Ah hullo, Magnus.' He smiled wearily. 'Well, there we are! We've had pubic hair on the small screen at last. I suppose it had to happen. After all, it took a bit of time to come through in painting. Who was the first one to break the ice?'

'Modigliani,' Magnus said, collecting his breath. 'And he upset a lot of people doing it. How much did you get of her?'

The journalists had their notebooks out. Winters gave a grim laugh: 'The whole bloody lot, old boy. No one's fault. We were all too busy watching the time signal coming up.' He smiled humourlessly. 'You can quote me. She had it timed to the second.' He flung away his cigarette and looked up at Magnus: 'Who was she, do you know?'

Magnus found a certain irony in the question. 'Not the faintest idea,' he said truthfully. 'Will there be a lot of trouble?'

'For me or old auntie B.B.C.? You tell me.' He was already fumbling for a new cigarette. 'We've had the old four-letter word, so I suppose it won't be so bad. But the clean-up-T.V.

people are going to have a ball.' Magnus lit his cigarette for him, as he added, 'It looked to me as though it was organised. Not just a prank — that girl knew what she was doing. And some girl!'

More people were crowding out of the door towards them. It looked as though the Speak-In was breaking up — not under any pressure, but because the audience had had their climax. Not even Garth Scammell could cap this little spectacle.

Winters said: 'I think it would be better if we waited for an official statement.' He looked helplessly at the reporters. 'There's nothing more I can say at the moment.'

The rest of them began to drift away, and he and Magnus walked round to where Winters had parked his car. 'Got any ideas, old boy?'

'Should I?'

'I'm only fishing. But it looks as though somebody's been having us on. It could be some extravagant joke. Or it could be somebody who just doesn't like the B.B.C. Perhaps the girl was a disappointed actress or dancer. Some of them'll do anything to get a spot on the telly. And my God, she did too!'

They walked in silence. If it hadn't been for the glimpse of that balding head in the doorway a few seconds before it had happened, Magnus would have treated the incident lightly enough; at least it provided him with copy for tomorrow's edition. But the momentary appearance of Mr Jan Steiner had given the whole incident a new, more sinister dimension.

He said to Winters: 'You mentioned that it might have been someone who didn't like the B.B.C. What made you say that?'

Winters shrugged. 'It's a sure way to put television back five years — if somebody wanted to do it. Anyway, I'll have to get back to the office and face the music. God knows what some of these mad Welsh bods are going to say about it! Can I give you a lift?'

'Thanks. I'd better get another word with Platt and the others.' He waved goodbye, feeling an uncomfortable sense of guilt. But even if he had told Winters about Steiner and the girl, what good would it do? He hadn't a shred of evidence, he didn't even know her name. All he did know was that she was no cheap stripper out for free publicity. She had done it in cold blood, and in deadly earnest. Magnus wondered why.

The town that night was full of furious speculation. They said it had been a student rag; an impromptu stunt by a rival channel; a private joke by Scammell and his friends. Later, the police confirmed that enquiries had been put in hand, but the Superintendent was evasive; the Reardon Smith Lecture Hall was a public place, and the incident might therefore constitute a breach of the peace. The Cardiff civil authorities were more outspoken. There was a chorus of resignations from the Festival Committee, followed by the threat of wholesale resignations from the Welsh B.B.C. Service whose switchboards had been jammed all evening by more than eight thousand calls of protest. Two local M.P.s announced that they intended to bring the matter up in the House; one public-spirited lady sent a telegram to the Prime Minister; and Peter Platt, while disclaiming all responsibility, thought it 'rather a giggle'.

Meanwhile, the one person in the whole drama who really mattered, and whom everyone wanted to interview, had vanished. Magnus had his own theories about her, but he kept them to himself, and that evening he dined alone in the Royal Hotel, drinking a bottle of wine and three brandies. When he left it was nearly midnight. He had thought of asking

Reception if they had a room for the night; but changed his mind at the last moment. Somewhere, among the events of the last two crazy days, there had to be a meaning, a motive; and he now had an exciting suspicion that the key to the whole plot — for plot it was, he now felt certain — might lie in that shabby little hotel on the other side of the railway tracks.

The front door was again unlocked, the same dim light over the desk. This time Tom Meredith was behind it, reading a book. He looked up at Magnus, then reached back and handed him his key. As he did so their eyes met, for a full five seconds. Magnus noticed how the man's were a grey-blue, strangely reminiscent of Skliros's, only less alert, less intelligent. Meredith would belong to the other ranks; an efficient thug who could be hired and let loose, to be swiftly brought to heel again.

He swung the key in his hand and said: 'Tom Meredith, isn't it? I saw you box once — for the Regent's Park Sporting Club.'

'Yeah?' The grey eyes were dead.

'You won,' Magnus said; and suddenly Meredith smiled. His teeth were tiny and very white, as though snipped out of orange pith, lighting up his long face with the animation of a Halloween mask. 'That's right — Mr Owen.'

Magnus nodded and was just turning, when Meredith added: 'I heard there was a spot o' trouble this evening? Some girl stripped starkers on the telly?' The Halloween smile was still there. 'Bloody cheek!'

Magnus looked at him for a moment, then shrugged: 'Goodnight, Mr Meredith.'

Meredith nodded, turning back to his book, and Magnus had just time to see the title, *Britain on the Brink*, by John Austen

Cane. As he came level with the lounge, he looked back and called: 'Where's the stair light?'

'End o' the passage on the left! You can't miss it.' His eyes did not look up from the book.

When Magnus reached his room, he again locked the door and wedged a chair under the handle. For some time he lay in bed, his head whirring with wine and bewilderment. The darkness was disturbed by visions of Maya's body, big-breasted, deep-buttocked, slipping away from him now as he lay listening to the groaning of water pipes and trains passing in the night: seeing girls in dark glasses bending down in all their vulnerable nudity, while Peter Platt called for quiet and the mob closed in.

He woke suddenly. An angry voice cried, 'Go screw yourself!' — and there was a peal of laughter. Someone slipped with a crash and a girl called breathlessly, 'Ah c'mon, for Chrissakes!' then giggled, and the first voice shouted again: 'Sally-Jay baby, I'm gonna screw you tonight like you never been screwed before!'

Magnus blinked and sat up, as the girl answered playfully, 'You're too goddam drunk to screw anybody, Chuck!' The voices were outside his door now; more footsteps came clattering down the corridor and Garth Scammell's voice rang out, 'I'm stoned! I'm stoned! I'm blind!'

'You're stoned, baby! But you're still beautiful!' It was Bernie Berliner's voice this time, as the door to the next room banged open. 'Blind out of my mind!' Scammell sang. 'How's that for music?'

The door slammed shut; but the voices and laughter carried on, muffled through the wall beside Magnus's bed. He looked at his watch: nearly half-past two. He was pondering the wisdom of making further acquaintance with Messrs Berliner,

Scammell and Company, when he heard more footsteps down the passage, then a loud knock next door, followed by a familiar voice: 'You people know what time it is?'

There was sudden silence in the next room. The harsh Cardiff accent carried clearly through the walls. 'I can hear you from right downstairs!' Somebody murmured something and Meredith snapped: 'What did you say? Say that again!'

Magnus switched on the light and leapt out of bed, as several voices now began shouting next door. He could hear the girl calling: 'Hey, it's all right — now leave 'em alone!'

Magnus was pulling on his trousers, kicking on his shoes without bothering about his socks, dragged the chair from under the door handle and stepped into the passage.

Meredith's tall back filled the lighted doorway of the next room. Bernie Berliner, Garth Scammell and the girl with the ponytail were in the background, while the Great Destroyer, Chuck Ortiz, stood just inside, facing up to Meredith, squaring his shoulders in their T-shirt, his eyes slightly red under his low brow.

Meredith swung round, saw Magnus and nodded, as though he had been expecting him: 'You heard the bloody racket up here?'

Magnus looked at him levelly: 'You've got thin walls in this hotel. I could hardly help hearing it.'

'I bet you couldn't.' He turned back to Chuck Ortiz. 'You feel like repeating what you said just now?'

'Oh forget it!' the girl cried behind them.

'I don't feel like forgetting anything,' Meredith said, balling his fists; and as Magnus watched he was aware of an acrid bitter-sweet smell from inside the room. Meredith did not move. 'You called me a bastard just now,' he said, to Chuck Ortiz.

'Forget it!' Berliner shouted, his white face peering nervously round Ortiz's shoulder; but the big man waved him back, and took a step towards Meredith.

'Don't push me, buster! So we were makin' a bit o' whoopee! So we disturbed the gentleman next door! So we say we're sorry, huh! So will you get your arse out o' here! We got a lady here and she don't like snoopin' bell-hops.'

Meredith did not move. 'You've got more than a lady in here,' he said at last: 'You've got a funny smell too.'

'What?'

Meredith sniffed loudly, then laughed: 'I think you boys have been smoking something in here.'

'What!' They all moved closer. Chuck Ortiz flexed his big shoulders, then lunged out and hit Meredith hard in the face. The impact was drowned by his voice: 'You great motherin' bastard!'

Meredith rolled with the blow, jerking his head slightly to one side, steadied himself, took a step forward, measured Chuck Ortiz, and hit him twice, very quickly, with a jab of his right fist, bringing up his left from below, and the Great Destroyer gave one grunt and went down with a crash. The girl began to scream and Meredith took another step forward, both fists ready.

The girl screamed again, 'Oh for God's sake, stop it!' She started forward, as Ortiz rolled over and kicked upwards at Meredith's groin.

But at the last split-second Meredith stepped sideways and grabbed Ortiz's foot, giving it a quick twist, and the man on the floor screamed — almost indistinguishable from the girl's scream — and flopped back on his stomach, moaning.

The girl then went for Meredith with both hands flailing. He took her round the waist and swung her round, backwards, while she went on screaming: 'Somebody get the police, for Christ's sake! He's crazy!'

'It's me who's going to be getting the police,' Meredith said, and pushed her back against Berliner, who stood white-faced in the middle of the room.

He now turned to Magnus. 'You smell it? They've been smoking pot in here! Right in my hotel. Would you believe it? I'm getting the police — right now, I'm getting them!'

'Wait!' The girl ran forward again, but Meredith was already striding back down the passage. She turned to Magnus, her prettiness gone, her face streaked with tears. 'Oh Jesus, he's crazy! We haven't been smoking pot! He's just crazy! You see what he did just now to Chuck?'

But Garth Scammell pushed her aside. He gave Magnus a long stare from behind his wrap-around dark glasses. 'So what the hell are you doing here, Owen? You in on this too?'

Magnus looked stonily back at him. 'You woke me up, Mr Scammell. You were making a lot of noise.'

'You saw what happened,' Scammel said, he seemed quite sober. 'You'll back us up?'

Magnus nodded: 'Yes, I saw what happened. I saw your friend hit the porter, and the porter hit him back. Right?'

He glanced down at Chuck Ortiz, who still lay curled on the floor nursing his foot, when Bernie Berliner gave a shout:

'Hey, look at this!' He was holding up an ashtray spilling over with thin squashed cigarette stubs. 'These weren't here before! We ain't been back here since yesterday.' He leant down and sniffed them: 'Jesus, that bastard's planted them!' He came forward, holding out the ashtray as though it might explode in his hand. 'This isn't ours! We never smoked the stuff in here!'

He turned his small brown eyes towards Magnus, and repeated imploringly: 'I tell you we never smoked the stuff! None of us have been back here all day.'

Magnus looked down at the ashtray and said: 'Is that stuff pot?'

'Jesus, it's not ours!'

'How did it get there, then?'

Chuck Ortiz was beginning to climb to his feet, bleeding from the mouth. The girl led him to the basin and ran the tap. Scammell came over beside Berliner and said to Magnus: 'I don't know what the hell this is all about — but you've got to help us. Go and see if that nut downstairs really did go for the police.'

'He went for them all right,' Magnus said quietly; and Berliner looked at him and nodded, still holding the ashtray. 'Then we'd better get rid of these things quick,' he said. 'They're not ours — we didn't put them here.' He was already walking towards the window.

'They've been planted on us,' Scammell said. 'That big bastard down there planted them on us! Who did you say he was?'

'He's the night porter,' Magnus said.

Berliner reached the window, paused, and started back across the room. 'I'm going to put this stuff down the can!'

'I wouldn't do that if I were you,' Magnus said.

Berliner stared at him, beginning to sweat. 'Why the hell not? This stuff's not ours, I'm telling you!'

'The night porter saw it — and so did I.'

'Bloody Press!' Scammell yelled: 'It's always the same with you bastards, you love a bit of dirt, love to see people in the shit, don't you?' He took a step forward. 'I ought to block your mouth, Owen!'

'Try,' Magnus said.

At that moment Meredith returned. His face held the grave but satisfied expression of a job well done; and then he saw Berliner holding the ashtray. 'Oh no you don't! That's hotel property. And what's in is police property. Put it back!'

'You called the police?' Berliner cried.

'Bloody right I did!' Meredith looked at Chuck Ortiz, who was drying his face on a towel. 'You're lucky, boy! I don't like people who try to kick me in the balls. It's as well for you I was on duty, or I might have hurt you.'

Ortiz muttered something through swollen lips, and the girl said softly: 'You'd better sit down, Chuck.' She helped him over to the bed and sat down beside him. Meredith was still holding the ashtray when the police arrived.

There was a uniformed sergeant, a constable, and a florid man in a tweed jacket who stomped in, paused, then bawled: 'Right! — what's been going on here?'

'Drugs,' said Meredith, nodding down at the ashtray. 'Indian hemp, I'd say.' They were all looking at him. 'I used to work down in the docks and there was some boys there — coloured they were — that smoked it. That's how I know the smell,' he added; and Magnus had to admire the way he covered his tracks.

The florid man stepped up and took it from him, sniffed at it and handed it to the sergeant. 'We'll be needing that. Now!' He looked them all over quickly, his eyes resting last on Magnus, as Meredith said: 'He's the guest next door. Woken up by the noise.'

The girl stepped forward and cried: 'He'll tell you what happened!'

'You'll all tell me what happened,' the big man said cheerfully. 'Let's have your names.' The sergeant already had his notebook out. 'Now, who's in this room?'

Berliner gestured towards Chuck Ortiz and gave their names. The detective eyed them both disapprovingly. 'Bernard Berliner? I've heard of you, haven't I? You're the one with the exhibition?' He did not sound like one of Berliner's fans. 'All right, and who's in the next room? You two?' He glanced at Scammell, then at the girl.

'Are you charging us?' Scammell cried.

The detective smiled. 'I'll charge the bloody lot of you if you don't give me your names double-quick.'

It was the girl who did so. When she gave Scammell's name, the detective nodded again and said: 'Oh yes, I've heard of you too, haven't I? You haven't by any chance got that stripper in here, have you?' He glanced suspiciously at the girl, then turned to Chuck Ortiz: 'What's the matter with your face?'

'That bastard of a porter hit me!' Ortiz mumbled.

'Oh yes? Is that right?' He turned to Meredith.

'In self-defence, sir. He hit me first, and I had to hold him off. Then I'm afraid he tried to kick me when he was on the floor, sir. The guest here will confirm that.'

The detective looked at them all thoughtfully, then turned to the sergeant: 'I think you'd better take 'em back to the station, sarge. Get full statements made. I'll stay and have a look round.'

The sergeant took a step forward and the girl cried, 'Are you arresting us?'

'We just want you to come along to the station, miss.'

'All of us? We haven't done anything! Those cigarettes aren't ours! They were planted there! They weren't here before, I swear on Christ they weren't here before!'

'Yes all right, we'll sort that out at the station.'

'But we haven't done anything!' She began to sob. 'That man just barged in and picked a fight here with Chuck, and he hit him in the face and twisted his ankle when he was on the floor!'

'Yes, all right,' the big man said patiently. 'Now come on. You can explain it all at the station.' He looked at Magnus, then back at Meredith. 'He was just next door, was he?'

'That's right, sir,' Meredith said.

The detective looked at Magnus and nodded. 'I'd just like to take a brief statement from you here, if you don't mind, sir.' He turned to the constable: 'Have a look round in the next room. The porter here'll go with you.'

The sergeant was already shepherding the others into the passage. The girl was weeping, Berliner dumb and quivering. As aliens they had more to fear than Garth Scammell, who turned at the door and snarled: 'You're making a bad mistake — all of you! Don't think I'm going to take a frame-up from a lot of Fascist fuzz!'

'Take him out, sergeant!' the detective roared, and the sergeant pushed Scammell through the door, with Meredith and the constable following. The detective turned, glowering at Magnus: 'Your name?'

Magnus told him, but did not mention *The Paper*.

'Just a visitor, are you, Mr Owen? You know any of those clowns?'

'Only by reputation.'

'What happened?'

Magnus repeated what he had seen, remembering not to refer to Meredith by name.

The detective sat down on the bed and took out his notebook. 'Just an ordinary scuffle, eh? Open and shut, I'd say, unless this fellow Orteeze tries to bring a charge of assault against the porter. You never know with these foreigners, they can be bloody crafty sometimes, if they get a good lawyer.'

He sat writing in ponderous longhand, until the door opened and Meredith and the constable came back from the next room. The constable was holding something wrapped in newspaper, which he began to unfold carefully on the bed beside the detective. Inside was a pile of what looked like dried grass. 'Found it in the bedside drawer, sir.'

The detective stood up. 'Better take it all back to the station and charge the four of them.' Magnus noticed that the newspaper was the *International Times*. So they thought of everything, right down to the last perfect detail.

The detective handed his notebook to Magnus. 'I've just written that you were awakened by excessive noise during the night, Mr Owen, and that you then witnessed a dispute between the night porter and Mr Orteeze, and saw Mr Orteeze strike a blow at Mr Meredith, to which he retaliated in self-defence. You also observed Mr Berliner pick up the ashtray full of smoked cigarette stubs. The ashtray was in the room when you entered. Now, if you'd just sign there, sir. And put your address. You live in London, I suppose?'

Magnus wrote his address in Battersea. 'Is it a serious charge?'

'That'll be up to the Court, sir. Not for me to comment. Goodnight, sir. I'm sorry you were disturbed.'

Magnus and Meredith watched him return down the passage to the stairs. Meredith did not move. Magnus turned: 'A good night's work, Mr Meredith.'

Meredith nodded, expressionless. 'I'm glad you were around, Mr Owen. If they'd all decided to go for me I could've been in trouble.'

'I don't think so. Remember, I've seen you fight before. You're good. You're damned good.'

'Thank you, Mr Owen. Well, it's late, so I'll be getting along. Goodnight.'

Magnus went back to his room and closed the door. But he no longer bothered to lock it or wedge the handle. Tom Meredith's job was done.

CHAPTER 5

There was a dead thump as the medicine ball came rumbling towards them across the coconut matting. Cane skipped clear, but Magnus, with his bad leg, was not quick enough and it caught him a painful blow on the ankle.

'Careful with that thing!' Cane shouted, as a young man in a tracksuit bounded up to retrieve the ball.

'Sorry about that, Colonel Cane.' He ignored Magnus, who had stopped to rub his ankle, while Cane strode on round the indoor swimming pool and sat down in one of the canvas chairs opposite the diving board. Magnus limped up and took the seat beside him. Cane smiled. 'Well, how was Cardiff?'

'You were reading *The Paper*?'

'As always. I thought your stuff was first-rate.'

Magnus watched a young man in bathing trunks climb to the high board, balance himself with his heels over the edge, then swoop backwards and disappear with hardly a splash in the green luminous water.

'Oh well done!' Cane cried; and there was a rustle of applause from a number of other men down the row of chairs.

Magnus waited till it was over, then said: 'It was such wonderful material. I just couldn't miss.'

'You've got something on your mind. Tell me about it.'

Magnus hunched his shoulders, watching the next diver hit the water with a clumsy smack. 'Ah come on, John. We've been through the introductions. We did the groundwork last time, remember? Now we're in business.'

Cane's face showed no expression. 'Go on,' he said quietly.

'I congratulate you on Tom Meredith. He's good — damn good! Except for one small detail.'

'Yes?'

'I caught him reading one of your books, John. Careless — especially if someone had been snooping. But otherwise it was a beautiful piece of contingency planning. I congratulate you.'

'You flatter me.'

Magnus grinned: 'As an ex-colonel of Military Intelligence? No, I just think you did a very successful job. But now I want you to come clean, John. What's it all about?'

It was some moments before Cane replied. He sat watching another group of youths in bathing trunks appear at the far end of the pool and spread out in squatting positions along the edge. A whistle blew and there was a multiple splash. Cane's voice was soft but tense: 'What exactly do you want to know?'

'The truth. Next week I'm going down to Cardiff again to give evidence for the prosecution on a drug charge. Whatever I say isn't going to make much difference — not alongside the police and young Meredith — but I'm still not very happy about it.'

Cane raised his eyebrows: 'Your conscience troubling you?' Magnus laughed grimly: 'Oh, nothing so delicate. Don't think I'm going to lose any sleep if Scammell and his friends spend a few months behind bars. In fact, I'd be pretty surprised if they didn't smoke pot — at the very least.'

'Then what is worrying you?'

'I know I can't prove anything — you made damn certain of that! But I'm not fool enough to think we all found ourselves in that dump of a hotel last week just by chance. We were put there.'

Cane said nothing.

'All right, let me spell it out for you, John. I was put into the hotel last week for a purpose. You wanted to test me — find out if I fell for your little plot, then see how I reacted. You'd probably nobbled the big hotels and made sure Scammell's party didn't get any rooms, then when you found out where they were finally booked in, you got that upstanding lad Meredith to apply for the job of night porter. The rest was plain sailing. I'm going into court next week to say my piece — say I saw Chuck Ortiz assault Meredith, and that Meredith hit back in self-defence — and then confirm his story about finding the ashtray full of smoked reefers. There's no problem of conscience — I'll be telling the truth.'

'So what is worrying you?' Cane said again.

'The person who booked me into the hotel. Hugh Rissell.'

'Rissell?' Cane frowned.

'The News Editor of *The Paper*?'

'*The Paper*?' he repeated woodenly.

Magnus nodded. 'The booking was done through his secretary, at the last moment. That's why they couldn't get me into one of the decent hotels — or so they told me. And that's why I'm worried.' For a moment he thought he saw a look of fear in Cane's face. 'I'm not quite with you, Magnus.'

'I'm talking about *The Paper*. I've got a good job with them, they pay me good money, and if in some way *The Paper*'s involved in all this, I want to know how and why.'

Cane's hand jerked up as though warding off a blow. 'Just a moment.'

'Not just a moment, Mr Cane. This is important to me. I want to know how Hugh Rissell knew about the Bute Hotel.'

'I don't know anything about this Mr Rissell. And that's the truth, Magnus.' His voice was still low and steady, but he was clearly troubled; and for the first time since they had met,

Magnus felt a curious psychological superiority. Cane had admitted nothing; and while their talks together had been suggestive, they have never been compromising. But now, with the mention of *The Paper*, all that had changed.

Magnus knew that Cane had now reached the moment of decision: he must either bring their dialogue to a close, denying all knowledge of what Magnus was trying to insinuate; or he must take a dangerous gamble and confide in him entirely.

For a long time he sat gazing down into the pool where the young men were competing with swift breast-strokes. These were his legions, part of a voluntary regiment of healthy-minded citizens dedicated to cleaning up Britain and the world.

When he spoke again, his words had a slow solemnity as though delivering a prepared speech: 'When you were in the Army, Magnus, did you ever try to query the orders of your superior officers?'

'Never. I was a blind obedient conscript.'

'But you would agree there are moments in the life of any soldier, especially in combat, when he must expect to receive orders which he does not understand, or with which he disagrees?'

Magnus sat very still, feeling his heart begin to race. 'It never happened to me.'

Cane nodded gravely. 'That is why I asked you, Magnus. Because in the next few weeks you may find yourself under combat orders, and when you do, don't try to seek an explanation.'

So this was it. Cane had decided to commit himself. The effort of decision showed clearly in his face: his eyes deep and weary, his breathing slow.

'I'm not suggesting that I don't trust you, my boy, but honesty is not an absolute virtue. We are a small organisation fighting terrible odds — against a huge amorphous enemy to whom honesty and fair play mean nothing.

'The sewer that flows under our public life — which for centuries, except for a few brief and miserable interludes, has succeeded in flowing underground — is now bursting out and swamping the decent life of our nation. This week that sewer was flowing broad and swift through Cardiff — though, God forbid, Cardiff didn't deserve it! We, as an organisation, weren't able to shut down the floodgates completely — all we could do, and did do, was drop in a few nets and pull up some of the sewer rats. You, Magnus, had the honour to be there when it was done.'

He was leaning out of his chair now, his face still gaunt, but his eyes smiling with a feverish inner light. 'I know what you're going to ask me. What about the law? Well, Magnus, the law is like honesty. Both have qualified values, and they must command qualified respect. We are at war. And in order to win that war, we cannot afford to be sentimental. We must be ruthless and steel ourselves to duties which may often be distasteful, even dangerous. For this is not a clean front-line war. The enemy have seen to that — they've called the type of fight it is to be. A dirty subversive guerrilla war. So we too must be guerrillas. Our tactics must be their tactics, our weapons their weapons — but turned against them, with a vengeance!'

He settled into his chair, and for a moment the tension seemed to leave him. The swimmers had gone, the rest of the spectators were drifting away. The baths were quiet now.

'You will be familiar,' Cane went on, 'with the elementary precautions that any secret organisation must take to protect itself against infiltration and exposure? Well, I have to admit that you find yourself in a somewhat privileged position.

Entirely on my own authority, and at my own discretion, I have allowed you to know more of our organisation than is normal at this stage. I have done this because I believe in you, Magnus. I believe that with a measure of restraint and guidance you would come to serve us — serve your country, indeed the whole of western civilisation — to an extent which you cannot at the moment fully appreciate. I have great hopes for you, and I would be a fool to pass you up out of some faint-hearted doubt.' He paused.

'There is one last thing, Magnus. If you want to opt out, it's not too late. If you have any doubts, any fears — tell me now.'

For a moment Magnus almost laughed in his face. He realised now that the man was not only mad, he was also dangerous. Yet in his madness there was a certain consistency. He had decided to trust Magnus, and nothing would now shake that decision. Whatever his other sins, Cane did not suffer from self-doubt.

Magnus, however, enjoyed no such serenity. As they walked back round the swimming pool, up the concrete stairs to the street, he felt a heaviness in his belly. Until now it had all been a game, an intriguing puzzle which had begun only lately to have sinister undertones. Magnus had played along out of idle curiosity; but in the last hour all that had changed.

By making him his confidant, Cane also made him an accomplice. Magnus was not sure what the crime would be — conspiracy? perjury? But worst of all, he was no longer sure which side he was on. Certainly not the Nesbitts and Scammells and Berliners. But that didn't mean he was on Cane's side either, along with Pym and Sir Lionel Hilder and clean young thugs like Meredith. Of only one thing he was sure — that he had gone this far, and it was his duty, moral duty now, to see the thing through.

They walked out into the square near Regent's Park. Cane stopped beside him, watching him closely. 'Well, any last questions?'

'Yes — the girl. Who is she, John?'

Cane shook his head. 'No, Magnus. There are some things…'

'And Steiner?' He felt a nerve jerk in his bad leg, and as though to support him Cane gripped his arm, squeezing slightly.

'I'm sorry, Magnus. I've told you enough already. To tell you too much at this point would not only be foolish, but dangerous for yourself, as much as for us.' He started down the street, still holding him by the arm. 'You're a fine journalist, Magnus, but for goodness sake, do watch that demon drink!'

Magnus stopped short. 'Drink?' he muttered.

Cane nodded gravely. 'It's the little weaknesses, my boy. From small failings grow great failures.'

For the second time that afternoon Magnus almost burst out laughing. To switch from criminal conspiracy to the language of a Victorian temperance play was a thing not to be taken seriously; yet Cane was serious.

'You may not think it any of my business, but your weaknesses are now our weaknesses. And don't tell me you haven't been drinking. Down in Cardiff — I've been hearing stories, you know.' Magnus walked on, nodding slowly. They had spied on him once before — a shabby little fellow who had passed himself off as the gas man. At least the second time he had enjoyed more sophisticated attention. He took a deep breath. 'So it was the girl?'

Cane said nothing.

'I don't like snoopers, John.'

'That's our privilege.' He waved at a cruising taxi. 'Want a lift?' But suddenly Magnus wished to be rid of him. 'I'll walk.'

Cane paused as the taxi drew up. 'Remember what I told you. When there's something for you to know, you'll be told in good time. You must trust us, Magnus. We trust you.' He climbed in, and Magnus heard him give the address of Albany.

He waited till the taxi was out of sight, then headed for the nearest pub.

PART 2: FRAME-UP

CHAPTER 1

The Air France Caravelle boomed down through the dusk, its jets sweeping up drifts of rain as it taxied round the apron to where the bus came crawling out from the Europa terminal.

The first-class passengers were released from a door close to the nose, descending past the toothpaste smile of the air hostess. The last of them emerged some moments later. He was a tall young man with a shelf of dark blond hair that flopped over his eyes, his jaw rough with several days' stubble. He wore skin-tight jeans, faded almost white round the buttocks and knees, scuffed leather boots and an open-necked checkered shirt.

The steward came out behind him, holding his LOT overnight bag, helping him on with a lumber jacket, as they began to manoeuvre their way down the steps. The young man seemed to be having difficulty articulating his legs. By the time they reached the tarmac the air hostess from the first-class compartment had retreated to join her companion, who was seeing the tourist passengers out of the tail of the plane.

The young man splashed through the puddles to the bus, steadied himself against the door, then very deliberately spat on to the tarmac below the steps. The steward came up quickly behind him and pushed him aboard, hurrying him into a seat against the window.

A girl in uniform got on, holding up a grey card. 'Will all passengers not holding a British passport please complete this form for Immigration.'

The young man looked at her and grinned. He had a long slack mouth and thick eyebrows that were startlingly dark under his blond hair. His eyes were grey and fierce, spoilt only by an orange glare at the corners. The steward, who had taken special charge of him on the plane, had filled in his Immigration card, as well as holding his passport for him.

For most of the fifty-five minutes' flight from Orly, passenger Krok had been reasonably well behaved. It was only when the signal flashed up for fastening seat belts before the descent over Heathrow, that he had begun to grow troublesome. He would not fasten his belt, insisting that the stewardess did it for him; then, as she bent down to do so, had pressed a wet kiss on to the nape of her neck. (The steward had already noted, with some misgiving, that passenger Krok had taken liberal advantage of the free champagne offered to first-class passengers, making up a fair portion of the difference in price between a tourist ticket and his own — which he had not had to pay for in the first place.)

The bus doors closed and they began to move. For a time the young man peered through the misty window, then rested his head on the back of the seat and began to sing. He had a rich bass and the song he sang was a tragic Slavonic love song, bellowed through the packed silence, his eyes closed, his neck muscles bulging and quivering, while the steward sat poker-faced beside him, waiting anxiously for the bus to stop.

They were again the last to leave. It was 6.45 when passenger Krok climbed the ramp to the two segregated entrances marked 'British Passports Only' and 'Foreign and Commonwealth Passports'. It was here that the steward's responsibility ended and he gratefully handed over his charge to an airport official who would accompany the young man through Immigration and Customs, then on to the V.I.P. press lounge.

The official looked him uneasily up and down, then smiled timidly, deciding at the last moment not to offer him his hand. The young man was flexing his fingers in rather an odd manner, and his mouth was stretched back in a grimace of mock pain. 'Mr Krok? Hope you had a good journey.'

Krok hung his head and belched.

'Is something wrong?' the official asked.

'I am non-British,' Krok said. 'Does that mean a non-person? An un-person?' He looked up and glared dangerously. 'And if I had a British wife? She would go through a different door — she would be segregated, I think?' His voice was surprisingly steady, but with a heavy accent.

The last of the foreign passengers had passed through Immigration, and it was now Krok's turn to move up to the desk. The airport official simpered nervously: 'No, no! It's just a formality, Mr Krok — it hurries things up, you see.'

Krok seemed mollified by this explanation, and passed obediently up to the Immigration Officer, a young man in a blazer who examined the Polish passport with some interest, noting the details of Pan Bogdan Krok, born in Warsaw 1936, Profession Author and Film Director. His visa was in order, and he did not ask any questions; arrangements had been made to hurry Bogdan Krok through as smoothly as possible.

He stamped the passport, and Krok and his escort passed into the lounge to wait for the baggage to come up. Krok sat down in morose silence, swinging his hands between his knees. The airport official kept his distance until they were called through into the Customs hall.

Here the formalities proved less pliable. The Customs men, disguised as naval officers, moved down the benches performing their polite inquisition, warning of the penalties for smuggling, opening suitcases, feeling through clothes, lifting out books and bottles. By the time Bogdan Krok was approached he was showing impatience.

The officer was a sallow man with a clipped moustache. The airport official handed him Krok's passport, and he took his time leafing through it, while Krok began kicking his boot noisily against the bench. After a moment the airport official murmured: 'Mr Krok is being met outside in the V.I.P. lounge.'

The Customs man seemed unimpressed. He closed the passport at last, handed it back to Krok and said, 'Is this all your luggage, sir?' On the bench in front of him stood a battered leather holdall and the LOT overnight bag. Bogdan Krok nodded and went on kicking the bench.

'Have you read this?'

Krok looked at the plastic notice behind the man's shoulder, and shrugged. 'No, I haven't got anything.'

'Will you read this notice, please.'

Bogdan shrugged again, without looking at the notice.

'Please read it,' said the man.

Bogdan Krok squinted at it for a moment, drew in his breath, and began to read it, aloud, in his ringing bass: 'H.M.'s Customs and Excise…!' He had stepped back, his left arm flung out in the pose of a Victorian actor declaiming: 'All articles purchased abroad…!'

'That's enough, sir!' the Customs man snapped, his cheeks reddening.

Bogdan Krok's audience consisted of perhaps a hundred other passengers — all now looking in his direction — as his Slavonic bass bellowed on: 'Tobacco, spirits, perfume…!' He swung round, pausing dramatically; and as he did so, the Customs man noticed his right hand — a thumb and single forefinger tapering from his wrist into a fleshy prong.

'The penalties for smuggling are severe!' Krok roared, oblivious of the hubbub of voices round him; then saw the Customs man looking at his hand. He stopped and gave a bellow of laughter.

The man bent his head and began busily opening the holdall. It was stuffed with old clothes, a half-empty bottle of Rémy Martin, piles of paperbacks in Polish and French, a loose razor and a hot-water bottle. While the Customs man was looking through the books, Krok lifted out the bottle, uncorked it and drank greedily. The officer looked very angry, but said nothing.

People were still staring as Krok was finally shown through to the main hall, stumbling head and shoulders above most of the crowd, into the V.I.P. reception lounge.

A thickset balding man advanced towards him, smiling: '*Dobry wieczór, Panie Krok!*' He turned to a glossy little man in a pearl-grey tie: 'This is Mr Loman, who is responsible for the publicity of Satellite Films, Pan Krok.' His accent was faint, but familiar. 'I am Jan Steiner — East-West Cultural Association. We are honoured to be at your service during your stay in Britain, Pan Krok.' He held out his hand, and Krok took it with his left, showing ill-concealed distaste.

He had lived for more than two decades under Communist rule, and he recognised the type — probably of German extraction from the Western Territories, stolid and impersonal, with that flat Teutonic accent.

'Mr Loman has made all the arrangements,' Steiner explained, and Loman added: 'I hope you're not too tired after your journey, Mr Krok, but we've arranged a press conference for you. It's to catch the morning papers. Then afterwards we'll take you on to dinner. Will that be all right?'

'I'm drunk,' Krok said.

There was a moment's silence. Loman cleared his throat and chuckled: 'Well never mind, we'll get you some coffee.'

'Get me some cognac. Good French cognac!' Steiner murmured something in Polish, and Krok glared. The airport official took advantage of this exchange to withdraw; he did not envy the task ahead for either Mr Steiner or Mr Loman.

Loman, meanwhile, had slipped away to the bar, and now returned with a moderate measure of brandy which Krok disposed of in one swallow. The three then made their way through the lounge, into a bright stuffy room with perforated walls and rows of steel-tubed chairs. There were about a dozen journalists present, already equipped with a handout listing Krok's achievements, prepared by Loman's publicity department.

An orphan from the war, he had started work in the mines, then drifted into the Polish Merchant Marine. Later, after the 'thaw' of 1956, he had won a place in the Film School at Lodz. He had since made two international prize-winning films, the latest of which, 'The Tram', was about to open in London. It was known to have run into opposition from the Polish authorities, and only after a good deal of manoeuvring had it reached the West.

Loman's handout was succinct, but omitted the more lurid episodes of Bogdan Krok's biography, such as a six-month spell of imprisonment in 1961 for assault with a broken bottle in a Warsaw bar; and later, his short-lived marriage to one of Poland's leading film actresses, which had driven him one evening to slice off half his hand with a meat cleaver, then walk five kilometres through the snow, almost bleeding to death, before seeking asylum in a Catholic hermitage on the outskirts of Crakov. The dramatics of his private life, combined with the irreverence of his work, had established him as the idol of Polish youth; but not so of Poland's leaders.

Loman now led him to a chair at the end of the room facing the journalists. Only one of these had shown any excitement when the group entered; but it was not at Krok that he was now looking, but at his balding escort who remained standing by the door.

Magnus Owen had known that eventually Jan Steiner would reappear. It was ten days now since Bernie Berliner and Chuck Ortiz had been fined £250 and deported, and Garth Scammell — who had a previous conviction on a drug charge — had been sent to prison for nine months. Magnus, meanwhile, had received no further word from Cane since their last meeting at the baths of the Regent's Park Sporting Club; but he had been told that sooner or later, in their own time and their own way, the organisation would make contact. Steiner was the signal.

The conference began with a formal introduction by Loman. Krok listened restlessly, twisting his fingers together and staring at the ceiling.

The first question came from a smartly-dressed woman critic with a great deal of lacquered hair. 'Mr Krok, do you have any plans to make a film in England?'

Krok hunched his huge shoulders, and looked at her with half-closed eyes. 'I want to go to Hollywood.'

'Hollywood?' She sounded a little dismayed. Western progressive film circles held Krok in high esteem.

'I want to make a million dollars,' he said mournfully, 'then maybe I go back to Poland, or maybe I go to South Africa.'

There was a puzzled silence; then a leading film critic asked judiciously: 'May we ask, why South Africa, Mr Krok?'

Bogdan grinned like a cat. 'Because I want to be able to walk through a door marked "Whites Only" instead of one of your bloody doors in London Airport saying "Foreign Passports Only".'

There was some polite laughter and the woman with the lacquered hair said: 'Now seriously, Mr Krok —'

'I can't be serious, madam. I'm just a stupid Polish peasant boy.'

The woman gave a coy laugh, and went on: 'You've won prizes at Venice and Cannes, but I understand your films have also run into a certain amount of official criticism in Poland. Can you comment on this?'

Krok did not answer at once. He spent several moments groping in the hip pocket of his jeans, and finally pulled out a slim grey booklet which he began waving above his head. 'Oh I'm a national hero in Poland! Our beloved People's Government even gave me a passport so I could leave!'

The next question came from Magnus: 'Mr Krok, does that mean you intend to defect to the West?'

There was a moment's silence; then Loman, who had been standing with his hands folded on his stomach, stepped forward: 'I don't think Mr Krok need answer that question.'

Krok turned to him: 'Get me a cognac.'

Loman blinked with surprise. 'Get me a cognac!' Krok roared, and Loman nodded and hurried down the side of the room towards the lounge.

Krok sat scratching his stubble. 'Why should I defect?' he said at last. 'They love me in Poland!'

'Do you have any comment,' Magnus persisted, 'on the recent personal attack made on you in Warsaw by General Roman Morowski, suggesting that you be deprived of your Polish citizenship?'

Krok glared down at him with eyes like hot coals. 'When did Morowski say this?'

'Last week, at a speech to the Warsaw Academy of Political Science.'

'I was in Paris last week,' Krok said, scowling. 'I didn't hear about it. What did he say?'

Magnus glanced at his notebook. 'He called you — and I quote — "an agent of degenerate Western culture whose disciples are the beat-bands and hooligans who do not wash or cut their hair, and who have no place in Socialist Poland".'

Krok put his head back and let out an empty laugh. 'General Morowski is a Russian dog! He is not a true Pole. He is like one of Pavlov's dogs — when Moscow shouts, Morowski jumps! He is a —' he snapped his fingers, searching for the word '— as we say in Polish, *kurva!*'

Steiner, standing impassively at the back of the room, made no effort to interpret. Then, as though to break the tension generated by the last question, the woman with the lacquered hair said:

'Mr Krok, as a leading member of the Polish younger generation do you have any message for the youth of this country?'

Krok grinned, as Loman came padding back with a glass of brandy. He took it without a word and stood up: 'Madam, I give you this message for the British youth. When you drink, don't fuck! When you fuck, don't drink!' He emptied the glass in a gulp and sat down.

There was a loud titter round the room; but the woman critic was disconcerted. She had been expecting something rather more intellectual of Krok. In a last attempt to bring him back to serious matters, she asked: 'Mr Krok, can you tell us anything at all about your ambitions for the future?'

Slowly, as though uncoiling himself from the chair, Krok rose to his full height — careful to keep his right hand out of sight — swayed for a moment in the lights, then roared: 'My ambition, ladies and gentleman, is to ride down Piccadilly on a Soviet tank!'

The journalists laughed and scribbled in their notebooks, and Magnus's neighbour muttered, 'The man's arseholes!'

Magnus shrugged: 'Nothing to what he was like at a reception in Venice when he got down on all fours and ran round the room barking like a dog.'

Steiner, meanwhile, had moved up beside Krok and declaring the conference closed. He and Krok then disappeared through a side door, and Loman came forward to answer any further questions.

Magnus did not stay. What he really wanted to know about Bogdan Krok could not be answered by an ingratiating P.R. officer; and as he left the Europa building, walking through the rain to the car park, he sensed with weary despair that Krok would be next.

Jan Steiner was the contact, and behind Steiner was John Austen Cane.

It was after eleven o'clock. The story of Bogdan Krok's arrival had been written, sub-edited, passed by the legal department, typeset and locked into the machines. Any moment now the first editions would be on the streets, proclaiming with all the ponderous gravity of *The Paper* that Poland's leading film director wanted to ride down Piccadilly on a Soviet tank.

Magnus was tired. He reached the third floor, pausing to find his keys; then froze, feeling the sweat start up on his face and neck. There was a light under his door.

He stared at it, trying to reason clearly. He had left the flat that morning, and there had been no lights on then; the last girl to whom he had entrusted a key had drifted out of his life months ago; the only other person who had one was his char, and she only came in the morning once a week.

He remembered that long face, ghost-white in the chair against the wall; and he took out his keys, fitted them between his fingers in the form of a crude knuckle-duster, crept up to the door and listened.

From inside he could hear piano music — Chopin's sonatas played by Dinu Lipatti. It was an old record he had had since Cambridge, badly scratched — scarcely the sort of thing that would appeal to a man like Tom Meredith. Unless, of course, Cane had converted him. Cane was a music lover, he remembered, as he raised his free hand and knocked twice, loudly.

For a few seconds all he heard was the music; then a voice called cautiously: 'Who is that?'

'It's me, damn you!'

The door opened at once. 'Oh thank God!' She wiped the hair from her eyes and smiled. 'I thought you'd let yourself in. Have you lost your key?'

'No.' He showed her his fist with the improvised weapon. 'But since you've moved in, I thought it only polite to knock.' He walked ahead of her into the sitting room, noticing that it was conspicuously tidier than when he had left it that morning. He took off his coat and sat down. 'Right, now tell me how you got in, how long you have been here, and what you're doing here?'

'Would you like a drink? I saw you've got Polish vodka in the kitchen.'

He nodded: 'You get it — since you know where it is.'

So they were checking up again, he thought, as he watched her walk out of the room, moving beautifully under a plain skirt and black sweater. He tried to remember how she had looked under the television lamps, but the image was preposterous, unreal. He heard the refrigerator door slam and she was back with two thimble glasses and the frosted bottle of Vyborova. She held it up and smiled approvingly: 'I can see you know how to drink vodka. This bottle's so cold I can hardly hold it!'

She sat down on the floor near his chair, put the glasses down beside her and began to pour them to the brim with the icy spirit that flowed as viscous as oil. 'I didn't give myself one earlier, I thought I'd wait for you,' she added.

'You're very polite, Maya. Now answer my questions.'

'I came to talk to you.' She handed him his glass without looking at him. 'I owe you an apology for last time, running out on you like that.'

'You ran out twice — the last time getting away in a sports car, I think? I admired your act, by the way. I thought you came over very nicely.'

'Thank you.' She screwed up her face and stared at the ceiling.

'The police didn't get on to you?'

'No.'

'Who told you to do it? Steiner?'

She picked up her glass and turned it in the light, watching the vodka quivering on the rim. 'I hope you noticed,' she said, 'that I put all your records back in their covers? You spoil them if you leave them out. And I made your bed.' Her voice was controlled and detached. 'Do you have many girls up here?'

'Dozens. I keep a whole stable of them down near the Battersea Dogs' Home. Who told you to do it, Maya?'

She sipped her drink slowly. 'I can't tell you that. You didn't really expect me to, did you?'

He leant back and let out a moan. 'Oh God, we're back on the old see-saw! But if you don't want to tell me, don't! Just what's good for me, all in your own time. How did you get in?'

'I used a strip of celluloid under the lock. Anybody could have done it.'

'Why didn't you call me at *The Paper*?'

'I did, but you were out. You were at London Airport meeting Bogdan Krok. How was Bogdan?'

'Wild. You can read all about him tomorrow morning.'

'Did he make a fool of himself?'

'He was drunk.'

She nodded: 'He usually is. He won't be able to work over here even if he wants to. Nobody'll work with him. Back in Poland, at the Lodz studios, they had him on a cure during the whole of his last film.'

'From what he said this evening, I'd have thought the Communist authorities would have encouraged him to drink himself to death.'

She shrugged: 'He doesn't work for the Communists. You must know how it is in Poland — the number of true Polish Communists you could fit on the top of a London bus. Bogdan's a Party member, but that doesn't mean a thing. In the bad days before '56 it was the only way to survive.'

'You seem to know him very well?'

'I've met him.'

The Chopin record came to an end; Maya went over and changed it to Beethoven's Piano Sonata No. 7 in C Minor. 'You like the piano?' Magnus said.

'Would you prefer something else?'

'Cane sent you here tonight, didn't he?'

She sat back with her legs curled under her, absorbed by the music. 'I've never met Cane,' she said at last.

'Like hell you haven't!'

'I'm telling you, honestly.'

'Honestly?' He held out his glass. 'Let's have another, Maya. If it wasn't Cane, it was Steiner. Steiner told you to take your clothes off on the small screen, and you took them off. But you won't tell me why. Well, perhaps you'll tell me why you agreed to meet me for dinner that evening, then stood me up, and now break into my flat, and tidy everything up and make my bed, and then talk about Bogdan Krok as though he was a childhood chum?'

She refilled his glass and said, 'Perhaps I could ask you something. You know John Austen Cane. Why?'

The question took

him aback. She had laid so many puzzles that it never occurred to him that she might find something mysterious about his own behaviour. Her eyes were on him, her hand floating to the rhythm of the music. 'Well?'

'I'm a friend of Cane's. We've met a couple of times, that's all.'

'All?' She gave a hard little smile, and there was something in her eyes now that he had not seen before: a faint, growing contempt. 'What do you do when you meet? Talk? Talk about what, Mr Owen?'

He gave a helpless gesture which ended in a gulp of vodka, and she laughed cruelly: 'You talk about the sad state of Britain, don't you? About how decadent and degenerate you've all become, and how something will have to be done to put the old country back in order.'

'Like putting nudes on television,' Magnus murmured. 'Why did you stand me up in Cardiff?'

'I couldn't make it. If we'd been seen talking —'

'If who'd seen us talking?'

She shook her head. 'I couldn't, that's all.'

'Couldn't even leave a telephone message?'

'Oh God!' She cried, 'is it so serious? I'd like to have seen you, but I couldn't. That's all — I couldn't!'

He nodded. 'So you came here instead. Because you were told to come — by Jan Steiner.'

'It has nothing to do with Steiner!'

'Nor Cane?' He grinned at her discomfort. 'Or what about Sir Lionel Hilder? Or Mr Henry Deepe?'

She frowned: 'I've never heard of them.'

He looked at her closely, and for some reason he believed her. 'Sir Lionel Hilder's a big industrialist. An old man — a millionaire — probably writes Cane a blank cheque every now and again. Henry Deepe's another of Cane's friends. A civil servant — works in the Home Office.'

'One of those bastards!' She reached for her vodka. 'I can't stand government officials — even if they do have nice suburban titles like "civil servant". What was it Churchill said about them? That they're neither civil nor servants?'

'The Home Office!' she went on bitterly: 'In Poland we call it the Ministry of the Interior. Doesn't sound so nice, but at least it's more honest.'

'So you work for Steiner?' Magnus said at last.

'Not entirely.'

'Who then?'

'I teach in an infants' school up in Camberwell.'

He started to laugh: 'Oh that's beautiful, Maya! That's the best touch so far. A pretty young social worker who does amateur stripping on the telly, and a bit of spying on the side for John Cane and his friends.'

She seemed not to hear him, as she held the bottle out to refill his glass. But he shook his head. 'I'm sorry, Maya — I'm going to try and stay sober this time. I don't want you telling any more stories about the drunken Magnus Owen of *The Paper*. Now what have you come to talk about?'

'Bogdan Krok.' She watched him over her glass, the clear liquid trembling as she spoke. 'Leave him alone. Please!'

The Beethoven record ended and the gramophone switched itself off. The room became very quiet.

'What are they going to do to Krok?' he asked, in a dull voice.

'I don't know yet. Please believe me, I don't!'

'So what have I got to do with it?' he asked, feeling her fingertips on his knee. 'All I did was ask him some questions at London Airport today.'

'Oh God!' There was suddenly a bleak stricken look in her eyes, like a terrified child. 'You can't be so stupid! You know what's going on! You knew what was going on before you went to Wales. What did you think it was all for? Some charade put on to give you a good story for *The Paper*?' She was leaning forward, both hands on his knee now, all control gone. 'Magnus, just leave him alone!'

'Leave him alone?' He thrust his glass towards her, watching her as she refilled it. 'So you're the one who drove Bogdan Krok to slice half his hand off, are you?'

She leapt up. 'You idiot!'

He shrugged, and drank.

'I was never Bogdan's wife! If I had been I might have been able to help him. He's just a nice boy who needs a break! They've allowed him to come to the West, and if he was only given a chance —! But you bastards won't let him!'

'Me?' he began, and she yelled at him: 'You won't give him that chance, will you? You'll destroy him!'

'Me?' He watched her from his chair, feeling cold and sick. 'Yes you, Magnus Owen! All of you! Trying to clean up the world — save civilisation! You hypocrites!'

He had closed his eyes, thinking, *you shouldn't be talking like this, Maya. You shouldn't be here at all. If Steiner knew* ... He said miserably: 'Who the hell's Bogdan Krok? What's he got to do with you and Steiner and Cane?'

She was on her feet, collecting her coat, while he sat with his eyes still closed, and said again: 'All I did was interview him.'

He did not even hear her leave the room. The outside door had slammed before he was on his feet. He stumbled on to the landing and shouted: 'Maya!' Her footsteps, clattering down in the dark, did not stop.

He began to chase her, but his bad leg was no match for her. He heard the door to the street open when he had only gone down one landing; then a car engine snorted outside, and he was suddenly too tired even to look out and see whether it was a Humber, a sports car, or whatever they had given her this time.

She works for Cane, or Steiner, or both, he thought, as he limped back upstairs. *She works for them, yet she hates them. A teacher in an infants' school in Camberwell who's met Bogdan Krok and wants to protect him.*

It still made no sense. No sense at all.

Back in his flat he sat down and drank the rest of the Vyborova alone.

CHAPTER 2

Maya arrived five minutes late. *That was as it should be*, she thought: *a girl should never be too punctual — always leave her partner room for doubt, even in a cold-blooded business like this.*

He was alone at a table by the window. The nearest people to him were a couple of frowsty girls eating cake, and a filthy old man with a blotched face and sleep-dirt at the corner of his eyes who sat over an empty cup muttering to himself.

The man by the window was already on his feet, pulling out a chair for her. 'Good morning. I hope you didn't have too far to come?' He did not smile or shake hands. His voice was toneless, disinterested; his face neat and clean, and very young, like a serious child. Except for his youthfulness, he was very much as she had expected: soft white collar, Gannex raincoat, fair hair shining in the light from the window.

'I'm sorry if I kept you waiting,' she said, sitting down.

'I only arrived a moment ago myself.' She watched him put a spoonful of sugar in his tea. 'I won't keep you long. It's just a matter of routine. You know the gist of it, of course?'

'Of course. I wouldn't be here if I didn't.'

He nodded, stirring his tea. When he looked at her his eyes were dry and distant, not looking at her as though she were a girl at all. *He would look at every girl in the world like this*, she thought. *Girls weren't important to him; he was schooled by higher thoughts, trained in perfect self-control; he was a neuter.*

'I understand you usually take your orders from Mr Steiner?' he said at last.

'That's right. I've always dealt with Steiner until now.'

'Mr Steiner has not been brought in on this operation,' he said, sipping his tea. 'That is why I am dealing with you directly.' His eyes flickered sideways, at the two girls who were collecting their bags and going. 'I'm sorry if you had to come so far out of your way.' He lowered his voice: 'You're perfectly happy about going through with this, are you?'

'Quite happy, detective sergeant.'

'I'd prefer you didn't mention my rank, if you don't mind. I'm only interested in the operation being a success,' he added, taking refuge in his tea. When he put the cup down, his mouth had a pinched look about the corners. Then he began to talk, in a soft flat voice, with no emotion, and as she listened, she knew she had turned pale.

She did not look at Peter Skliros. She sat with her shoulders hunched under her coat, staring desperately at a smear on the tabletop, longing for a cigarette — a drink — anything to break the monotony of that voice droning across the table. With Steiner it had been different: Steiner was an organiser, a time-serving bureaucrat. This man was an automaton.

At last it was over. When she looked up at him, he had taken a folded sheet of paper from inside his raincoat, and was handing it across to her.

'That's the timetable. I want you to read it carefully, memorise the details, then destroy it. Put it down the —' he was about to say the lavatory, but checked himself in time — 'dispose of it in the Ladies before you go.'

Oh you're so beautifully well-mannered! she thought hatefully. His gentility reminded her of that concentration camp commandant who had always insisted that prisoners be clothed for the sake of decency before they were flogged to death.

She unfolded the sheet of paper. A column of figures ran down the left side, against notes written in ballpoint on the right. These notes were stark but explicit; almost nothing was left to chance.

Skliros said: 'The only important factor is the human one. That is your responsibility. If for any reason he fails to co-operate, or the schedule is upset by his behaviour pattern, then the operation is to be called off at once.'

She began to read through the timetable again, more anxious to conceal the look in her eyes than to refresh her memory. 'You're not giving us much leeway?' she said at last.

'A maximum of half an hour one way or the other. It should be enough. But if it isn't, as I told you, we call it off and try another time.'

She heard his chair scrape back. 'Very well, you're all clear now?'

She nodded, folding the paper up again.

He looked at his watch. 'I'll have to be getting along now. How long will it take you to memorise it?'

'Not long,' she said. 'Five minutes perhaps.'

'Remember to get rid of it immediately afterwards.' He glanced round, at a coloured woman who was settling two children down at the next table. 'Very well, good luck then.'

She watched him walk towards the stairs, knowing that in that last moment Cane and his gang had made their first serious mistake. They had allowed the opposition the one opening they were looking for — a trial before a British court of law. Nesbitt and Scammell and the others had been on their own, and the set-up had been foolproof. But this time there would be witnesses, and there would be evidence.

She waited five minutes, in case he returned to surprise her; then got up and went into the lavatory. She could not be certain that someone — some little man queueing up for the tea urn — had not been left there to watch her.

After thirty seconds, she pulled the chain and walked slowly out into the street.

Magnus was not feeling well that day. It had taken him even more than the usual amount of black coffee, Vitamin C and saline solution to restore him to working order.

At six o'clock, just before the evening editorial conference, Rissell appeared at the door of his room, beckoning. Inside, everything was just as it had always been. The gas fire stuttered, Rissell stood sucking his pipe, eyes downcast. 'You're off at seven, aren't you, Magnus?'

He nodded, knowing the routine. He would not be off at seven: this was Rissell's standard prologue to keeping a reporter on several hours after his shift was officially finished.

'It's your friend Krok,' Rissell mumbled round his pipe. 'There's a reception for him in Bloomsbury somewhere tonight. You might get a few quotes, bearing in mind some of the things he said last night. Conflict of interests and so forth.' His eyes flickered sardonically under their long lashes, as he gave him a Roneo-typed handout, again on behalf of Satellite Films Ltd.

Magnus knew that it would all now follow with frightening simplicity. Yet he could still not quite accustom himself to thinking of the stately precincts of *The Paper* as being a menacing part of the plot.

The handout said that the reception, to be given by the East-West Cultural Association in honour of Bogdan Krok, would be held at the Radcliffe Hall, off Red Lion Square, at 7.30, with drinks, buffet and dancing. Rissell said casually: 'Just drop in and have a look. It might be quite fun — and he gave us a good run last night.'

It was true — the morning's Press had treated Krok proudly. His face, wild-eyed and windswept, glared from the pages of even the more serious papers, above at least one caption that seemed in danger of catching on: 'The Red Beatnik'.

Rissell had gone back to clipping together a pile of telex sheets. There was no more to be said and Magnus left him. Rissell would have been well briefed, and it was no part of Magnus's function — whatever that function exactly was — to pry into Rissell's inner motives.

Magnus left the office a few minutes before seven o'clock — little knowing then, as he stepped down into the marble entrance hall and acknowledged the stiff nod from R.S.M. Bostock, that he was leaving *The Paper* for the last time.

He took his car to the meeting, intending to phone his story through over dinner, and return directly to Battersea afterwards. He found a parking space a few yards from the Radcliffe Hall.

The room upstairs was bright and drab, with rows of chairs round the walls as though for a village dance. About two dozen people stood about, talking quietly. Jan Steiner was waiting just inside. 'Glad to meet you, Mr Owen. Mr Krok's not here yet — he had to see some film people at his hotel in the Gloucester Road. I expect he's been held up by the traffic. Come over and have a drink.'

'Only a small one,' Magnus said, following Steiner to a table laid with an unexpectedly lavish stock of whisky, gin, Polish and Soviet vodka, plates of red caviar sandwiches, ham, salami, and pickles.

'Vodka?' said Steiner.

'A small Vyborova.' He grinned: 'Since it's the national drink.'

Steiner did not react; his face was closed, betraying nothing.

He was not drinking himself, and moved off to welcome more guests who had just arrived. A gramophone began to play songs by the Red Army Choir.

Magnus was standing by the table, fingering his glass despondently, when a beaky-faced girl moved up beside him and began picking about among the hors d'oeuvres.

'Hello!' she said, glancing sideways at him with a keen smile. 'You're a new member of the Association?'

'No. I'm from *The Paper*.'

'Oh, a journalist.' She hesitated, long enough for her plucked eyebrows to remind him of blackheads. 'My name's Marlene Almar,' she added. 'How do you do?' Her hand felt like a small fish. 'I suppose you're waiting to see Bogdan Krok?'

He nodded, glancing round for a chance of escape, but she had already begun telling him what a great admirer she was of the Polish cinema. 'They've got such a lot to teach us, you know. There's a real spirit of creative endeavour over there — so wonderfully refreshing after the sickening commercial tripe we get from America!'

Magnus nodded dutifully. 'But I understand the Party line on Krok's is rather reserved?'

'Reserved?'

'His latest film has been more or less banned over there.'

'Banned? But it's just about to open in London — he's been allowed to come to the West and publicise it!'

Magnus nodded glumly, having no stomach for argument with the girl. But she spared him by introducing a shiny-faced man in a brown suit and red woollen tie. 'Mr Owen — meet Mr Leslie Tyler. Mr Tyler's our London representative for the East-West Cultural Association.'

Tyler shook hands vigorously. 'Glad to meet you. Can't say I read *The Paper* very often — I'm not much of a highbrow — but I'd be glad to give you any gen you want about our work.' He wore a badge on his lapel — a red banner with the heads of Lenin, Marx and Engels overlapping in relief. Here at least was no enigma, and Magnus was grateful for the man's honesty.

'You got a drink? Give yourself a refill,' Tyler said, turning to the table. 'Careful though — this Polish stuff's got a real kick! Ever been in Poland, Mr Owen?'

'Never.'

'I was there last year. Cheers! Plucky little country — got real guts. Those German bastards razed her to the ground and she really pulled herself up right by her bootstraps. More than you'd get for this country with all the bigwigs stuffing themselves on three-hour lunches and spending six months a year on the Riviera.'

'Have you seen any of Krok's films, Mr Tyler?'

'Oh yes, saw his first. Marvellous technically. That's what they've got over there, you see. Technique. They allow a director to experiment. None of this penny-pinching you get here. Because in the socialist countries it's government money — that is, the people's money. That's to say, it's the people who go to the film who pay for it. The director just takes over from there — you see?' Magnus said he saw, wondering if Bogdan Krok would have agreed. He looked at his watch. Krok was now more than an hour late. The gramophone was still playing the Red Army Choir, as Magnus became aware that Miss Marlene Almar had insinuated herself again at his side. 'Wonderful, isn't it?'

'What?'

'The music — "Song of the Fields". It's one of the great hymns of the Revolution. Just compare it with something like "The Dam Busters March".'

Magnus listened to the soldiers' chorus rising to a slow crescendo, and had to admit that she had a point — although he was not quite sure what it was. But as the record came to an end, the temptation to rile her became too much for him.

'It's a rousing old tune, but I think it's just as well you played it before Bogdan Krok arrives.'

'What do you mean?' She gave him a sharp, eager stare which made his heart sink.

'The Poles aren't reputed to be very pro-Russian,' he said lamely, noticing Tyler closing in to defend the girl.

Unfortunately she did not need defending. 'There you go again!' she cried exultantly. 'What you're talking about are the old traditional hatreds that any intelligent Pole has forgotten long ago. There may have been differences with Russia in the past, but at least the Russians today don't go around arming the Germans and threatening to seize back Poland's eastern territories.'

Oh she knows it all, he thought despairingly, and gave himself another vodka.

Tyler butted in between them, his tie beginning to come undone. 'Mr Owen, I want to be honest with a serious newspaper like yours. Now I admit that before 1956 the Soviet Union made mistakes…'

Magnus looked up and saw Maya at the door, shaking hands with Steiner. The gramophone began to play jazz. Marlene Almar broke in: 'Thought we might get a bit of dancing going.' She turned to Tyler: 'Recognise it, Les? That new Czech band from Prague.'

Tyler smiled: 'Very nice, Marlene. A lot better than these screaming nits with long hair.' He looked round demandingly at Magnus: 'That's one thing they've stamped out in the Socialist countries. The young people over there have better things to worry about. They're interested in building up their country, instead of dressing up in fancy clothes and taking drugs and listening to all this pop music!'

Magnus saw Maya still talking to Steiner.

'That's right,' Marlene said. 'Over there you don't have to look twice to see who's a man and who's a girl. Of course, they've got a few hooligans — youth's always a problem, especially in an industrialised society.'

But as Magnus listened, it seemed that he had heard all this before — that he were back in that private banqueting room, with Sir Lionel Hilder ranting on about British youth and the Long-Haired Lilac Brigade, and how the Soviet Union knew how to deal with the problem — no messing about — they packed their hooligans and intellectual delinquents off to labour camps or lunatic asylums.

He turned and saw Maya standing beside him. She smiled at Tyler and Miss Almar, and Magnus said to them: 'Excuse me a moment.' Miss Almar eyed them both with undisguised malice, as they moved to the end of the table.

'What are you doing here?' Maya said.

'I was sent by *The Paper*. Is Krok with you?'

'Why do you want to know?'

'I'm here to interview him.'

'You interviewed him last night.'

'That's right. So why don't you ring up my News Editor and ask him why he's sent me out to interview Krok two nights running?' Her expression did not change. 'Is he coming here?' he asked again.

137

'He's here already. In the lavatory.'

'Sober?'

She laughed, with no humour. 'Oh he's got a hard head, Bogdan. Like me.' She glanced down at the glass in Magnus's hand: 'How have you been doing?'

'Steady as a rock. Wonderfully restrained, considering the temptation.'

She looked round the room. 'What's it like here?'

'Swinging. The whole fifth column from Marble Arch have come in force. He should love it.'

There was a stir from the door, and Magnus caught a glimpse of Krok's blond head swaying in above the crowd. He still wore his checkered jacket and jeans, but he was shaved now and looked superb — *like a fully paid-up god*, Magnus thought.

His eyes were clearer than they had been last night, but they held a dangerous glint as he looked round the room, making up his mind whether he liked or disliked what he saw. It was evident from his expression that he hated what he saw. Tyler, very red in the face, had rushed forward with a glass of vodka, handing it up to him with the cry of: '*Nazdrovye tovarich!*'

Krok was looking at the badge in his lapel: 'So you speak Russian?'

Tyler beamed: 'Thanks, Mr Krok, but I was having a bash at Polish!'

'*Tovarich* is Russian,' Krok said. 'And I am a Pole.'

An uneasy hush fell round him. Tyler grinned stupidly, still holding the glass of vodka he had offered to Krok. A big Jewish woman stepped between them, smiling busily. 'Ah, Mr Krok! — you've met Mr Leslie Tyler?'

But Krok was not listening. His eyes had fixed on Magnus and Maya, who were still standing at the end of the table. The Jewish woman was saying, 'You must meet our other friends in the Association' — but Krok pushed past her and started down the table.

'You!' he cried, pointing his left hand at Magnus' chest. 'You are the one who told me at the airport about General Morowski?'

Magnus swallowed hard and nodded. Krok took a step forward. 'Why do you do it? — in front of all those people.' He was now touching Magnus, his voice thick and menacing. 'So you can write in your newspaper that in Poland they call me a degenerate hooligan?'

'We didn't print anything about you and Morowski,' Magnus said quietly.

'Are you a Communist?' Krok cried; but Maya interrupted in a flow of Polish. Krok listened, frowning; then looked up at Magnus and gave him a painful slap on the shoulder. 'O.K., I am sorry! Since I leave Poland I look everywhere for enemies. I am confused, you see. Last night I was drunk. Completely drunk since I have come to Paris. But now you will have a drink with me?'

Maya poured three vodkas and they drank each other's health. 'That's my trouble,' Krok said. 'Drunk. Always drunk, that's what my doctors say. In Warsaw they said to me, "Bogdan, if you go on drinking, you will kill yourself!" So I said to them, "O.K. sure, in maybe thirty or forty years." And my wife, she said the same. Always that I am drunk. O.K., I like drinking. I like to drink and drink, because what else is there to do except make love to a pretty girl?' He smiled at Maya, and she smiled back, and Magnus felt an unpleasant pang in his stomach.

Behind Krok's shoulder, he saw Steiner, alone, watching them; and suddenly he wanted to be out of this gruesome congregation. The evening would not even rate a paragraph in

The Paper, and even the presence of Maya, smiling at Krok, was far from being a consolation.

It was the appearance of Miss Marlene Almar that stopped him. Less daunted than the others by Krok's rudeness, she had slipped her beaky face under his elbow and cried: 'Mr Krok, our journalist friend here didn't want us to play any Russian music for you. He thought it would offend you.' Her eyes gleamed spitefully at Magnus.

Krok shrugged his enormous shoulders: 'What Russian music?'

'The Red Army Choir! Would you like to hear it?'

'No.'

Miss Almar puckered her bare eyebrows. 'Mr Krok, as a Pole of the younger generation, what do you honestly feel about the Russians?'

Krok turned slowly, studied her, then leant down and said, 'My dear young lady, my country has had a bad history. You know that?'

Miss Almar's flat chest heaved with excitement.

'On one side,' Krok said, 'we have the Germans, and on the other we have our friends.'

Miss Marlene Almar smiled uneasily, beginning to realise there was something wrong with this answer, when Tyler interrupted them, armed with an enormous drink, to propose a toast to 'closer cultural relations between Britain and the People's Republic of Poland!'

Krok growled something into his glass, which was empty; but before Tyler could refill it, the big Jewish woman was clapping for quiet: 'Ladies and gentlemen! I'd like to introduce a group who've come here this evening especially for our entertainment. The Stratford East Morris Dancers!'

She stepped back to a burst of applause, as a troupe of elderly men in breeches and buckled shoes came hopping into the middle of the floor, smacking their thighs and shaking handkerchiefs at each other in what Magnus recognised as 'traditional English folk-dancing.' He was embarrassed that Bogdan Krok should have to watch it.

Krok, however, took little notice. He stood bowed over a tumbler of vodka, while Tyler plied him with infamous details about the British film industry. He did not interrupt; but several times Magnus saw him look up at him from under his dark eyebrows and smile at Maya; and each time she smiled back, with that wide beautiful smile that sent a pang through his bowels.

He wondered again, why the hell don't I get out of here? She wasn't interested in him — she wanted Krok. She'd even gone to the trouble of warning him last night to stay away from Krok. He should take her at her word and clear out.

His glass was empty and he gave himself one more — his last. He heard Tyler still holding forth, his eyes growing moist with the thought of a State-subsidised film industry. He sighed: 'It's the wonderful sense of release you must get, Mr Krok, knowing that you're not working simply for profit — for a sordid criterion like sex and violence.'

'Excuse me,' Krok said suddenly, 'but what do you know about the cinema?'

'I'm an electrician, Mr Krok. But I've worked down at Pinewood a few times. I take a lot of interest in films.'

'Do you own a Mercedes Benz 300 SL?'

The smile went from Tyler's face. 'Christ, on my salary? You're joking!'

'I'm not joking. Do you own a Mercedes 300 SL?'

Tyler gulped at his drink: ''Course I don't!'

Krok nodded and held out his hand: 'In that case, sir, we do not speak the same language.'

Tyler stood with his mouth open, so muddled with vodka that he shook Krok's hand, while the faces round them expressed pained surprise. Krok turned to Maya, leering malevolently. Magnus heard her say something in Polish and his face went slack, almost ugly, with a look of despair. The next moment he swung round, pointing at an unopened half-litre bottle of Vyborova on the table.

'Is that vodka?' he roared in a voice that brought the room to silence. Even the Morris dancers stopped their ludicrous cavorting; the whole crowd turned and stared.

'Is that vodka?' Krok stood glaring round, as though to dare anyone to contradict him. No one did, although one voice called nervously, 'Go on, chum, have a drink!'

Bogdan Krok was still pointing at the bottle. 'Give it to me!'

Tyler gave it to him. Krok studied it for a moment against the light, then unscrewed it, tilted it back above his head, then, closing his eyes, began to drink dramatically. He drank for perhaps thirty seconds, without a break — at first in almost dead silence, then with his throat muscles beginning to contract violently, issuing a sound like irregular gargling. When he at last put the bottle back on the table it was more than three quarters empty.

The guests were clearly awed; a few giggled their appreciation, and Tyler actually applauded: 'My God, you boys can certainly put it back!'

Bogdan Krok glared round him, speechless. The Jewish woman begun whispering to Steiner, who now looked at Krok and nodded.

Krok had steadied himself against the table and was frowning down at his hands. Apart from two dark spots on his cheeks, he looked remarkably composed. Magnus was wondering how long it took for the human system to react to one-third of a litre of 85 per cent proof spirit, when he heard Maya whisper to him: 'Oh God, he'll go berserk!'

A couple of seconds later Bogdan Krok accordingly went berserk. His movements, although rapid, reminded Magnus afterwards of a film in slow motion. He leant down and seized the tablecloth in both hands, then, with a great howl, lunged backwards, dragging the whole table to the floor with a crash of broken glass, bottles, pickles and tangled wet linen. The guests stood back and gaped, their bourgeois sensibilities shocked rigid.

Krok was now running sideways across the room, bellowing like a beast in pain, and still pulling the tablecloth on which a solitary bottle of whisky rolled unscathed in a sludge of ham and caviar. He only let go when he reached the door; and then the shouting started. A few guests began picking their way through the wreckage like dazed survivors after a bomb disaster; someone laughed and someone else cried, 'Get the police!'

Magnus had a rare scoop for *The Paper*. Besides a man from *The Morning Star* — which had already gone to bed — he seemed to have the place to himself. There remained twenty minutes till the deadline of the first edition; and now he had only to phone the story through. But at the moment he was not thinking of *The Paper*. His mind was concentrated on one thing — Maya had disappeared with Krok.

He had just started towards the door, when he came face to face with Steiner. Throughout all the chaos, Steiner alone had remained unperturbed, standing against the wall, surveying the shambles with his stolid piggy-blue eyes; but at the sight of Magnus trying to leave, he stepped out and said, 'I'm sorry about that, Mr Owen. Our guest seems to have had too much to drink.'

Magnus began to laugh, rather wildly, as Steiner added, 'You'll be writing it for *The Paper*, I suppose?' His hand plucked at Magnus' sleeve: 'There's a telephone just through on the left of the stairs.'

'Very kind of you, Mr Steiner!' Magnus cried, breaking away from him and reaching the door.

Too bloody kind of you by half! he thought, not even glancing to see where the telephone was, as he started down the stairs, swinging his left leg out, taking two steps at a time. Steiner hadn't batted an eyelid — not even when a reception given by his East-West Cultural Association had been wrecked by the guest of honour. Instead, he had gone out of his way to tell the only journalist present where he could find a telephone.

There was something wrong there, he thought, as he reached the street and heard car doors slamming. He began to run, in long kangaroo hops that must have looked grotesque if anyone had been watching. But he no longer cared. She'd made off in a car twice before, and he wasn't going to let it happen a third time.

It was a big dark Mercedes, parked about fifty yards beyond where he'd left the Citroën. This gave him a small start on them, although he was going to have to hurry. As he clambered in and started the engine, he wondered if the car had been hired by Maya or Krok. She'd used a Humber and a sports car before; but Krok was known to favour the German firm — a perverse joke he enjoyed playing on his more conventional compatriots.

The Mercedes had already pulled away and he caught a glimpse of its rear lights swinging away at the end of the street, as he crouched forward with his foot down on the floor; and then he saw Steiner.

He stood alone in the door of the Radcliffe Hall, watching as the Citroën swept past, picking up speed, and for the first time that evening Magnus felt a great wave of relief. Until now he had been impelled by a number of emotions — curiosity, jealousy, frustration — but the sight of Steiner had changed all that. Steiner was decisive. He meant trouble — he had always meant trouble — and as Magnus reached the end of the street and swung the wheel over after the Mercedes, he knew it was no longer Maya he was pursuing, but Bogdan Krok.

For some reason which he still did not understand, they were planning to trap Krok. The whole evening had been an elaborate trap from the start — the obsequious Tyler, with his red woollen tie, and all the other fawning fellow travellers, set against the abundant booze and the seductive Maya. Magnus had been summoned merely to record Krok's behaviour, and in this Krok had obliged generously. The rest was now up to Maya.

But what was she up to? Was she working for Cane and the others, helping to trap Krok? Or was she doing what she had begged Magnus last night? — trying to help him, rescue him before he got into deeper trouble? Or again, had her visit the night before been merely another trick to test Magnus' loyalty? And if so, did it mean that Cane had begun to suspect him?

But in any case he had now given himself away. In that moment of running out in front of Steiner, he knew he was irrevocably committed. Cane had told him not to seek explanations; and while he might plead that he had chased after Krok just for a few last-minute quotes, the excuse was a lame one, and he knew it.

The Mercedes had turned into Southampton Row, a good hundred yards ahead of him now, driving fast but steadily; and although he could not see inside the car, he knew it could not possibly be Krok at the wheel. He wondered if she had seen him run out after them, or how suspicious she was of being followed; but he could not risk losing her again. He raced up after her into a dark street, riding on his sidelights now, as they started west across that drab but uncrowded stretch between Euston and Oxford Street.

The going became easier and he began to relax, trying to work out where she might be taking Krok. As far as he knew, Krok had still had no dinner; and while he was hardly dressed for the smartest places, there were always those mushrooming discotheques where they were not fussy about people in jeans and no tie, providing they were famous.

Ahead, the rear lights of the Mercedes glowed at him like hot eyes in the dark; and as he followed his mind began to react with dull obedience, as though the mechanism of consecutive thought had in some way been short-circuited, until there were just the two thoughts: Maya is in the car ahead with Bogdan Krok, I must keep my eyes on the car and not lose it.

They were across Oxford Street now — into Mayfair. The traffic down Park Lane was five abreast, and at one of the lights he was forced to draw up almost alongside the Mercedes. He had a glimpse of Krok's head lolling on her shoulder, while she sat in profile, eyes on the road ahead. *Just a drunken man being driven home by a pretty girl*, he thought; and suddenly he felt a great weariness creep over him. Supposing that was all it was? — that there was no plot, no mystery, and she were simply driving away from the party because he was drunk and she wanted to get him out of trouble?

She leapt away from the lights as they changed to amber, leaving him standing; and soon she had drawn far ahead of him. Round Hyde Park Corner, where he was only just able to get back on her tail as she swept past St George's Hospital and down towards Knightsbridge.

They were coming into Detective Sergeant Skliros's 'manor' now, and the pain began in Magnus's leg. He passed the turning to the Congreve Club, driving down Brompton Road towards Kensington and Fulham, he remembered Steiner's words as he had entered the Radcliffe Hall — 'Mr Krok's been meeting some film people at his hotel in the Gloucester Road.' So it was that, after all. A nice conscientious girl driving Krok back home to bed.

But he stayed on their tail. The worst that could await him now was an embarrassing encounter with Maya. In any case, he didn't owe her anything.

Then suddenly he realised they were past the Gloucester Road, heading for Putney. He crossed the river, where he had to slow down in a line of cars — the Mercedes about half a dozen ahead of him. A pair of headlamps came on suddenly behind and dazzled him in his mirror. *Some half-drunk bastard trying to get past him*, he thought: but he wasn't going to let him! He felt his blood quickening, as the car behind began to hoot angrily. A glimpse of a black family saloon: only one man in it, driving.

And then they were out of Putney, with the traffic thinning and the city lights falling behind, as they climbed the empty rise to Wimbledon Common. It was a black spring night, and he was forced to turn on dipped headlamps.

He had his foot down flat again, as the red lights of the Mercedes now began to draw away fast. The Citroën was touching fifty, fifty-five, the speedometer needle creeping higher. He still did not dare to put his headlamps on full, although the Mercedes was several hundred yards ahead and gaining rapidly.

There were the headlamps of another car somewhere behind; lights of houses sprinkled along the edge of the Common; but otherwise he was alone with the Mercedes.

He turned on the radio, and Handel organ music swelled ominously through the car. Then suddenly he was afraid. It came in a hot rush from his belly, unexpected and totally irrational. Like Cyprus all over again: a night patrol on an empty road, waiting for an ambush. Only in Cyprus he'd had others with him; there had been none of the loneliness of this drive — the organ music within, and Krok and the girl racing away from him into the black silence outside.

He shook himself and wiped his palms round the steering wheel. He was a grown man driving at night on Wimbledon Common — and he was getting as jittery as a young girl.

The Mercedes' rear lights were only a faint smudge of red now, and he knew that any moment he would lose them. He tried to remember the geography of the Common — whether the direction they were taking led to one of the trunk roads — when he saw the headlamps of another car coming up fast behind him. Its indicator winked in his mirror, and a moment later it passed him, very fast. *Probably 'hotted up'*, he thought. A black Hillman Minx saloon — one man in it, driving. He couldn't be sure, but it looked very much like the car that had tried to overtake him on the bridge.

The road was flat and straight. He had switched the headlamps on to high-beam and was driving at seventy now, watching the lights of the Hillman as it swung out again, this time to pass the Mercedes. He was thinking, *Whoever that is, he's in a damned hurry!* — when both sets of brake lights ahead glared angrily — almost simultaneously, it seemed — and next moment flicked to the left and vanished.

Magnus saw the bend when it was less than fifty yards away, under a screen of dark trees. He had been too intent on the rear lights to notice the warning sign before it was already racing past in the arc of his headlamps. He began to brake violently, feeling the back of the Citroën swing round, and he was wiggling the wheel frantically to correct the skid; and then, even through the closed windows, he heard the shriek of brakes ahead. He was going round the next bend, still braking, and saw the Mercedes a moment after it hit the verge, bouncing back almost at right angles to the road and pointing down like a ship in a heavy sea.

His own reactions were not fast enough. There was a blind turning among the trees on his right, and out of this the black Hillman had driven straight into the road. There was nothing he could do — nothing anybody could have done. He had his foot down full on the brake, bracing his arms against the wheel, and his last clear thought was that someone had got out of the Hillman; then he closed his eyes and waited for the crash.

It came like a paper bag bursting beside his ear, followed by lights spinning and swirling in the darkness. He could hear voices too, but they seemed a long way off. There were people in the road and doors slamming. He put his hand out and opened his own door, put one leg out and stood up with his hand still on the door handle.

There was a girl watching him from across the road; then she became two girls, then three, and something hit him hard across the shoulders. It was the Citroën roof as he stumbled backwards, and it made him very angry. He began to swear loudly, and someone swore back like an echo.

'Owen! What the bloody hell are you doing here?' It was a man's voice, sharp and tight, and it made him straighten up, trying to focus properly. Something warm was dribbling into his eyes and there were two lights shining down at him, blinding him.

He put his hand up and said feebly, 'I can't see anything. What's happened?' It was extraordinarily bright all round, with two lights that glared down at him like arc lamps. A girl stood silhouetted against them, hair over her shoulders, shouting above the organ music: 'Now you've done it! You've really done it this time!'

'Shut up.'

There was a movement in the light, and Magnus wiped his eyes and thought, *That's no way to talk to a girl.* But she gave a triumphant laugh: 'So what are you going to do now? You've got the wrong man, you stupid bastard!'

'Shut up!' His voice had cracked into a falsetto, almost a woman's voice: 'I'll have you in too if you're not careful!' He took a step forward. 'What are you doing here, Owen?'

Magnus stood looking at the Hillman. It was jammed sideways against the sloping snout of the Citroën all crooked and hunchbacked with its windscreen shattered like crushed ice. The door on the driver's side, away from where the Citroën had struck, hung open. He turned, blinking at the headlamps of the Mercedes which still pointed down into the road.

'I couldn't help it,' he murmured, 'you came straight out —'

'What the hell are you doing here?' His face had a white naked look with eyes that seemed to have no pupils, like a pair of burnt-out flashbulbs. Magnus peered at them, and the face became dim. 'I was behind you and you came straight out —'

A door opened somewhere and a tall figure wobbled down into the glare of the road, his legs throwing shadows as though he were walking on stilts. Above the organ music the man's voice cried: 'Krok! Bogdan Krok!'

The girl laughed again: 'I tell you, he wasn't even driving!'

'Shut up, you little bitch! Krok,' he shouted, 'I'm a police officer. There's been an accident and I'm having you in. You understand that? I'm charging you — unfit to drive…'

Krok was stumbling about and swaying his arms. Magnus felt sick and dizzy. He leant against the Citroën, trying to focus on the three figures in the road. There was a lull in the music from the radio, and he heard Maya's voice, clear and mocking: 'You won't get away with it this time, detective sergeant. This time we've got evidence.'

'Evidence?' Skliros turned to Krok, who stood beside Maya, his huge hands still swinging at his sides. 'Don't tell me he hasn't been drinking! I can smell him from here.'

'He wasn't driving,' Magnus called feebly. 'I can swear to that. I was a witness.'

'You keep out of this, Owen! Just keep out of it, or I'll have you in too!'

'Why don't you have us all in!' Maya shouted, 'then we'll see what the court has to say when they see that timetable you gave me this morning —'

There was a loud smack as Skliros hit her across the mouth. Her head jerked back, but she made no sound. He was bringing his hand up again, fist clenched this time, when Bogdan Krok raised both arms and swooped down on him, folding the slim young man in a crushing embrace, his right hand slamming into Skliros' neck, while his truncated left, with its single finger and thumb, stabbed at the man's face like some obscene blunt instrument.

Skliros was still very fast, trying to resort to every trick he had learnt in the gym at Hendon; but he could never quite recover from that first paralysing blow on the neck. He went down backwards with Krok rolling on top of him — Skliros kicking out, trying to bite the massive hand that pressed him to the road — while the prong of Krok's left drove down like a stave into his throat.

Maya was shouting in Polish, trying to drag Krok away. Then for a few seconds the two men lay side by side, motionless.

Krok was the first to move, crawling over Skliros and spitting into the grass verge. Maya had run forward and began to help him up, leading him back across the road to the Mercedes. Magnus followed, walking carefully like a man entering a crowded room with all eyes on him. He climbed into the front seat next to Krok. Maya got into the driver's seat, the engine started and the car lurched down off the bank and swung round, pointing back towards London.

There was a cold wind on Magnus' face and he felt the blood growing tight and sticky round his eye. He remembered that he had left the keys in his car, the radio still on.

'My car's back there,' he murmured. 'With all my keys. I can't get into my flat — unless you can break in for me.' But there was no answer, just the powerful hum of the engine. He looked sideways at Krok, whose head lay back, relaxed as though in sleep. He said to Maya: 'I'm sorry I followed you. I shouldn't have, should I?'

'I don't know. You tell me.' Her voice was small and unfriendly, and he suddenly felt miserable.

'I hit my head. I don't feel too good. I suppose we'd better go to the police.'

'Police! Bogdan nearly killed one back there.'

Magnus considered this for a moment, watching the lights growing larger along the edge of the Common. 'That man's not a real policeman,' he said dully: 'he's a raving nut. I know all about him. He's one of Cane's boys. He did this because Cane told him to.' He paused; Maya had turned to look at him. 'Cane told him to,' he repeated.

'I know that. But why did you follow us tonight?'

'Didn't think you were safe with Krok. Thought you'd be safer with a chaperon.' He suddenly giggled: 'Safer with Magnus Owen! — that's a laugh, isn't it?'

'I told you to keep away from him,' she said. 'Now, are you well enough to listen to me?'

'Ready and willing!' he said, trying to concentrate on the lights ahead. They meant traffic, people, police stations. South-West Central.

'Magnus, whose side are you on?'

He leant back and closed his eyes. 'Whose side are you on, Maya?'

She ignored the question. 'The important thing is that Bogdan's in bad trouble, and you're involved. You can't get out of it now.'

'I rammed Skliros' car,' he said thoughtfully. 'We'll have to go to the police.'

'We're not going to them yet. Not until I've talked to some people who'll be able to back us up. I've got written evidence against Peter Skliros, a timetable he gave me, the idiot!' She turned to him again, her eyes harsh in the lights ahead. 'But you know all about that, don't you?'

He shook his head, which was slamming with pain. 'I can guess. Another little frame-up? Dangerous driving while under the influence? It's a criminal offence, so he'd probably have been deported — like Duzinska and Berliner and Chuck Ortiz. Only this time it's gone wrong?'

'Very wrong. But not just for them. Bogdan's still in trouble. He can now be charged with assaulting a police officer — and the police will be inclined to back Skliros up. That's why we need friends to discredit him before he can give his own version.'

'What friends?' He heard Krok stir beside him and growl something in Polish. Maya ignored him.

'You'll find out,' she said. 'But first we've got to clean you both up and give Bogdan a chance to get sober. And while you're doing that, I'll go to these friends and explain what's happened, and then we can all go together to the police and tell them everything — about Skliros and Steiner and Cane, and the party tonight, and why you ran out, and all about the crash, and how Skliros hit me when I mentioned the timetable. You understand, Magnus?'

Magnus understood very little. He said simply: 'Anything you say, Maya. Any place, any time. Just clap your hands and Magnus Owen comes running.' He remembered that the first edition of *The Paper* would be away, and there would be nothing on Bogdan Krok's previous escapade. Instead, his evening's work had consisted of leaving a crashed car with his fingerprints on the ignition keys, next to a plainclothes police officer who had been beaten senseless in the road.

He wondered what Hugh Rissell and Sir James Broom would have to say when they heard about it.

PART 3: NIGHT RIDE

CHAPTER 1

Magnus felt safe. Safe, because she and her friends were looking after him, seeing he came to no harm. He was in London, and London was safe. Safe as this big dreary hotel off the Gloucester Road — a Victorian retreat for retired officers and elderly ladies with small private means. Hardly the place to put a man like Bogdan Krok; but then the funds of the East-West Association were probably not lavish; his first-class air fare from Paris had been paid for by his French sponsors.

He found he could think almost clearly now, although it was easier when he turned his head from the wall, which was a churning pattern of crimson and mauve. The floor was gentler — a well-trodden carpet. The room contained a single bed, washbasin, table and chair, a wardrobe and a small sofa.

It was on the sofa that Magnus was now lying, his knees hooked up uncomfortably under his chin. It was not a large room, and Bogdan Krok was pacing it like an animal in a cage.

Magnus began to sit up. He said painfully: 'Bogdan, where is she? Where's Maya?'

Krok's long legs swung past him, pausing at the table where he drank something from a bottle. 'She's crazy! She went to the embassy.'

'What embassy?'

'Our embassy. The embassy of the great Polish People's Republic.'

Magnus knew that he should be surprised by this: but all that happened was a great roaring in his ears like a train going into a tunnel. When it stopped he was lying on his back again looking up at Krok, who towered above him swinging a brandy bottle like a club.

'Maya went to our embassy, so now you have a drink and then we go to the newspapers.' He thrust the bottle at Magnus, who began to struggle up again, trying to avoid the giddy wallpaper. He remembered the Citroën's nose buried into the side of the Hillman; remembered again that he'd missed his deadline, missed his scoop on Krok, that he might even get the sack; and all Maya had done was run off to solicit help from a Communist embassy. 'Oh my God!' he groaned.

Krok had resumed his pacing, five strides to the wall, five back. 'We go to the newspapers and tell them the story. You saw what happened. Maya told us — they were trying to get me arrested for driving a car when I was drunk.'

'And you beat up a police officer. That's worse, Bogdan. G.B.H. Grievous bodily harm.'

Krok growled and sat down on the end of the sofa. 'So what do I do, huh? Lie on my back and wait for them to come and destroy me? I'm not a sick dog with one testicle, I tell you! And I'm not an idiot! We go to the newspapers and we tell them everything. We telephone them and they come here and we hold a press conference.'

'At one o'clock in the morning?' But he conceded that allowing for Krok's limited knowledge of England, the idea had a certain bold logic. 'We ought to go the police,' he added, with no conviction.

'Police? Are you crazy too? You think I'm just some idiot Pole! Well I tell you, I know things now about your beautiful England that I did not know yesterday. What Maya tells me!' He pushed his face up to Magnus', eyes glaring: 'Before I come here, I think this of England — skies low, living standards high, freedom wide!' He flung both arms out, almost smashing the brandy bottle against the wall.

'But now I know more. I know that the blond man I have beaten tonight was a policeman. An English policeman!' He stood shaking his head: 'So I keep away from the police. We telephone the newspapers now and tell them everything.'

'It's too late for the newspapers,' Magnus said. He sat up on the edge of the sofa and looked at his watch. Maya had been gone nearly an hour now, and had not even telephoned.

'We can't go to the newspapers, Bogdan,' he said thickly. 'We can't do anything. We're screwed!'

'You have a drink, then you'll feel better, huh?' Krok handed him the brandy again, but he shook his head.

'There's only one thing for it — unless that girl comes back damned soon. We have to go to the police.'

Krok brought his foot down with a stamp that shook the floor. 'I tell you, I'm not going to any bloody police! You say that again and I break your head!' He stood above him holding the bottle by the neck, and Magnus remembered the man already had some experience in this form of combat. He waved his hand feebly and said, 'All right, Bogdan, just put down the bottle and we'll have a drink.'

They were drinking when the knock came on the door. Krok did not seem to hear it. It was repeated, more loudly. It was Magnus who got up and answered it.

The man outside had a narrow pointed face, rimless glasses and a pale-blue uniform with the hotel insignia stitched to the lapel. He stood in the doorway looking at Magnus with visible displeasure; then said, in a strong foreign accent: 'You are disturbing the hotel.'

'Tell him to go shit himself!' Krok called from inside, and the man's face went very red, but he did not move.

'You are a most insulting man, Mr Krok. You will be reported in the morning to the management.'

Krok came lurching across the floor, elbowed Magnus aside and leant against the door jamb, leering at the porter. 'You know what,' he said at last: 'I want to piss! And I can't bloody well have one in this hotel of yours because you haven't even given me a bathroom! Not even a place to piss!' he shouted. 'What sort of hotel do you think it is?'

The porter had backed prudently into the corridor and now began to tremble. 'Mr Krok, this is outrageous. It cannot be tolerated.' But as he spoke, Krok pushed past him and headed noisily down the corridor.

The little man stood for a moment, undecided whether to follow or not, then seemed to choose the line of least resistance. He turned to Magnus. 'I must ask you to leave, sir. At once —'

Krok's footsteps were now pounding unsteadily down the stairs. The porter glanced nervously along the corridor. There was a toilet only a few doors away; if the Pole was heading downstairs, it could only mean more trouble.

Magnus looked at him and hesitated. The man was a night porter, a foreigner, and he worked in the improbable hotel where Krok was staying. 'Are you Polish?' he said suddenly.

'I am not. Now please, you will leave my hotel!'

'German?' Krok's footsteps were nearing the lobby.

'I am from Switzerland. Now please —'

Magnus nodded: 'Oscar Wilde was right! — you all look like waiters, including the mountains.'

The Swiss stiffened. From the dark well of the staircase there now burst the voice of Bogdan Krok, carrying round the silent corridors the refrain of a Russian drinking song. Within seconds he had a captive audience reaching for house telephones, pushing bells, opening doors.

The Swiss had turned and was hurrying towards the stairs where a couple of dim figures in dressing gowns were leaning over the banisters. Krok's voice rolled into a magnificent crescendo, and a man called across the stairway, 'What's going on? Will someone stop that noise at once!'

There were voices all round now, lights going on, slippers shuffling; and then suddenly the singing stopped. Magnus had reached the first landing when it happened. Below him the lobby was dim and quiet; the solitary light behind the reception desk shone on a poster advertising London theatres.

In the middle of the floor stood the Swiss porter. He was glancing rapidly around him, hands fidgeting at his sides. A door opened, then swung shut in the darkness, and a man in a raincoat walked briskly past him, turning up his collar as he reached the revolving doors into the street.

Magnus hurried down the rest of the stairs. The Swiss looked up and started to say something, his face grey with anger. 'You are leaving my hotel at once,' he said, keeping his voice as low as possible.

'Where's Mr Krok?'

'I do not know. Now will you leave.'

'What do you mean, you don't know?' From above, groups of faces were watching them round the well of the staircase.

'Leave!' the man hissed, 'or I shall be obliged to call the police.'

'I'm finding Mr Krok first,' Magnus said, 'and then we'll leave together.'

He looked round, at the doors to the bar and the restaurant; and for an instant he thought he saw a face watching him outside the revolving doors. It was very dark; his head was pounding; he felt groggy, half-drunk.

There was another door — the one that had opened a moment earlier — and while the Swiss was starting to say something again, Magnus moved towards it. The electric sign above it had been turned out, but he could just read 'Gentlemen'. He slammed it open, wasting a couple of seconds finding the light switch. It was silent inside, except for a slow tinkle of water, and he noticed a faint smell, both familiar and strange. Then he turned on the light.

It was the usual white-tiled room with basins and mirrors down one side, cubicles and urinals along the other. Krok had fallen against the urinals and lay with his face in the corner of the trough, touching a cake of germicide which had turned orange at the edges. Water rippled down from the nozzle above, flowing over his blond hair and growing pink as it soaked into the collar of his shirt.

Magnus looked at him for perhaps ten seconds. His shirt was still muddy from his fight with Skliros, and Magnus noticed how the water forked into two trickles behind his ears, one flowing into the trough, the other spreading out over his neck and washing clean a dark hole about half the width of a pencil … .22 calibre, he thought. Light and lethal at short range. The Japanese had used them in the capture of Singapore. This one would have been a pistol fitted with a silencer. Krok had probably not even turned. He would have been up against the urinal, singing at the wall, when someone had stepped up and shot him point-blank just below the skull. For a morbid moment he found himself wondering whether Krok's flies were undone. Then that puzzling smell of germicide and cordite became overpowering, and he was back through the door, past the Swiss and across the lobby, lunging through the revolving doors and tripping almost headlong into the street.

He steadied himself against one of the pillars outside, breathing cold air to clear the taste of bile out of his mouth. The street was quiet except for the swish of traffic from the Cromwell Road. The porter did not come after him; but he knew he did not have long. The Swiss would try the toilet first, then call the police. It would be a matter of minutes. But meanwhile Magnus' last doubts were resolved. He would go to the police himself and tell them everything.

He had begun walking unsteadily towards Gloucester Road, where he hoped to find a taxi, when he saw something that made him stop and go cold all over.

A few yards ahead of him, against the kerb, stood a Citroën. It was parked with its rear towards him. The light in the street was not good, but he could see that it was the same unwashed grey and could read the number plate. He read it forwards, then backwards, and there was no mistake. It was his car.

He stumbled round to the front and stood looking down at the dented bonnet which had come unhinged on one side, black paint scraped along the edge, one headlamp smashed. But otherwise the impact seemed to have been absorbed by the two rubber-nosed prongs jutting out from the bumper. He thought quickly: in the shock of the crash none of them had thought of trying to drive the car away. Or rather, neither he nor Maya had thought of it.

Somebody else had, though. He was looking up and down the street, as he groped blindly round to the door on the driver's side; found it unlocked; clambered in and saw his keys still in the ignition. He reached out to switch on and a voice behind said: 'Hello, Mr Owen. Nice of you to be so prompt.' It was scarcely recognisable: a hoarse croak as if he had laryngitis. Magnus could only see his mouth in the mirror: small and prim, with the collar of the Gannex turned up round his ears.

He turned in his seat. Skliros' hands were sunk in his pockets, his face pale and slightly lopsided; otherwise, apart from his voice, there was no sign of his encounter with Krok.

'Start her up, Mr Owen. And don't do anything stupid.'

'You think I'm in a fit state to drive?'

'If you take it slowly. We don't want any more accidents.'

Magnus turned back and switched on the ignition. 'Where to?'

'Down to the Embankment.'

'The Embankment?' His voice had become an echo of the croak behind. 'You're going to kill me?'

'I'm going to have a little talk with you, Mr Owen. Now get going. We've got plenty of petrol. And don't forget your lights!' he added — a copper still to his fingertips.

He flicked on the lights, slipped into gear, eased the car into the road. Not a soul in sight. Amazing how desolate London could become just when you needed it crawling with police, traffic wardens, prowl cars. He wondered dismally what good the police would be. *'Officer, I've got a C.I.D. man in my car and he's going to kill me!'* Man with a cut over his eye, nerves all shot to pieces, smelling of that last brandy with Krok. Krok dead in the hotel, and he the last person to see him alive. Or almost the last.

'Is this official, sergeant?' he asked, slowing for a red light.

'You might say so, Mr Owen.'

He drove stiffly, carefully. 'How did you know where to find me?'

'I didn't. You're just a bonus. Steady — keep your eyes on the road.'

Cruising taxi coming towards them; youth in a windjammer loping along the opposite pavement. Slow at the Fulham Road. Easy now. Hear what he's got to say, don't rush him, he's got a gun. Any moment now there'll be a police car. Ram it. Pulled in, drunk-in-charge, night in the cells, interesting tomorrow up in front of the Bench...

'I'm looking for the girl, Mr Owen. Where is she?'

Still not a damned car in sight. The King's Road as dead as a Welsh Sabbath. 'Where is she, Mr Owen?' The stiff croak was close to his ear and he could feel the stir of breath on his neck. He was running with sweat, face, thighs, groin, hands slippery round the wheel. 'Come on, I know she wasn't in the hotel.'

'How do you know?'

'The porter told me she left.'

'So you've got the Swiss eating out of your hands too?' Something hard touched the back of his neck, nudging up against the base of the cranium. 'Two-two, isn't it?' he murmured.

'Don't be impertinent, Mr Owen. I'm not joking. I'm bloody serious. I want to know where she is. And I want to know what you were doing up on the Common tonight.' The steel ring pressed harder. Skliros sat forward, watching him in the mirror. 'Come on, lost your tongue?'

'Good looking girl. Lovely. Too good for that Pole.'

'She's a bitch.'

He nodded glumly, trying to avoid the eyes in the mirror. 'I was a bit stuck on her, that's all. Shouldn't have trusted her — neither of us should. Never trust a woman, Peter.'

The gun jabbed painfully at his neck. 'Don't ride me, Mr Owen. I've had a difficult evening. I'm being very patient with you, as it is. I've taken a lot of trouble on your behalf — driving this car down from the Common. It could have been embarrassing if it had been found.'

I bet it could, he thought. 'What about the Hillman?'

'They can't trace it.'

'And the timetable you gave the girl?'

The gun jabbed again, Skliros' breath now coming fast against his neck. 'I give you just ten seconds to tell me where she is, Mr Owen.'

Slow for the Embankment; long-distance lorries hissing to a halt at the lights on Battersea Bridge. Jerk my head backwards — once — hard — then duck down in the seat and ram one of the trucks.

'Five seconds.'

I don't owe her a damned thing — not even loyalty to Krok anymore. 'I only know what Krok told me, and he was sloshed. He said something about her going to the Polish Embassy.'

Silence from the back.

'You want me to drive back?'

'Go on over the river.'

'The Polish Embassy,' he repeated, his voice dropping to a whisper: 'It's back in Portland Place, isn't it?'

'Go on over the river.' Skliros sounded oddly relaxed.

On to the bridge. Barges creeping below like whales through the black water. Skyline dark ahead. No witnesses. I'm being taken for a ride, and all so damned easy. I've handled guns myself, even used one in anger — a heavier one too — and this punk in the back thinks he can hold me up with a baby pistol, drive out to a quiet place and kill me because I'm a witness. Coming up to more traffic lights, turning green, not a car in sight, long mean street, dark shops and houses, sweltering chaos of a Cypriot cafe with dust and glass and bodies splayed crookedly in the sunlight.

'She told us both to wait at the hotel,' he said. 'She went to pick up some friends at her embassy — said she was going for evidence. That timetable, Peter. The one you gave her.'

'You're a real joker, aren't you, Owen? You think I'd be so daft as to give her anything in my handwriting? Just keep driving.' Coming up to Clapham with the road running into a sudden hollow of blackness. 'Where now?'

'Straight on.'

The gun had left from his neck and Skliros was sitting back in the corner, both hands sunk again in his Gannex.

'Must be awkward having me around?' Magnus said at last. 'If it had just been Krok and the girl...'

No answer.

'I'm a witness. I can still cause you a lot of trouble. You realise that?'

'I'm not a halfwit, Mr Owen.'

'Then get it over with!' he yelled. 'What's stopping you? Worried about your career? I can ruin your career — I can break you, Peter Skliros!'

'You're not going to break me, and I don't give a damn about my career. First left now — then on to the A2.'

'You don't like the police?' he asked desperately. 'C.I.D. — I thought that was an interesting job?'

'"Interesting job"!' Skliros mimicked, in his tight croak: '"And don't you think our police are wonderful?" God, another bloody intellectual! You lot either think we're a bunch of fascists or we're doing a fine job protecting society. Well I can tell you, Mr Owen of *The Paper*, we're not fascists and we're not wonderful. We're just a herd of glorified pen-pushers and uniformed civil servants. Be nice to the public, nice to the nobs, nice to the foreigners, nice to the thugs and drug-pedlars and queers — because they've all got rights, you see, and there's Judge's Rules, and with a sharp lawyer and a soft magistrate, you get a rap in court and the super's on to you, saying, "Got to watch it, sergeant, can't afford to get the station a bad name." And then we're supposed to fight crime. Laws, lawyers, bloody intellectuals — you make me sick, the lot of you! Turn on the radio.'

Magnus turned it on — syrupy music late into the night. 'What about Krok?' he said. 'What had that poor sod done that you had to blow his brains out in a lavatory?'

'Careful, Owen. Careless talk costs lives.'

He nodded: straight road now, little traffic. Nearly thirty minutes' drive, and Skliros hadn't done it yet — unless he was waiting for open country. But he'd had enough time between the crash and the killing to contact Steiner or Cane; and if he had been acting under orders, and the orders had been Cane's, Magnus still had a chance. Cane might be mad, but he was still a man of principle. He would allow Magnus his defence.

Skliros said slowly: 'You're a cheeky bastard, Owen. Maybe you've got guts, or maybe you haven't, but you've kept driving this car. Or maybe that just makes you stupid? But I'll tell you something — nobody ever crosses Peter Skliros and gets away with it. I don't care if it's some toffee-nosed nob in court trying to pull a fast one or a drunken hooligan like that Pole. I get level with them all in the end. I'll get level with that girl too. Just see if I don't!'

So that leaves me, Magnus thought. *A bloody intellectual, sole witness to a murder*. He began to grip the wheel in fury, his fear draining away as he thought again of Krok gunned down in the trough of a urinal with water dribbling through his hair into a cake of germicide. But his rage was impotent, he was helpless. Skliros was cool and confident, an expert, or he wouldn't be using a silly little gun like a .22. But Magnus still hadn't given up hope.

He twiddled the knob of the radio and found some classical music on a foreign station. From then on they drove in total silence. The road grew wider, emptier, faster.

For the past hour he had been driving almost by reflex; the shock had set in again with merciful anaesthesia, and the smooth hydraulic lilt of the Citroën had a certain drugging effect of its own. At least he was still alive. Only the glimpse of the prim mouth in the mirror adjusted him to reality.

They had bypassed Maidstone and were on a minor road that cut straight into the night, rising slowly above flat fields like a railway embankment.

'We're on the marshes!' Magnus said suddenly.

'That's right.' They were the first words spoken in more than an hour.

'The Romney Marshes?' He began to feel cold, although the heater was on full.

Skliros said nothing.

'A nice lonely spot for the end of the ride?'

Skliros still said nothing, and the road went on, with a mist seeping out of the fields, giving the night a ghostly greyness in the headlamps. He began to slow down.

'Keep your speed up,' Skliros croaked from behind.

He went on slowing and felt the cold of the gun against his neck.

'Keep driving.'

He said wearily: 'It's the mist! Can't you see there's a bloody mist?'

'Keep going.'

He kept going, leaning forward, his eyes beginning to smart. After a moment he said: 'Listen, Skliros, I've kept my side of the bargain. I didn't make any trouble back in London when I had the chance. So supposing you give me a break?'

'You're doing fine,' Skliros murmured: 'Just a few more miles.'

A few more miles, then a neat little hole in the back of his brain.

He watched the marsh mist growing thicker, swirling round the car like white smoke. When he spoke again, he was appalled to hear himself whimpering: 'Look, please, I can't go any faster. The mist, it's getting worse.'

He had slowed right down now, and heard the voice in his ear say, 'It's all right, Mr Owen. You're doing fine. It's not far now.'

It was then that Magnus decided to swing the wheel over and plunge them both into the marshy darkness. He calculated he would have a double advantage: he would be prepared and Skliros would not; and he could also brace himself against the steering wheel. It seemed a good chance — at least, a hero's chance.

But the next moment that chance was gone. There were hedges on either side and Skliros was saying: 'Easy now. There's a turning on the left.'

It was a farm track, scarcely wide enough for one large car and fenced in on both sides by strands of barbed wire. *A one-way track*, Magnus thought: *the point of no return.* 'Just here,' Skliros said.

The wire fences spread apart, then disappeared. Two red lights glowed out of the dark, and a dog began to bark. The Citroën's headlamps had picked out the reflector lights of a car parked in a muddy paddock. There were more lights beyond — the curtained windows of a house.

'Stop here,' Skliros said. Magnus drew up beside the car and sat resting on the wheel. 'Right — out!' Skliros laid a hand on his shoulder and Magnus said, without moving: 'Shut your mouth.' He leant against the wheel, breathing heavily.

'What's the matter?'

Magnus swung round with his fists up, and the man slunk back for a moment, both hands empty. 'You ever driven for two hours with a gun at your head — and you ask me if anything's the matter!' His words spluttered with fury, unintelligible: 'Get out yourself.'

Skliros sat watching him with a flat stare, then leant forward and took the keys from the ignition. 'Very well, take your time.' He opened his door and got out, his hands back in his Gannex. Without looking again at Magnus he began to walk towards the house.

Magnus took his time. He watched Skliros reach the house, a door open, then close. Outside, the dog went on barking. As he listened he began to feel an odd affinity with that dog. Finally he got out, his shoes squelching in mud. The night was cold and fresh and he could smell the sea. Once, when the dog paused, he heard the distant quacking of wildfowl. He began to make his way over to the house. On the way he looked back and noticed the car beside his own — a black Humber.

It was a rambling barn-like house. There was no one at the door. Inside was a tiled passage lined with gumboots, old coats, caps, walking sticks on pegs. Unconsciously he began to wipe his shoes on the mat. A door opened and Cane stood there, stooped under the lintel. 'Magnus! Come in.' He did not smile.

Magnus followed him into a low room with beams and whitewashed walls. There were antique clocks ticking and swinging on the walls and logs crackling on a brick hearth. The room smelt of woodsmoke and fresh coffee. There were two other men in the room — Skliros and Jan Steiner.

No one spoke. Cane pointed to a shabby armchair. Steiner stood at the far side of the fireplace; Skliros at the end of the room beside a grandfather clock.

Magnus slumped down heavily and looked into the flames.

Cane said: 'You'd like some coffee, Magnus?' He wore old trousers tucked into Wellington boots with the tops turned down — a gentleman farmer relaxing by his fireside.

When Magnus failed to answer, Cane made a quick gesture and Skliros slipped through a door at the end of the room. A little later Magnus felt a bowl of black coffee placed in his hands. 'You couldn't lace this with something — something medicinal — could you?' He looked up at Cane with a grin like death. 'I know it's against the rules — but I've had a hard drive.'

'Of course!' Cane made another gesture and Skliros was gone again. They listened to the logs crackling, clocks ticking, the dog still barking outside. Cane turned to Steiner: 'Do try to shut that animal up, Jan.' Steiner nodded and trotted heavily from the room.

'Nice place you've got here, John.' He sipped his coffee. 'Very peaceful.' Skliros returned with a bottle of pale brandy and poured some into his cup. 'Thank you, Peter.' Skliros recorked the bottle with a thump.

'Magnus, tell us why you left the meeting last night and followed Bogdan Krok.'

Magnus put his face down into the big coffee cup, thinking rapidly: *Must pull myself together; he wants to give me the benefit of the doubt; must help him.* He looked up at Cane and tried to smile. 'I'm sorry, John. It was damned silly — weakness of the moment, shall we say?' He knew he was too pale to blush, but he tried his best hangdog air: 'It was the girl. You know, I met her down in Cardiff. I rather liked her.'

Steiner came back into the room; the dog outside had stopped barking.

'Krok was dreadfully drunk, and when I saw she'd gone out with him I was worried. I went after them — I don't really know why. I suppose I might have been a bit jealous.'

Cane said: 'You realise that your moment of weakness, as you call it — what I would call a weakness of the flesh — has placed you in a very difficult position indeed?'

Magnus looked into his coffee and said nothing. All around the clocks seemed to be ticking chaotically. Cane's voice reached him like a voice on the edge of sleep.

'Magnus, on my own initiative I took you into my confidence. Indeed into the confidence of all of us. I did this because I saw in you a kindred spirit — someone whom I could not only help by sharing a common purpose, but who, with discipline and experience, could help us in turn. No man can be perfectly certain of his fellow humans. We are all fallible. But you, Magnus, are a little too fallible.'

He nodded wearily. The case for the prosecution. The death sentence will follow. Skliros is only waiting. *Get on with it. Get on with it! I'm so bloody tired.*

'You have behaved, Magnus, like an infatuated boy. What you hoped to achieve by following that girl and her drunken escort, I cannot begin to imagine. But there we are, the damage is done — and the damage is heavy.'

He looked up, his heart beating fast. Was it possible that Cane believed him? — believed that he had chased after Maya and Krok simply out of jealousy? But then he looked at Skliros, his face white and misshapen, at the end of the room — and he knew that Skliros did not believe a word of it. Nor did Steiner. They were just playing with him.

'What happened tonight,' Cane said, 'has been a shock to you. It has been a shock to all of us. Tonight we were betrayed.'

'Betrayed?' He was looking Cane in the eye now, arming himself again with that memory of water washing Krok's pathetic wound. He had played the dumb foundling long enough, he wasn't going to go down without a fight, even in front of this velvet-gloved fanatic. 'You talk about being betrayed!' he began, 'betrayed by a bloody girl —' when the whole room exploded in a cacophony of chimes and gongs striking four o'clock. When it was quiet again he had lost his impetus. He faltered.

'I'm sorry, John. You were betrayed. A man was also killed. That takes a bit of getting used to.' He sank back, his last moment of glory stillborn. Now they could kill him like a dog, just as they had killed Krok.

Cane nodded gravely: 'But I should not allow yourself to become too sentimental about Mr Bogden Krok, Magnus. You yourself saw his behaviour at the Radcliffe Hall — the behaviour of a lout, a worthless exhibitionist abusing the most basic hospitality. His behaviour has already become a national disgrace to his own country, and it would clearly have become the same here — except that in the present moral climate of our society, it was just this hooliganism that would have helped make him an international hero. People like Krok must be stopped, even if it does mean taking a few shortcuts across the law.'

Magnus looked at Steiner, then at Skliros. Neither had moved. Obedient hirelings, both of them; and he felt the rage rising again, exhilarating him. He turned back to Cane: 'So Krok was killed because he got drunk and insulted the East-West Cultural Association?'

Then Cane lost his temper. 'Are you just obstinate or stupid? We are at war. All of us in this room. You too! I warned last time that if you wanted to opt out you had the chance. You didn't, and now it's too late.' His eyes had that dark feverish look that made Magnus shrink a little in his chair.

'Yesterday an operation was mounted — a simple exercise to cut down a disreputable foreign impostor. But the operation went wrong. It went wrong because we were betrayed. And a man has been killed. But what do you think would happen if every time a fighting soldier saw a man die he paused to search his heart and weep? Why, he would go out of his mind! What has happened is regrettable, of course — all death is regrettable. But who was Krok, anyway? A degenerate drunk.'

Magnus finished his coffee. 'Well, poor old Krok. That just leaves me, I suppose?'

'Not quite. There's still the girl.' He had stretched back in his chair looking at the ceiling; and without moving his eyes, called out: 'Get Mr Owen another coffee, Peter. A strong one — with a little cognac again, if Mr Owen so wishes.'

Magnus nodded, as Skliros came soundlessly across the room and took his cup.

'Peter informs me that you claim she went to the Polish Embassy?'

'It's only what Krok told me — if you can believe Krok.'

'I think in this case we shall have to. Fortunately, the Polish Embassy represents a government that is technically hostile. Even if she is able to convince them, it is hard to see what immediate action they can take. Naturally, our own authorities will be concerned about the death of Krok —'

Skliros had returned with the coffee, which Magnus sat up and began to drink greedily. He had not seen Skliros put the brandy in this time, but it had the right bitter taste, hot and sugarless.

'Eventually,' Cane went on, 'since they will find no immediate clue, our police will be obliged to follow the only lead there is — even if it does come indirectly from the officials of an unfriendly government. This could prove embarrassing. Not least of all, for you, Magnus. For you do appreciate your position in all this, don't you?'

Magnus leant forward and nodded, trying to concentrate but feeling too tired, the fire suddenly too hot, as he tried to push back his chair, listening to Cane's voice which seemed very close to his ear now: 'You see, you're deeply involved. Fortunately, Peter here was able to remove your car from the scene of the accident. But you were there, weren't you? Even the girl will have to admit that. And then there's the hotel porter, the guests — seeing you go in, go out — and you admit you were jealous of Krok, you were seen last night chasing after him and the girl…'

Magnus nodded again, swinging his empty cup in time with one of the pendulums on the wall. He could not see Cane very clearly any more, and felt his head drooping, his eyelids sliding down with exhaustion. He shook himself, tried to focus on Cane, and was dimly aware that Skliros was standing beside him. He began to protest: 'Look, John, I'm all right. I know he's one of your privileged heavies, but for God's sake take him away!'

When he looked up again, Skliros and Steiner were gone. Cane's voice called to him gently: 'You're very, very tired, Magnus. You must try and rest.'

He nodded. 'But tell me what happens to me?' His voice seemed to be reaching him from a long way off; he tried to sit up straight, tried to look at Cane whose face was now rising and falling like a yo-yo.

'Magnus, it is necessary that we take you away — for only a short time — for a holiday.'

'Holiday?' He peered up through a thickening mist. All around he could hear the clocks ticking, louder and louder, while Cane's voice grew fainter and fainter.

'You've been overworking. There's nothing to be ashamed of, it happens to lots of people. Overwork. Don't worry about *The Paper*. I'll be getting in touch with them — they'll understand.'

Hugh Rissell. He'll understand. To hell he'll understand. His head was dropping. A great warm darkness was coming up at him and he thought vaguely, happily, *the bastards have drugged me*. Then he fell forward.

PART 4: RETREAT

CHAPTER 1

He came round without pain, as gently as he had gone out. He was in a narrow, tightly-made bed of cold linen. He was comfortable. He was dressed in pyjamas, loose silk, and for some time he did not want to wake up. The only thing that troubled him was the window. It was just above his head: a small window with a blind drawn, but the light seeped round the edges and hurt his eyes.

He sat up. There was a curious noise — a humming roar that came from all round him. The bed vibrated with it; there was also a metallic smell and the air was not quite fresh. He pulled himself up and released the blind.

The window was the size and shape of a television screen; beyond was the sky. It was a huge luminous grey, and below was darkness. He turned and saw that the other side of the bed was hemmed in by a curtain. He put his legs over the edge and found they were swinging in mid-air. Without bothering to pull the curtain back, he slid off the bed and dropped a few feet on to a pile carpet. He was in a gangway lit by dim blue lights along the ceiling. The floor vibrated. It was very warm, and his head felt thick and his mouth was dry with the aftertaste of barbiturates.

He looked at his watch: just after ten o'clock. There were curtains drawn down both sides of the gangway, with more curtains at either end. In his bare feet he began to pad along in the direction of the humming noise. He pulled the curtains aside and blinked at the sudden light.

He was looking into what seemed to be a glass room full of dials. A man with earphones sat with his hand on a lever next to another man who was making notes on a chart. This second man looked up at him with surprise, but did not move. Magnus stood for a moment gaping at them, then walked groggily back down the gangway. His mind was still slow and unclear, and after some fumbling among the curtains — during which he mistook his bunk and put his hand on a sleeping face which snorted but did not wake — he finally found his own bunk, clambered in and fell asleep again almost at once.

His next conscious moment was looking into Cane's smiling face, his jaw dark with stubble. 'Awake! Already?'

'Hullo. So I'm still alive?'

Cane chuckled: 'Of course you are. Like some coffee?'

Magnus grinned and the curtain flapped shut. He waited, peering again through the window.

It was a twin-engined aircraft with no markings which he could see. Below lay what looked like a wrinkled black carpet sliced up by grey and white channels that rose and dipped with the miniature fluctuations of the ground. There were no clouds, and the light puzzled him. He could not decide whether it was morning or evening, although Cane's hearty welcome indicated the former. In any case, Cane was hardly the man to go a whole day without shaving.

On the horizon he could see mountains, tiny and sharp as crystal against the dark spread below.

The curtain broke again and Cane handed him a paper cup of coffee — black and steaming — and memory became clearer. He swung his legs back off the bunk and said: 'I don't like to sound nosey or anything, but where are we going? Not Poland, by any chance?'

Cane smiled wanly. 'No, Magnus. We're going to Iceland.'

Magnus thought he must have heard 'Ireland'. Cane laughed: 'No, no! Iceland. Don't look so surprised — it's only five hours from London.'

Magnus glanced at his watch again: 'Leaving at six-thirty this morning? You must have been in quite a hurry!'

'We were. Now, I'll get your clothes. We'll be landing in about twenty minutes.'

'John, who undressed me?'

Cane looked disconcerted. 'I did. Thought you'd be more comfortable.'

'After you'd had me held up with a gun, then drugged me?'

'It was for your own good, Magnus. You were very overwrought.' He smiled and patted his knee like a doctor. 'Anyway, you seem to have made a splendid recovery! I'll see you when you're dressed.'

Magnus sat with his legs dangling over the edge and thought about Iceland. He found there was very little he could think about, except that the name was vaguely bound up with B.B.C. shipping forecasts. Dogger, Fisher, Bight — south-east Iceland. Then he began to wonder if he really was going out of his mind. He had read and heard the usual stories about brainwashing and amnesia after a knock on the head.

There was nothing to do but finish his coffee and wait for his clothes. These were brought, neatly folded in an overnight bag, by Steiner, his face as closed as ever. Magnus dressed slowly, noticing as he did so that nothing had been taken from his pockets. His wallet still contained £17, his driving licence, insurance, Press card, Scotland Yard pass and cheque book. At least they trusted him that far. All that was gone were his keys, and he did not think he would need them in Iceland.

The other curtains down the gangway had now been drawn and the beds folded up like couchettes in a train. In the seat across from him Peter Skliros was eating a breakfast of coffee, rolls and jam off a plastic tray. He did not even glance up at Magnus; his face was still pale and slightly swollen, but as smooth as though he had just shaved.

Cane and Steiner came through a moment later from the control cabin and sat down. There were no greetings. Cane had been the only one to show any enthusiasm, but now he sat stiff and hollow-cheeked, his eyes staring in front of him. His jollity on waking Magnus must have been an effort, and was short-lived. He now looked exhausted with worry.

The pitch of the engines changed; there was a slight lurch and the man Magnus had seen marking the chart in the cabin now came forward and asked them formally, in a Scandinavian accent, to fasten their seat belts.

Below, the black carpet was rippling into firmer contours, the grey and white channels growing broader, clearer, into great valleys of snow and ice. Somewhere in Magnus' mind it was all familiar: a painting he had seen somewhere, a glacier under the midnight sun.

The next moment they landed. Cane handed him his overcoat, but when the door was opened he was surprised how mild it was. The light was pale grey, and the air had a harshness that stung his nostrils and was deliciously invigorating after the stale cabin.

The runway was a stretch of what appeared to be cinders. There was a windsock flying from the roof of a prefabricated hut, in front of which stood a Volkswagen minibus. Otherwise, there was no sign of civilisation. Beyond the hut rose a wall of mountains stretching to the horizon. There was not a tree or house or blade of grass in sight. A dark, dead, alien landscape in which the only sound, as they walked towards the hut, was the crunch of cinders underfoot. Cane came up beside him and took his arm. 'Not long now. I expect you're tired?'

'I'm curious. How did we get out of England? No passports, no Immigration?'

'Ah!' Cane gripped his arm tighter: 'I'll explain everything later.'

As they reached the hut a tall man with thick grey hair and a face creased like an autumn leaf came forward to greet them. He wore mountaineering clothes and hobnail boots. Cane introduced him to Magnus as Mr Erik Pallson.

Pallson shook hands all round, then withdrew to speak to Cane, while the others climbed into the minibus. Again no Immigration, no Customs; but Magnus had ceased to wonder any more. He found himself sitting opposite Skliros, their knees almost touching. For an instant he met those bright grey eyes, and was glad when the other two came aboard — Pallson in the driving seat — and they started off.

Beside him Steiner began to snooze noisily. Magnus turned to the window and watched the black cinders crawl by. After a time the landscape became a desert of pumice stone, ridged into static waves that flowed out and swelled into strange cones and towers. A prehistoric land forced up through the earth's crust by volcanic action — a landscape on which modern Man seemed to have only the slenderest foothold.

At the back of the bus Cane sat impassively, hands in his lap, his eyes as dark as the scene outside. Magnus did not disturb him. Only one thing mattered for the moment: he was alive. If they had wanted to kill him, they could have done so easily enough back on the marshes. But instead they had decided to take this elaborate trouble to spirit him away. The plane, he guessed, probably belonged to Sir Lionel Hilder; he also remembered that in Cane's corner of Kent there were several airfields — Lympne, Lydd, Manston — and the sound of aircraft taking off in the early morning would attract no attention.

Nevertheless, to be able to fly a private plane from England to Iceland at a few hours' notice was no mean feat. This was a strange and daunting organisation. And again he began to wonder who was behind it. Surely not Cane? He was too open, too informal. Sir Lionel Hilder was probably just old moneybags, and the rest were no more than subalterns, hatchet-men.

He dozed off, his head bumping against the window. They had been driving for nearly an hour when he woke. The mountains had become lower, flat-topped, along a valley where the lava fields had crumbled to ash, sprinkled with tufts of brown grass and dwarf trees that reached no higher than a man's waist. As he looked out, he saw a great trail of sheep, perhaps a thousand of them, winding in single file across the lava; and for the first time he understood the expression 'following like a sheep'. There was no shepherd, not even a dog in sight. They were following one of their kind. A leader among sheep. A considerable achievement, he thought drowsily: perhaps Cane and his friends could have something to learn from that first plodding beast.

He fell asleep again, and when next he woke the bus had stopped.

Once again the landscape had changed radically. They had reached the end of a broad plain between mountains, and were now in the neck of a steep valley. On either side the lava sheered dismally away into that curious cloudless sky that was a hybrid-light between dusk and dawn.

At the foot of the valley, alone in the black wilderness, stood a house. Indeed, it was more than a house — it was a folly.

Built of bricks hewn from the lava, it rose five storeys under crenellated battlements and pointed black towers with leering gargoyles fashioned out of pumice stone and gables honeycombed with birds' nests. All the windows above the first floor were shuttered. The entrance, above a sweep of balustraded steps, led under a Gothic arch with a door built to resist a battering ram, studded with nails each the size of a man's fist. The only rational signs of civilisation were two Beetle Volkswagens parked in front of the steps, and a single electric cable that reached back down the valley on poles that disappeared with the horizon.

Magnus got out and stared wonderingly. He had seen houses in England that tried to be like this — houses built by eccentric gentlemen in the nineteenth century, to decline into the premises of some prep, school or nursing home. But nothing quite as preposterous as this — an ogre's castle set down in the midst of a Nordic desert. For a moment he wanted to laugh.

Cane was beside him, with a smile: 'You find it amusing?'

'Amazing! Who was responsible?'

'A Dane in the last century. They tried to turn it into a tourist hotel after the war, but —' he waved his hand with a shrug '— it's hardly a tourist spot.'

'So you took it over?' Above them the doors had been swung open by a tow-haired youth in a dark suit.

'We got it for a song,' Cane said vaguely, 'and it comes in very useful. It's out of the way, and you can get a lot of people in. Getting supplies up is the problem but there's always the airstrip.'

They entered a dim baronial hall with cathedral windows and shrouded furniture; chandeliers hung far above them, and Magnus could just make out huge paintings of stags and

184

reindeer and landscapes that reminded him of the one in Cane's room in Albany.

'What do you use it for?' he asked, bewildered.

Cane looked at him absent-mindedly: 'This place? Oh, it's a kind of holiday resort. It's called the Haëli — Icelandic for "retreat". We also use it for conventions.'

'Conventions?' But Cane did not seem to have heard; he had signalled something to Pallson, who was bringing in the luggage. Pallson nodded and Cane said, 'Right, Magnus! If you'll follow me —' He was already leading him away across the hall through a second Gothic arch, up some winding steps through a padded door, into a bright modern corridor stuffy with central heating. They came to a self-operated lift. The control panel had seven unnumbered buttons. Cane pushed the one from the top and Magnus remembered the five rows of windows outside. The house must have two floors of cellars.

They stopped in less than three seconds, and came out into another bright corridor lined with plain doors of honey-brown pinewood. There seemed to be no daylight anywhere. Magnus supposed the house had its own power plant. The cables down the valley would only connect the telephone.

Cane strode ahead, round a corner, down another corridor with doors on either side, impersonal as a hotel. He opened the last door. 'I think you'll like this room.'

It was white and spartan, with the fresh smell of pinewood. The bed was covered with a thick duvet and the double-windows were closed, the outer panes steamed up. Cane opened a second door and showed him the bathroom: shower curtain, towels, wrapped soap, box of tissues. 'I'll have some shaving things sent up for you. Anything else you want?'

'Only to know what I'm doing here.'

Cane closed the door and stepped back into the bedroom. 'I thought I explained last night.'

'I was confused last night. All I know is you put something in my coffee and I woke up this morning over Iceland.'

Cane looked at him kindly, a little sorrowfully. 'We've taken you here for your own good, Magnus. Believe me. Just while things are a bit difficult back in London. Now I suggest you have a little more sleep, then I'll have some lunch sent up, and afterwards we can have a talk. Do you want to shave now, or wait?'

Magnus gave his hang-dog grin: 'I'll wait.' (*What's the hurry, anyway?* he thought. *Why bother to shave at all?*) 'Am I under open or close arrest?'

'Don't be melodramatic — it doesn't suit you.' Cane swung on his heel, then paused: 'We're taking a lot of trouble over you, Magnus. I'd like you to appreciate it.'

'You mean the Conrad Hilton treatment? Oh I appreciate it. It's just that I'm a little worried about young Peter Skliros.'

'He's none of your concern.'

'Sure he's not. Except that he's been brought here to kill me.'

'Oh don't talk rot!' Cane was angry, but his anger was oblique; it did not seem to be directed at Magnus. He was frowning at the wall, as he added, 'Skliros is under my orders. You have nothing to fear.'

'Did he have orders to kill Bogdan Krok?'

'You're being impertinent. We've had this out before, Magnus. A soldier does not question the decisions of his superiors.'

Magnus held his tongue, knowing that Cane was not only worried, but undecided. Skliros was a murderer and Magnus the prime witness; both were an embarrassment, and both had to be kept out of the way. The question was, for how long?

Krok had been destroyed. That, in one degree or another, had been policy. But Magnus had become involved and that was not policy. Logically, Magnus must be destroyed too; yet for the moment Cane seemed to want to protect him. Cane was not a cruel man. A fanatic, deluded, but not wicked.

Whatever I do, he thought, *I must play along with Cane.* His shoulders sagged and he said lamely: 'I've been talking like a fool, John. I'm still overwrought after last night.'

Cane's face cleared. 'I know, I know. Don't worry, we're all a little overwrought. Just you get some more sleep and then we'll try and get matters sorted out.'

'Just one thing,' Magnus said. 'About *The Paper*?'

Cane gave his warmest smile 'Oh that's been settled, don't worry! I've left a letter telling them you're ill — that you're ill and need a rest — several weeks' rest.' His smile became almost roguish, 'I said I was a doctor.'

'Rather short notice, isn't it? I was only in the office yesterday evening. Supposing they check up?'

Cane chuckled: 'That's the least of our troubles. Sleep well.' The door closed softly behind him.

Magnus waited till he would be safely gone, then stepped over and tried the handle. It was unlocked. Outside the corridor was empty and silent. He closed it again, and went back across the room and unfastened the double casement, throwing open the outer misted windows.

What he saw puzzled him. In the lift Cane had pushed the button one from the top, which indicated the fourth floor, yet he was now looking out on to ground rising less than twelve feet below the window. He wondered, had the lift been some kind of trick? Then he realised the house had been built against the slope, and he must now be at the back of the building, looking up the funnel of the valley above.

He looked up that valley with a sense of awe. In the half-light, distances were hard to calculate, but perhaps a mile away there began what appeared to be a vast grey staircase climbing between the mountains into the sky. He was looking up a gigantic glacier. The mountains were high and shining white against the greyness, and everywhere there was silence. It was magnificently weird.

He looked sideways, along rows of shuttered windows, like a hotel in the off-season. There was no sign of life. No bars on the windows, no railings or traps below. Just this great house in the wilderness where they held conventions with planes summoned in the night to fly from Kent to the rim of the Arctic Circle.

It was too huge and confusing for him, and he moved away, leaving the windows half-open, stripped off his clothes, climbed under the duvet and collapsed into sleep.

CHAPTER 2

He was woken by a sing-song voice calling: 'Hello! You have slept well?'

Magnus peered up into the lean brown face of Erik Pallson. 'I have brought you things to shave with.' He smiled and put a pigskin case on the bedside table. 'You are quite comfortable? Your lunch will come in half an hour.' He disappeared without a sound.

Magnus' watch said four o'clock. He turned it back two hours, got up and walked naked into the bathroom. In spite of the open windows, his throat and nostrils were raw with the central heating, and he had a headache. The bath water came on steaming hot but with a sickly stench of sulphur. He filled it deep and lay soaking in it for a long time, trying to collect his thoughts. Cane had said he was not a prisoner, that he had been brought here for his own protection. This strange organisation had taken him into its shelter and he was not to worry.

But as he basked in the steaming heat, he did worry. The awesome sight of that glacier outside had left him with a nasty presentiment which he tried to fight off with wild thoughts — by thinking of Maya, closing his eyes and drawing her long body down against him, warm and naked in the water. Maya had escaped them. It was she who was their problem now, not him.

He got out and shaved listlessly, and had just finished dressing when there was a knock on the door. Pallson reappeared with a tray of food. 'Mr Cane will be coming soon,' he said, smiling, and was gone again. Magnus looked at the tray

— spiced herring, potato salad and tinned peaches. He began to feel more like a patient in hospital than a prisoner. He began to eat, without appetite.

They had spared him, he thought, because although he was a dangerous liability to them, his elimination would pose an even greater danger. Bogdan Krok had been one thing — a wild drunkard, a foreigner without roots, a man whose death would be lamented only by the professional film world and by his fans. But to dispose of Magnus Owen of *The Paper*, cause him to vanish overnight, would create impossible complications.

He was trying desperately to convince himself, thinking aloud now. He could disappear for a few weeks, a few months perhaps, but then the questions would begin to pile up, the rumours and paperwork — bills, tax, back insurance stamps — not to forget his wife's solicitors. Cane might be able to square Hugh Rissell with a bogus doctor's certificate, but he dared him to take on his wife and her family!

But there was yet another reason why he had been spared. Cane, in his fanaticism, had decided he was a valuable recruit: a man with his own passions and prejudices, but with faults and failings that made his conversion all the more challenging. Cane had not only found a novice in his own image — he also had the pleasure of initiating him. The lapses, the 'small weaknesses' — they were all part of the challenge.

The door had opened silently, without a knock. Beside the bed stood the tow-haired young man who had first let them in when they arrived. 'Please come,' he said, in stiff uncertain English.

'Where to?'

'Please come,' he repeated. He was thin and wiry, and probably very strong, Magnus guessed. He followed him out, walking just behind him to the lift. They rode down in silence.

Magnus began to feel uneasy. Pallson had said that Cane would be coming. Had Cane changed his mind, been overruled by the others? Magnus suddenly saw the feebleness of his earlier reasoning. All those people who would fuss over his disappearance — colleagues, creditors, solicitors — they were all a long way off, and the lava fields and the great glacier were very close and quite as good as anywhere on the Romney Marshes.

Down in the baronial hall the chandeliers had been lit against the grey light, and the sheets stripped from the furniture. In a far corner Steiner and Skliros were playing snooker.

Cane had risen from an armchair, his voice ringing across the hall: 'Ah there you are! Slept well?'

'Fine, thank you.' He watched Skliros chalking his cue, while Steiner played a red ball.

'I thought we might take a little walk. Feeling up to it?' He glanced at Magnus' feet. 'We'd better get you something to wear.' He called out in Icelandic, and the tow-haired youth scuttled away like a fag in a public school. In fact, it was all very like a public school — the dim frowsty atmosphere of the Common Room, with the masters relaxing round the billiard table. Only the Head Master was not there.

The young Icelander returned with an anorak and a pair of heavy boots which Magnus put on in the entrance hall, where he found Cane also booted and wearing a red woollen pixie-hat. He was also holding a stick of knotted rosewood, varnished black with a silver spike. Next to the pixie-hat it had an oddly evil appearance; and as they were leaving he swung it casually, but with such force that Magnus felt the air swish past his face. 'Ready?' Cane opened one of the studded doors and led the way down to the forecourt where only one of the Beetle Volkswagen cars was left.

'So the bus went back?' Magnus asked.

Cane nodded, striding towards a steep path that climbed round the buttresses of the house.

'And the plane?'

But Cane was already several feet ahead of him and did not seem to hear. Magnus scrambled up beside him: 'Did the plane go back to England?'

Cane turned, shaking his head: 'So many questions, Magnus, and so many answers to be given. Suppose you just leave me to give them in my own time?'

Magnus said no more. They climbed round the house and started up the slope he had seen from his room. The view, no longer confined to the frame of a window, now opened up as wide as the sky. Cane pointed up with his stick at the great ice-floe above. 'The Vatnajökull! The largest glacier in Europe. There are three active volcanoes under it, and when one of them goes up you get floods for hundreds of miles!'

'Great place for a country house,' Magnus muttered, and shouted: 'Whereabouts is it?' He did not ask the question idly: all he knew about Iceland, besides its fishing dispute with Britain, was that its capital was Reykjavik somewhere in the south-west.

But again Cane made as though he did not hear. He was climbing fast, with the ease of a young man, and Magnus' bad leg was already drawing out the distance between them. Apart from his limp, his boots were sinking into the lava shingle, and his face was streaming with sweat despite the brittle air that caught in his lungs with a panting wheeze.

For the next half-hour they climbed steadily and almost in complete silence. Off the shingle, up a steep gully where a fat grey moss now began to spread out underfoot like fungus.

'Careful!' Cane called back: 'It's treacherous stuff — if you go through you can break a leg!'

'How far are we going?' Magnus cried breathlessly; but just then a wind moaned round him and he did not catch the answer. Cane had started up a slope on one side, using his stick as a prop, and was soon a good fifty feet above him. Magnus pressed on, crouching on all fours, gasping and cursing Cane's vitality. He had not yet begun to be frightened.

Cane stopped at the top of the slope and stood waving down at him. 'Take your time! There's a glorious view up here!'

Magnus rested again and looked back, past the folds of moss and lava, to the Haëli far below, shrunk to a miniature castle out of a fairy tale. The wind had grown sharper and now that he had stopped he could feel it biting into the sweat on his face.

It took him another ten minutes to reach Cane, who was leaning on his stick, holding something in his hand. It was a bar of chocolate. 'Tired?' His eyes were shining with exhilaration. 'A few days of this and you'll be as fit as a fiddle!'

'So I'm here for my health, am I?' He accepted the chocolate.

'For your safety, Magnus. You must be patient.'

'I'd find it easier if you'd just tell me what's going to happen.'

Cane had turned with a deep sigh: 'I don't know. Honestly, Magnus. None of us does. We must wait.'

'Wait for what?'

Cane leaned on his stick, his head bowed. 'You must understand,' he said at last, 'that at this point the most important thing is to be out of the way — to lie low until something can be worked out.'

'And this walk?'

Cane gave a small grim smile. 'It'll be worth it when we get there. You see!' He had turned as he spoke, striding on, using his stick to prod the crust of moss which was now beginning to crumble under their boots in little clouds of grey dust. A horrible leprous vegetation, dead as the lava.

Suddenly he shouted over his shoulder: 'I'll know more this evening. We're expecting a visitor. Somebody important.'

'From England?' Magnus gasped.

'That's right.'

'The head of the organisation?'

Cane swung round, his face grey under the pixie-hat. 'What do you mean, head of the organisation?'

Magnus paused, panting for breath. 'I assume somebody must be the head. And I don't think it's you.'

'You want to know too much.'

'I already know too much. Don't I?'

Cane looked down at him for some time, and Magnus thought he saw his knuckles whitening round the top of the stick. 'That may be so,' he said at last. 'I'm only trying to protect you, Magnus. God man! Don't you realise that by now?' He turned back to the slope. 'You'll learn the answers soon enough,' he added; and again they plodded on in silence.

Beyond the next ridge they began to pass hollows of snow. Magnus could now make out in detail the edge of the glacier — a jagged wall of ice darkened with lava dust whipped up by the wind. A little farther they reached the snow line. Cane was moving carefully now, feeling each step with his toe, while Magnus followed exactly behind, the snow creaking under their boots.

They were about five hundred yards from the glacier when suddenly, from behind them, the whole landscape flared up in brilliant light. They swung round, shielding their eyes. Just above the horizon the sun had appeared, hanging so low in the sky that for a moment it seemed to be almost beneath them, reflected off the snow in a yellow dazzle that made their eyes ache. When he turned back, Magnus saw that the glacier above was filled with a peculiar glow, and he remembered the three buried volcanoes Cane had talked of. He shuddered, pulling his anorak close round him.

Cane was standing a few feet above him. 'Oh my God, the beauty of it!' he cried. 'The sheer peace and purity!' His eyes caught splinters of sunlight as his lips parted in a smile of childlike innocence. 'Purity. Peace. Great good words — once. But now they're sneered at, despised. But, Magnus, I am proud to be one of those last fools who hold them dear.'

As he spoke the sun faded as suddenly as it had come. It was as though the lights had been turned down in a huge auditorium, while above them a great shadow seemed to have settled down that icy staircase, and the mountain peaks were dim against a dark sky. The wind had fallen and Magnus was filled with a cold dread.

'In such moments one begins to feel a little of the power and communion of the human spirit,' Cane went on. 'This is the way it was in the beginning — the way it was always meant to be. And what have we little men made of it? We've plunged the world into torment, savaged it with lust, filled it with materialism and false gods!' His smile had been as fleeting as the sun: his face grey now, with not even a glow in his cheeks after the climb.

The wind came up again, tugging at the edges of his hair under the pixie-hat. 'Let's walk on a little farther. It's really a splendid sight!' He turned and headed on into the snow, which was becoming deeper, more uneven, rocking under their feet the nearer they came to the glacier.

Magnus saw the danger at once. Without a stick he could only move very slowly, and although he still picked his way along in Cane's footsteps, several times he felt his boots sink to the ankles and stood balancing himself like a tight-rope walker. He was about to ask if they couldn't call it a day, when Cane stopped again, leaning forward with both hands on the stick.

'Magnus.' A look of sudden pain crossed his eyes. 'You don't really understand? You don't understand at all, do you?'

'I'm sorry, John, but I'm not quite with you.'

'I told you before, they're everywhere. They know no bounds of race, creed or politics. They're international. The sickness, Magnus — the green sickness. The Queers' Charter — the little land of Sodom.'

Magnus said nothing; he was watching the stick under Cane's hands — strong piano-playing hands.

'But we're different, you see. We discriminate. We're not sick, and we do not invite the sick. We have what they will never have. We have moral fibre — a purpose in life. The purpose to recapture greatness and truth and purity!'

Magnus nodded and shivered — but not just because of the wind this time. The man's mad, he thought: and he's got that stick. The snow felt very unsteady under his feet, as he waited for Cane to go on:

'But there are things you do understand — understand perhaps better than any of us. How they percolate down from the highest in the nation to the very dregs. How they work in politics, Press, theatre and television, the Foreign Service.' He paused. 'Even the Intelligence Service. But of course, Magnus, you know that?'

Magnus just nodded again, and for a moment missed the point. He was thinking that when he'd heard Cane before he had found him strangely impressive. Perhaps it would all have sounded better in the calm of Albany, but here, on the tip of a glacier in Iceland, it was a nonsense conversation, in a nonsense landscape.

He said, in a controlled voice: 'Let's go back, John. It's getting dark.'

'It never gets dark at this time of year. We can take our time. Besides, I want to hear something about the British Intelligence Service.'

Magnus felt suddenly sick. Cane was looking down at him, almost pityingly, holding the stick now in both hands. Neither of them moved.

'I knew all about you, Magnus. Right from the beginning.'

'Well done.' He felt his mouth drying up, as Cane took a step forward. The snow crunched under his boot, but held.

'But what made you do it, man? You're not a professional agent, you're just an amateur. Did they offer you money? But you had a good job with *The Paper*. You wrote well. Why did you have to throw it all up, just to have a go at us? What have we ever done to you?' He was almost pleading. 'We never did you any harm, did we?'

'Come on, if you believe I'm a British secret agent, you're as mad as a barking hatter, but I'm ready for you. Come on!' He did not trust himself to step back into the snow, but crouched down, arms out at his sides, still watching the stick. There was no definable expression to be traced in Cane's eyes: when he attacked, Magnus would know it only from the swing of the stick. He was still out of range, but he felt his bad leg going, taking his weight on the other and tensing his muscles. 'Try and take me without the stick, John!' he yelled.

Cane's eyes dropped for an instant to the knotted weapon in his hands. When he looked up he was frowning.

'Unarmed combat, John. Didn't they teach you it in the war, in Military Intelligence? Poland, wasn't it. You must have used it against the Germans? Or was it against the Poles?' He was playing for time now, bluffing wildly, remembering that a man made angry is sometimes easier to fight than one cold-sober.

'What do you mean, against the Poles?' Cane's voice had changed entirely — no longer plaintive or accusing, but full of quiet fury.

Round One, Magnus thought, and gave a loud laugh that echoed up the ice. 'You just called me a traitor, John. Well I'm calling you one. You say you knew about me from the very beginning. You're a bloody liar! You were an Intelligence officer yourself. You wouldn't be such a damn fool as to trust an unknown amateur like me. Your sort hate amateurs.'

'My sort?' His frown had now forked from the bridge of his nose to his hairline; and suddenly the truth dawned.

'You're in Intelligence yourself!' Magnus cried, and felt the sweat growing icy under his collar.

There was no expression in Cane's face now. His brow was smooth again, his eyes black. 'Very clever, Magnus. I congratulate you.' He took another step forward, his foot holding again, and Magnus took one back, and mercifully that held too. 'We must be on different circuits,' Cane said. 'They're clever devils — don't even trust each other. Who's your contact, by the way? Briggs?'

'You're mad.'

'Briggs or Machell?' Cane tried to smile, and Magnus thought, *No, he's bluffing too. Hot and cold, on and off, trying to trap me one way or the other.*

'Briggs,' Cane repeated: 'Old fellow. Seconded from the War Office. Come on, you must know him — he deals with you younger fellows —'

'You're talking a lot of balls!' Magnus shouted, his eyes back on the stick.

'I'm talking about our job,' Cane said suavely. 'Relax. There's no one here. You could hardly have a quieter spot for a talk.'

Magnus felt one of his boots sink an inch deeper into the snow. It was not a good omen. Apart from the stick, Cane still had the advantage of higher ground. The only thing Magnus could do was play for time.

'The others wanted you dead,' Cane went on. 'I was the one who persuaded them to keep you alive. Or at least to keep you on ice — almost literally.' He attempted a chuckle that sounded as though he were clearing his throat. 'It wasn't easy for me, Magnus, believe me.'

'I bet it wasn't.' As he spoke Cane took another step, and the snow cracked under his boot. He steadied himself at once, but his eyes never left Magnus' face. Another step, and he'd be in range with the stick.

'For God's sake, man. We're on the same side. Can't you understand that?'

Magnus watched and waited for the stick. Either way Cane would use it — if he really did work for the Service, or if he believed that Magnus did — it would make no difference now. It was still bluff and double-bluff, and one of them would have to call it. Magnus decided to leave that initiative to Cane. He had the stick, after all; he might even have a gun.

'You're a liar,' he said again. 'Purity — peace — all that from you, and you drag me up here to play some childish game of cowboys and Indians, pretending we're both secret agents. I've told you, I'm ready for you. If you're really working for British Intelligence you'd better earn your pay. Come and get me!'

For a second Cane's body went stiff, his knuckles white again round the varnished joints in his hand; then suddenly he flung the stick down in the snow. Magnus stared at it for a moment, then remembered in time to keep his guard; if it was to be clean hand-to-hand fighting, so be it. Cane was twenty years his senior and Magnus had a bad leg: the odds were about even.

'All right,' Cane cried, 'I'm sorry.' He raised both hands, palms upwards. Magnus was still watching him warily, conscious now of the sweat trickling under his clothes. 'My boy, I nearly made a bad mistake. But I had to do it. I had to be sure. The others, they weren't so sure. They insisted that I put you to the test. I did only what I had to do —' He stepped forward and they were almost touching. His next words were no more than a whisper above the wind:

'I must tell you that for a moment I thought I'd been wrong. I thought you'd betrayed us.' He seized his arm. 'But I know you too well, Magnus. And in my case, as you said, the Intelligence Services don't employ amateurs. No offence, mind. Rather, it's a compliment. They prefer good steady drudge-horses — except in war, of course, when they take in all kinds of odd bods — like me, for instance!' He laughed: 'I used an old trick on you — one of the simplest in the book. If I pretended to be one of their lot, I knew I'd have to draw you one way or the other. It would be very difficult for you to remain neutral — unless, of course, you were professional. But you're not professional and you didn't remain neutral. In fact, you acted very much the other way and made me very angry indeed. When you accused me of having betrayed the Poles — my God! I nearly went for you then!' He was chuckling now, quite happily. 'Well, I don't mind saying I'm glad that's been cleared up.'

He still held his arm, as he helped him down between the treacherous humps of snow. Magnus felt loose and weak all over, but still retained an element of wariness: Cane's method of interrogation might be simple enough, by Secret Service standards, but Magnus remembered that often when a man relaxes he is at his most vulnerable.

'John,' he said steadily, 'you said the others wanted me dead. Is that true?'

Cane let go of his arm and stepped ahead of him. 'I don't say they wanted you dead but they were very suspicious. You do realise that we're all in a most delicate position?'

'And supposing they change their minds?'

Cane stopped. 'My dear boy! You don't suppose I have that little influence?'

'I don't know what influence you have. Obviously not enough to prevent Skliros from putting a gun in my neck.'

Cane gripped his arm again. 'Look, Magnus, that business with Krok and Skliros — let's put it all behind us. It's over. When things go wrong, people tend to act out of character. You must know that from the Army. The C.O. gets shot, the company's routed, and some junior officer loses his head. Well, that's how it was with Skliros.' He was talking quickly now, swinging the stick at his side, but still holding Magnus by the arm.

'But I never really doubted you. You were quite right to taunt me for playing cowboys and Indians just now. In fact I'm rather ashamed of it. Because I know you too well, Magnus. I've followed your stuff in *The Paper* and I know you couldn't have simulated all that. You feel as I do. You hate them as much as I do.' Then his voice became grave: 'But while you're one of us, you must also learn to live with us. I know you don't care much for some of the hard boys you've come up against. I don't expect you to. You're in quite a different class. And frankly, I don't altogether care for them myself. But these people are necessary. When battle has been joined, and time is short, one cannot always choose the purest of allies. You know that in the last war some of the bravest regiments were drawn from the scum of our jails?'

'Is that how you think of Meredith and Skliros?'

'They're not mercenaries. They believe. They hate what we hate but they lack the sensitivity and perception of people like you.'

He was talking now with a passion that excluded all doubts. He had made his decision and nothing, for the moment, would prove him wrong. His vanity, Magnus reflected, was astounding. Magnus was his recruit, his personal acolyte in a class far above the Merediths and Skliroses of his retinue. A man of letters whose readers numbered hundreds of thousands, many of them high and influential. He had been right: Cane would not discard him so easily.

Yet the danger was still there. Magnus realised that although he might know only a tiny part about this organisation, that part was already lethal. Cane still believed in him; but the real question was whether he could convince the others back at the Haëli.

They were well below the snow now, picking their way down the spongy moss towards the final slope to the house. And as Magnus looked at its shuttered windows, he realised it was the perfect spot to hold him until they made up their minds.

'What will you tell them?'

'Simply that I'm satisfied.'

'And the man who's arriving this evening from England?'

'I shall tell him the same.'

'There's still the girl,' Magnus said.

Cane was ahead and Magnus could not see his expression, but his voice had a dull tone now: 'Yes, the girl. I admit that she presents a problem.'

'And the Polish Embassy in London?'

Cane walked on as though he had not heard.

'Is she a Communist?'

'What do you call a Communist?' he called over his shoulder, and hastened his steps towards the Haëli.

'It's a fairly precise definition, isn't it?'

'A label, it means nothing.' The next moment he was running down on to the forecourt, and Magnus thought he was destined never to know anything about Maya.

He saw that the minibus and both cars were back in front of the steps. Cane was waiting for him at the bottom.

'Magnus, I'm afraid this evening I'll have to ask you to eat again in your room. It's nothing sinister, don't worry. But we're having rather a private business dinner. I'm sure you'll understand? Anyway, I expect you'd like to have an early night?' He led the way up into the front hall, taking off his pixie-hat and anorak as he went. The tow-haired youth had appeared silently from inside the door, carrying Magnus' shoes. Cane said cheerily: 'Jorgensen here will see you to your room. Is there anything I can get you?'

'Books,' said Magnus, 'and a drink.'

Cane laughed. 'I can find you something to read, but you're out of luck with the other. Iceland's dry. Even the beer's non-alcoholic.'

'Send some up, anyway. I can always pretend.'

Cane raised his hand: 'Will do. See you tomorrow, then.' He left Magnus still pulling off his boots.

The hall was deserted now, as Jorgensen led him to the lift and up to the fourth floor. They did not speak. Jorgensen took him to his door and unlocked it from a ring of keys in his pocket. He pushed it open for Magnus to pass, but Magnus stood where he was, holding out his hand. 'The key, Mr Jorgensen.

Give it to me.'

The boy looked puzzled. 'Key?' he repeated, in his wooden accent.

'That's right. The key.'

He looked down at the ring in his hand, then back at Magnus, and shook his head. 'Mr Pallson has the key.'

'So you're locking me in?'

'No. The door is open. Mr Pallson has the key.'

Good old Pallson, Magnus thought. He went in and shut the door, and Jorgensen did not lock it. He turned on the light and went to the window. Outside, the glacier lay in heavy twilight, although it was only five o'clock in the afternoon. His bed had been tidied and someone had arranged his things in the bathroom. He wondered who did the housework, realising that not once in his dealings with this organisation had he ever seen a woman. Except Maya.

He sat down on the bed and rested his head in his hands. His walk with Cane had only shifted the emphasis of his predicament; it had done nothing to remove it. He was scared — scared of ignorance, of the mounting atmosphere of mystery that was like a child's fear of darkness.

There was a knock and Pallson came in carrying a pile of books. His face was creased into a smile and Magnus noticed for the first time that he had two gold teeth at the corners of his mouth, like tusks. 'Mr Cane asked me to bring you these books.' He put them down on the bedside table. They were old hard-backed volumes that looked as though they had been bought in a sale.

'Mr Pallson,' Magnus said, 'I'm afraid I'm very ignorant about your country. Where exactly are we?'

'At the foot of the Vatnajökull, Mr Owen. Did you not go there this afternoon with Mr Cane?'

'Yes, but where is the Vatnajökull? Where is it from Reykjavik?'

His toothy smile widened: 'Oh a long way, Mr Owen. Half across Iceland.'

Magnus nodded, trying to look indifferent. 'And what's the nearest town?'

Pallson shook his head. 'There is no town by here. Not for a long way. You see, we are a big country but very small in our population.' He gave the hint of a bow. 'Is there anything else, Mr Owen?'

Magnus shook his head and Pallson withdrew.

It was clear now. There was no need for locked doors or bars on the window. They had him where they wanted him, in a nice centrally-heated room, with a lava desert on one side and a glacier on the other.

He sat down on the bed and looked at the pile of books. *A Life in the Alps* by E. M. Storey; biography of Savonarola; a couple of early Cronin novels; Thomas Mann's *The Magic Mountain*; a Dorothy L. Sayers detective story, and *Men of the Hour* by John Austen Cane. He had hoped there would be something on Iceland — a travel book, with perhaps even a map. But there was nothing closer than the Alps.

He chose Thomas Mann, propping himself up against the pillows, and prepared for a long night.

A couple of hours later he threw the book down. The last ten pages of Mann's tortuous prose had not registered at all. Beyond the window the twilight had grown no darker.

He went into the bathroom and plunged his head under the cold tap with its stinking gush of sulphur; then went back into his room and opened the door. No sound from outside. He walked down the passage to the lift, pressed the call button and waited. The lift arrived; he pushed the bottom button on the control panel, watched the numbers flashing down the dial. He had no plan, no idea what he expected. The lift stopped.

He was in a concrete passage lined with pipes, like the boiler-room of a ship. There was a humming all round, suggesting that he was close to the power plant. Behind him the lift doors slid shut. He walked round a corner and saw ahead a pair of green-baize doors. Somewhere above the noise of the generator he thought he heard a mutter of voices.

He had almost reached the doors when they swung open and the voices stopped. Three men stood in front of him. He recognised Pallson, his silver head rising a good head above the other two. The second man was Steiner; he was out in front, holding the door back for the others. But Magnus was looking at the third man, who looked back at him as though they had never met before.

For a few seconds no one spoke. Beyond the doors Magnus glimpsed a panelled room, table lined with leather chairs, ink-blotters along the table, several telephones. A comfortable conference room, two floors below ground. What were they expecting? he wondered: a nuclear attack?

'What are you doing here, Mr Owen?' It was Steiner's voice.

He shrugged: 'I'm sorry, I seem to have lost my way. Must be on the wrong floor.'

'Where were you going please?' It was Pallson this time.

'I thought I might find someone for a game of billiards.' He looked at the third man: 'Mr Henry Deepe, isn't it? We met a couple of months ago, at a dinner for the Regent's Park Sporting Club.' He stepped forward, his hand out: 'Magnus Owen, of *The Paper*?'

Still none of them moved. Magnus was close enough to shake hands with Henry Deepe, but Pallson slipped between them. 'I am sorry, Mr Owen, but we are busy. Please go back to your room.' Beside him that bland civil servant face had not flinched: had not even seen Magnus.

Magnus looked hard at Henry Deepe, then shrugged: 'Very well. Some other time.'

'Some other time,' Pallson said, guiding him deftly back to the lift. 'We would prefer you did not leave your room this evening,' he added, as he got into the lift after him and pushed the button one-from-the-top. 'I think Mr Cane already explained that?'

'All Mr Cane explained was that I was to have supper in my room. Does that exclude a game of billiards?'

'There is no one to play billiards tonight,' Pallson said, as the lift stopped. 'Your food will be sent up to you at eight o'clock.' This time he did not bow or smile. The doors shut and he was gone.

By the time Magnus was back in his room, he had made up his mind what he must do.

Half an hour later Jorgensen arrived with his supper: hors d'oeuvres of dried fish, chicken-in-aspic, more tinned fruit and a bottle of Icelandic beer. Again, he left the door unlocked behind him.

Magnus was hungry now and ate voraciously — but not only to satisfy his appetite. Proteins, carbohydrates: he needed all the energy he could store. He also still had the remains of the chocolate Cane had offered him on their climb; but he would keep that as a reserve.

He drank the sweet non-alcoholic beer and began thinking about Mr Henry Deepe. The incident in the cellars had been unfortunate, but highly instructive: he now at least knew the identity of Cane's important guest for the evening. His visit was no doubt to brief the party on repercussions back in London, and probably to advise them on the best way to react. Magnus realised there was also a danger. Henry Deepe was not a man who would enjoy being surprised on such a mission. Men in his position were schooled to avoid controversy, trouble of any sort, to cover up, prevaricate, play the role at all times of unimpeachable rectitude. His sort were rarely at a loss. Sometimes, under heavy fire in the Commons, a Home Secretary might be thrown to the wolves; but come what might, the permanent officials remained secure behind their walls of anonymity. Here in Iceland there were no badgering back-benchers, no prying journalists to spread embarrassing innuendoes in the morning papers, none, except Magnus Owen of *The Paper* and for a man like Henry Deepe *The Paper* would be the most dangerous of all.

He shivered. It was cold in the room, with the double-windows wide open, but he needed the air. He realised that for Henry Deepe the stakes must be very high indeed. Had he come voluntarily? Or been summoned by some higher authority? Or was it possible that this cold cagey little man could be the head of the whole organisation?

When Jorgensen returned at half past eight to collect his tray, Magnus was lying on the bed, pretending to read. 'I'd like some coffee, Mr Jorgensen. Black, with lots of sugar.' Jorgensen repeated the order and left with a bow — the perfect floor waiter.

Magnus now began taking careful stock of his situation. It was not encouraging. To begin with, his overcoat was downstairs, as well as the anorak, there were some things one did not think of, even in a crisis. He also had no map, no idea where he was, not a word of the language. On the credit side, he still had £17 in cash, his chequebook, Press cards and driving licence for identification. But they didn't amount to much. Above all, he had no weapon. He had thought of filching the knife from his supper tray — even the empty beer bottle — but they would almost certainly be missed. He had hunted through the wardrobe, empty drawers, in the bathroom; but there was only the razor blade — a weapon strictly for an expert, in cold blood. Magnus was looking for something handy, to be used in an emergency.

By the time Jorgensen returned, Magnus was undressed and under the duvet. He wanted nothing to arouse their suspicions; at this stage even the smallest deception could make all the difference. He watched the Icelander put down the tray with the coffee and bowl of wrapped sugar cubes. He moved with a grave guarded air, like a well-trained dog.

'Is there anything more?' he asked.

Magnus shook his head. 'I'll put the tray outside,' he said drowsily. 'You don't have to come back for it.'

He waited till Jorgensen had left, then lay back and drank the coffee, without sugar. The four wrapped cubes he put in his jacket pocket — the pocket of his best worsted suit, the one that passed muster with R.S.M. Bostock, which he still wore with his black walking shoes. Hardly the most practical costume, but it was too late to worry about that now.

He spent the next hour reading; but Thomas Mann's claustrophobic tale of the mountain sanatorium was not restful. He turned out the light and tried to sleep. There was no sound at all — even the wind had dropped — and he wondered if Henry Deepe and his friends were still in conference? Or whether they were through and their verdict reached. Either way, he knew he had little time to lose.

But he managed to hold out till after midnight. It was not a restful wait. The climb to the glacier had left him aching and exhausted, and he kept dozing off, only to shake himself back to consciousness for fear of falling into a really deep sleep and not waking till morning. But just after ten o'clock he dropped off again, and this time it was something else that woke him.

He sat up listening. At first there was just the dead stillness of the Arctic night which glowed dimly beyond the open windows. His watch told him it was just after twelve.

Then he heard it again. A slow creaking sound, like an old door being eased open. But it was from nowhere in the Haëli; it came from far away, in the direction of the Vatnajökull, and went on for several terrifying seconds, before dying out in a faint rumble.

He kicked off the duvet and ran to the window. Outside there was silence again. The glacier rose huge and unnatural in the twilight; and as he looked at it, beginning to shiver, he realised that what he had heard must have been the ice moving.

He turned and went into the bathroom, careful to close the door before putting on the light; then gave himself a quick shower, turning the water suddenly on to cold, and stepping out with his whole body braced and taut, as he rubbed himself down and scraped at his beard for the second time that day — a tradition he had learnt in the Army: always to be clean and shaved before action. He went into the bedroom and dressed in the dark.

There was a single sheet on the bed under the duvet. He tore it off, took hold of the end of the bed and pulled it across to the window. He was smiling as he tied the corner of the sheet to one of the legs, thinking of all those yarns he had read as a boy about this very situation. Only then it was usually a hundred foot drop on to rocks or into a river full of alligators. This was almost shamefully easy.

Now that the moment had come he was surprised how calm he felt. Action had brought a sense of relief and exhilaration. The waiting was over. He lifted himself over the sill, the sheet squeaking under his weight, as he slithered his feet down the rough brickwork outside. He went down a good deal faster than he had expected, with a searing pain across his palms, and landed with what sounded a very loud crunch. On looking up he was shocked at how white the sheet stood out against the black wall.

There was still no noise — not a breath of wind, not a creak from the glacier — as he pulled off his shoes, holding one in each hand, and began picking his way painfully in his stockinged feet round the buttress of the house, down to the forecourt. His luck was holding: the minibus and both cars were still there.

Above him the front of the Haëli rose like the set for some horror film. There were no lights anywhere. Only the three cars seemed real. He went to work on them, soundlessly and fast.

He had already decided on the minibus. It had several advantages: it would hold more petrol, be tougher, offer more shelter if he broke down, and he'd also had experience of one some years ago on a holiday in Spain. He moved up and tried the door. It was unlocked. He looked inside. There were no keys in the ignition — they'd hardly have handed him those, unless they wanted him to get away — and he saw it was one of the older models, with no petrol gauge. He left the door ajar and moved round to the back, carefully opening the engine cover. No problem here: it was the simplest of engines, and he had learnt most of the tricks in Cyprus, from jeeps to heavy trucks. He left the engine open, and hobbled over to the rear of the first car. The real problem now was the cold. It was biting under his light suit and his feet were numb, as he opened the back of the VW with one hand, fumbling for the sugar cubes with the other; unscrewed the petrol cap, his whole body shuddering with cold, grappling now with the paper wrappings as he tipped the first cube down the pipe. Two cubes for each tank — careful to crumple the paper up, put it away again in his pocket — closing the cover again as though the handle might break off in his hand. Softly, kneeling down by the back tyre, unscrewing the valve, with the metal like fire against his fingers, straightening up again to the steady hiss of air.

If it wasn't for this damned cold! he thought, and rubbed his knuckles together as he started on the front tyre. They'd probably have more than one spare, but changing two tyres would give a few extra minutes' grace.

Still no lights from the Haëli. He moved over to the second VW, letting both tyres down at once now, risking the double hiss as he dropped the last two cubes into the tank. This time he could hardly get the cover shut without slamming it; then hobbling back to the rear of the minibus, his hand plucking under the ignition wires, off with the distributor head, cross-contact the terminals — as easy as Maya breaking into his flat with a strip of celluloid.

The man must have come down the steps and across the gravel with extraordinary stealth. Magnus had heard nothing. He was still leaning over the engine with the distributor head in his hand — cup of hard steel, sharp edges — when the man spoke, so close they were almost touching.

'Well, well, Mr Owen, still a joker.' His face was a small blank oval in the twilight.

Magnus turned slowly and a hand gripped him just above the elbow. Skliros' fingers felt very hard. In the silence his action had an eerie quality, almost more frightening than open violence. But it gave Magnus a couple of seconds in which to think. If he had not had those seconds he might have shied off.

He remembered Krok — not with any sense of rage or revenge this time, but because Krok had been bigger than Skliros, and although Skliros was fast, what had counted against him had been that first blow. He thought of the light above the boxing ring, rows of dinner jackets, and the Scots boy sagging against the ropes, no fight in him, as Skliros went in for the kill. He swung his arm up and rammed the distributor head into the middle of that neat little face, the metal cup fitting like a clown's nose, with a crunch of cartilage, a squeak from Skliros as he jabbed again with all his force, thinking, *I'm a real joker, and I'm bigger than you and I'm not going to let you use any mere toy pistols on me, you bastard* — bringing his knee up into his groin — *and I'm no gentleman either, Peter, just another bloody intellectual* — with a final blow in the belly, the face growing dark, nose and mouth blotted out, groaning, beginning to sink. He took hold of him and let him down gently on to the gravel.

He had no idea how much noise they had made — like waking out of a nightmare and not knowing if one had been screaming the house down or just burbling in one's sleep. He thought vaguely, I ought to kill him now. Nobody ever crosses Peter Skliros and gets away with it, and he's been crossed twice now in twenty-four hours, and he's level with at least one of them. It's either him or me, now or later. He wiped the distributor head and replaced it over the crossed wires, touched the button on the starter motor and heard the engine fire first time.

He was beyond caution now, treading into his shoes and slamming the engine cover shut: into the driving seat, clutch down, into first, slewing the bus round to where Skliros still lay. Run him down — that's what he'd do. *And I didn't even go through him for a gun.*

He swerved round him and headed down into the valley. There was no need for headlamps; the twilight was strong enough to show him the straight unscreened track for at least a mile ahead. He had only one clear plan — to follow the telegraph poles. They kept abreast of him, about fifty feet to his right, stalking the land like thin sentries. Behind him he saw a light come on in the Haëli. He crouched over the wheel, waiting for the shots. But none came. The gravel purred smoothly under the wheels. He pulled the switch to the heater, feeling the warm blast round his legs and over his face. The fight had made him forget how cold he had been, and his body now began to react: stiff and clammy all over, his knuckles raw and sticky with Skliros's blood. But he felt clear-headed, and began to catch his breath and relax. More lights had come on in the Haëli, but they were growing smaller, as he drove faster, deeper into the great grey wilderness of Cane's Ideal. Peace and Purity. He was free, with a vengeance.

He now began to reckon his chances. At a conservative estimate he put them at no better than even. He had one main advantage, though — he had got away, and was still going. Against that, they knew he had gone, and they knew the country. They also had a telephone — although he didn't suppose there were many friendly forces in the area whom they could call up in this emergency. The Haëli meant the 'Retreat', and Magnus had broken out of it.

Then there were the cars. He assumed that in a country like this they would be well equipped to deal with their own breakdowns. They would find each car with two flat tyres; they might think he had punctured them, or they might guess the truth and simply pump them up. Either way, he gave himself a maximum of fifteen minutes' start. Then they would chase him: and it was here he was gambling. He had no idea how quickly it took lumps of sugar to dissolve in petrol. All he knew was that sooner or later the sugar would be sucked up into the injection tubes and stop the car in its tracks. Once this happened it would be hours before the engines could be cleaned out — and then, only after they had diagnosed the trouble. In theory, at least, he might seem to have the edge on them. But then there was always the unpleasant possibility of a fourth vehicle — a motorcycle perhaps.

He wanted to drive faster, but the black waste was deceptive in the twilight, and several times he narrowly missed running the bus into a bank of lava.

It was almost 1.30. No lights behind now. He tried to remember how long it had taken them to drive from the airstrip to the Haëli. It had seemed about an hour — but then he had been asleep most of the way, and he cursed himself now for having not been more alert. Even the smallest detail of that trip could now prove vital.

There was also the problem of petrol. He guessed they must have a supply back at the Haëli, and would refill the bus and cars when it was needed. But the bus had already made two trips to the airstrip that day. Would they have refuelled it on its second return? He remembered, from his experience in Spain, that a Volkswagen minibus held about forty litres, or nearly nine gallons; and in good condition it could manage thirty miles to the gallon. Taking a reasonably pessimistic view — that the tank was only a quarter full — he had something less than a hundred miles to run. But there was nothing he could do about the petrol. The important thing was that he was still moving — that the telegraph poles were still at his side.

Behind him there was nothing but a grey wilderness. He was on his own. If his fuel gave out he'd abandon the bus and walk. If they chased him, he'd fight. He began to feel reckless: a gambler on his last throw.

Then something disconcerting happened. A signpost loomed up ahead and the track divided in two directions. He turned on the headlamps. The sign was half rotten, like a stick of driftwood, and pointed only one way — to the right. He could just make out the word Helfoss, but nothing to say how far it was. But what worried him even more lay just beyond. It looked like a giant kirby grip sticking out of the lava, to which the single electric cable he had been so faithfully following now ended.

He stopped and got out, leaving the engine running to keep the heater on. It was cold and dark — far darker than up near the glacier. There were no stars, no sound. Far away on his left lay a rim of flat-topped mountains which he thought he recognised from the trip that morning up from the airstrip. He began to examine the two tracks. The one to the left, away from where the signpost pointed, was clearly the more used, its surface stamped down into black sand which still bore recent tyre marks.

The track to the right, however, was not encouraging: a pair of deep ruts, humped in the middle with small boulders, and leading away towards a great mass of mountain as black as ink. But however poor it might be, this one at least merited a signpost, and a signpost meant a destination.

He had wasted perhaps two minutes at the turning. Behind there was still nothing but the dusk and desert. He got back in, swung the wheel and started up the track towards Helfoss.

Two hours and seventy kilometres now gone. Just over forty miles of petrol and more than thirty of them since leaving the signpost to Helfoss. The track was very bad, and growing worse as it climbed, with the mountains closing all round like the sides of a great well. The weather was also changing for the worse: black clouds blowing up from behind with a wind that shrieked and shook the bus as it took the bends. The hump of the track was now rising perilously close to the axles. The floor scraped and jumped and crashed, and soon it became impossible to steer; the ruts held the wheels in a lock like inverted railway tracks. All he could do was keep his eyes open, ready to brake. The headlamps no longer shone across lava fields but off walls of volcanic rock, or swung out over the edge into darkness.

He was crawling now in bottom gear, and in spite of the heater, he could feel the cold seeping into the cabin. But there was no turning back. Helfoss, he thought. A faded name on a signpost in the wilderness. And now it was no longer the idea of pursuit and capture that frightened him — it was loneliness, desolation — fear beginning to tighten into panic, as he groped further and further into this land of ice and volcanoes, dependent only on a tough little bus and an unknown supply of petrol.

His back ached with tension, his eyes sore with concentration, as the bus strained on upwards, round shoulders of mountain that escaped the headlamps like bends in a tunnel.

Then he reached the snow — an icy mush that he could feel dragging at the wheels, while the engine whined behind him as though in pain. The clouds had covered the sky and beyond the headlamps the night was black. His teeth were chattering, he was stiff with cold; but he had one thought to comfort him:

If they come after me, and the sugar goes to work in time, they'll be stranded — they'll freeze to death. It was morbid comfort, but enough.

Then suddenly the track was level, broadening, growing smoother in the snow, and the speedometer needle jumped up to twenty kilometres an hour. He was beginning to descend. His whole body went slack, and he sat back and drummed his hands against the wheel and shouted, 'Helfoss! Helfoss here I come!' And at that moment the bus ran out of petrol.

At first he would not accept it. The engine missed once, twice, he pumped the throttle, heard it catch, stutter and go dead. The wheels dragged again in the snow, then stopped. There was silence.

He switched off the lights and got out. The cold was so intense that for a moment it was almost bracing, with a clean alpine bitterness. The wind had dropped and sighed around him like slow breathing. Without the headlamps the sky seemed lighter, a dome of frosted glass, its edges sharpened by the outline of mountains, grey with snow.

There was just the chance, he thought, that there would be some spare petrol cans in the back under one of the seats. He searched, but there was nothing. He had done his best and was through now. But at least it was better than being taken alive and turned over to young Skliros.

Then he stiffened, his face out of the wind, listening. After a moment it came again — a quick scuffling, just beyond the bus. He ran round to the front, peering down the track. 'Anyone there?' His voice startled him as though it were a stranger's. There was more scuffling, louder this time. 'Who's there?' he yelled, and this time it was quite close — someone running in the snow. He backed up against the car, pulled the door open and switched on the headlamps. A pair of eyes flashed, then vanished.

The next moment he saw them: crowding hurriedly down the slope onto the track, packed together in the beam like the humps of a giant caterpillar. A flock of sheep. 'Hello! Anyone there!' But there was only the scuffle of hooves, and they were soon gone and then there was just the wind. There had been no one, he thought. No one except the leader of sheep. Yet the very fact that there were sheep… And he began to reason vaguely: Like Columbus's first sight of seaweed. How far did these sheep roam in Iceland? There had been no sign of habitation that morning when he had seen them trekking across the lava desert.

Below the track he now saw what looked like an immeasurable valley full of dark mist.

There was nothing for it but to climb back into the bus, where there was at least a little warmth left, and try and hold out till dawn. He curled up shuddering on the seat, wondering what it was like to freeze to death. Would there be a final Nirvana, like the dreams of a drowning man? Or just a painful numbness, then nothing?

A little later exhaustion overcame cold, and he fell into a merciful sleep. He was dreaming of another bus now, rounding the bend of a dusty road in Spain. Late in the afternoon, leaving a bullfight in La Linea, full of bad wine and Fundador, in a foul temper with his wife, when they'd run out of petrol. They were on a bend of the road and there was nothing in sight, but somehow they had managed to get going again.

He sat up with a start, banging his knee against the gear lever, reaching down under the seat — and it was there, just as it had been in Spain. Instead of a fuel gauge, the bus was equipped with a reserve tank holding ten litres. He pulled out the knob, began to pump again furiously on the throttle, praying aloud as he got out and went to the back, opened the engine cover and groped for the starter button. His fingers were curled up, almost senseless with the cold, and he had to push five times before it fired.

He climbed back in and sat for a moment listening to the engine idling in the stillness, feeling the heater coming back on; and suddenly he laughed. The sound shocked him, as though he had laughed in church.

Slowly he let out the clutch and the bus rolled forward.

The light was coming up fast now and at the next bend he saw that the dark hollow of mist below was clearing, almost in front of his eyes, like steam rising off a saucepan. Some minutes later he was looking down at a great lake spreading out to the horizon, smooth as a sheet of tin. Skeins of birds swept low over its surface like shadows, and its shores were fringed with green, as though protecting it from the excrescences of lava that crept down from the snow-capped mountains all round. But even better, there was a town. Nothing much — just a huddle of huts along the margin of the water, with a track twisting up to it like a grey ribbon. But it represented civilisation, deliverance. He had taken on Cane and Skliros and Henry Deepe, and the great unholy alliance behind them, and he had won.

He began driving faster now, with the track flattening out between patches of coarse grass; then he came to another signpost, this time of rusted metal, and he read the name again: Helfoss.

There was only the one cinder street, bordered by huts with corrugated-iron roofs. It was still too early for anyone to be about. A wooden landing stage jutted into the lake, with a couple of rowing boats tied up at the side. It was very quiet and grey; only the birds moved, in swift rhythmic circles above the water.

The one building of any consequence was a barnlike structure standing back from the jetty, with a glass porch and a sign over the door saying Hotel Grimsvötin. There was a car parked in front of it — a red Volvo saloon splashed with mud. Magnus pulled up beside it, and as he got out, he heard music. He stumbled through the door of the porch, into a bare wooden room where a jukebox was pounding out a pop song. Chairs stood stacked on tables along the walls; there was a Coca-Cola sign in Icelandic, a framed photograph of an old man with a beard, an Espresso machine on an empty counter.

A large blond man in a lumber jacket leaned against the jukebox, thumping his boot in time with the music. He stared vacantly, as Magnus crossed to a door beside the Espresso machine and found the toilet. His hands were chapped and filthy, with Skliros' blood still clinging to the broken skin. He filled the basin with icy water, plunged his head in and stood up gasping in front of the mirror where his face stared back, hollow and wild-eyed with the scar standing out along his jaw like a strip of spaghetti. He did his best to smooth down his hair, then dried himself on a very dirty towel.

Next door the blond man was waiting for the record to change. Magnus looked at him and said, 'Do you speak English? English!' His voice was lost in a thunder of drums and electronic guitars. The man just stared at him, beginning to snap his fingers as well as thump his boot; his sense of rhythm was chaotic.

A second door opened and an old woman came in. She stood looking at Magnus with a face like a shrivelled walnut. 'You speak English?' he shouted hopelessly, above the din.

'Coffee — telephone.' He began to mime ridiculously: 'Telephone to Reykjavik. Reykjavik?'

She looked at him a moment longer, then shook her head and disappeared again through the door. The man in the lumber jacket was still watching him. The record came to an end, switched itself off, and he seemed suddenly bored — or perhaps he had just run out of coins. He gave Magnus another long stare, then ambled over to the porch and outside. Magnus saw him walk away along the cinder track, out of sight.

The place seemed deathly quiet after the jukebox. He looked at his watch: not yet six o'clock. He pulled a chair down off a table, slumped forward with his head on his arms and slept.

He woke with a start. A man stood in front of the table. He was very pale, behind square green-tinted glasses; dressed in a neat white polo-necked sweater, grey hunting jacket with shoulder-straps and button-down pockets. He held out his hand: 'Morning, sir. I heard you spoke English?' It was a soft American voice. 'You are English? May I sit down?' He pulled out a chair, smiling shyly. 'I heard the old woman talking about you. You just got in?'

Magnus nodded. 'I want to get to Reykjavik.'

'Uh-huh.' He ran his hand over the top of his head, as though stroking a cat. His hair was greying at the edges, cut square over a rectangular white brow. Everything about him, Magnus thought, was white and grey-green and symmetrical. 'Reykjavik's about two hours, I'd say.'

Magnus started: 'Only two hours!' And he glanced outside at the minibus.

The man's eyes must have followed his, invisible behind the tinted glasses. 'You're not thinking of going by car, are you?'

'That's the way I came.'

222

He shook his head and chuckled: 'I meant two hours by plane. Where have you come from, by the way?'

'The Vatnajökull.'

The man looked at him steadily, the green lenses exaggerating the pallor of his face which was like paper. 'You've come from the Vatnajökull?' he repeated.

Magnus looked across at the counter, his mind beginning to blur. 'I asked for some coffee,' he murmured.

'I'm afraid it's a little early for that. The machine's not working yet.' He leant closer, taking out a packet of Salem filter-tips and offering them across. Magnus shook his head. 'Whereabouts on the Vatnajökull?' the man said, lighting his cigarette.

'I don't know. All I know is I've been driving all night and I'm done in.'

He gave a slow whistle, blowing out smoke. 'That must have been a real rough drive. Listen, you can't get any coffee yet, but I've got a better idea. Like some Scotch? Johnnie Walker? You look as though you could do with some.'

Magnus lifted his head and blinked: 'Johnnie Walker?'

'Up in my room.' He had begun to rise, extending his hand graciously: 'And it's Black Label. I could lay you odds you won't find another in the whole of Iceland!'

'Johnnie Walker,' Magnus repeated: 'Just lead me to him!' He was shaking his head wonderingly as he followed the man through the door and up some stairs, to a small wooden room, very warm, with a round window like a porthole overlooking the lake. There seemed to be no personal belongings, except a rucksack against the wall strapped up and bulging.

'Sit down,' the man said nodding at the bed. He bent over the rucksack and brought out the square unopened bottle of Black Label. Magnus looked at it with much the same sensation as when he had first seen the lake and town far below. Or was Providence being just a little too kind?

The man fetched a tumbler and toothglass from the basin. 'You don't mind it straight? The water here tastes of sulphur.'

'Straight as you can!' He noticed that the man did not stint him. The Americans were a generous people he thought: God bless America!

'The way I feel,' the man said, handing him the tumbler, 'it's a crime to mix anything with good whisky.'

Magnus swallowed deeply, then leant back against the bed top, closing his eyes, feeling the liquid running warm from his throat down to his belly. No drink would ever be as good again, he thought.

The man sat down on a chair beside the bed and poured himself a smaller measure into the toothglass. 'Your health, sir!' His smile seemed to stretch his papery skin as though it would tear.

'You're American?' Magnus said, lifting the tumbler.

The man hesitated just a fraction of a second. 'That's right. Sorry, I should have introduced myself. George Novak, of Portland, Maine.'

'Magnus Owen — I'm from London.' He leant out and shook hands perfunctorily.

'Glad to know you, Magnus!'

'What are you doing here in Iceland, Mr Novak?'

'Bird watching. Not professionally, of course. Just a holiday.' He sipped his whisky. 'It's a wonderful country for birds.'

'You know it well?'

'So-so. I've been here a month now.'

Magnus was beginning to find those green-tinted lenses very disconcerting; the eyes behind them were like fish in a tank. He looked down into his whisky and said, 'How do I get to Reykjavik from here?'

The man put his glass on the floor and licked his lips. 'You in a hurry?'

'Yep.'

'Uh-uh. Well, Magnus, you're in luck! I'm planning to pull out myself this morning — by chartered plane. You're welcome to join me?'

'When?' Like the lake, the town, the whisky, it was all just a little too good to be true. He finished his drink, and the blood began to move again in his veins, with a pulse beating hard in the side of his head. George Novak was saying: 'I've checked to fly out this morning, but it depends on the weather. That's up to the pilot.'

Magnus nodded. 'We fly from here?'

'Just outside the town. Like a little more?'

Magnus held out his tumbler. 'What'll it cost?'

'Sixty dollars. That is, thirty each,' he added, with his shy smile. Magnus took a long drink. 'That's just fine. As long as you can get me to Reykjavik.' He touched the side of his head where he could feel the pulse like something alive under the skin. Novak came over and refilled his tumbler. 'You look as though you had a hell of a night, Magnus!'

'Not too good. You got some kind of map here?'

'Sure. Want to find out where you are?' He had knelt again by his rucksack, and Magnus got up suddenly and went to the window. The minibus was still there, alone beside the Volvo. The cinder track and jetty were deserted. 'Could I telephone Reykjavik from here?' he asked.

'You could try, but the plane might be just as quick. The phones aren't too good — sometimes you have to wait hours.' He came back to the bed, unfolding a large-scale motoring map. Magnus saw the Vatnajökull at once — a pale blue hand covering most of the lower right-hand corner. Helfoss was easy to find, the only town within miles, but still looking uncomfortably close to the glacier. Reykjavik, on the other hand, was at the opposite end of the island, several hundred miles away. He pushed the map aside and said: 'It's nearly seven, Mr Novak. When can we be out of here?'

Novak picked up his whisky again and said quietly: 'If the weather's O.K., and it looks O.K. to me, we can drive around there at eight. That's when the pilots check in. Got your luggage?'

'I haven't any luggage.'

Novak nodded imperturbably; and it occurred to Magnus, even through the euphoria of Black Label, that Mr George Novak took a great deal for granted. Perhaps it was shyness, or just the man's East Coast breeding. He added, to reassure him: 'All I've got is seventeen pounds in good old English sterling. Like me to pay you now?' Novak gave an enamel smile: 'You keep it till we get to Reykjavik. You never know — the weather here can change pretty fast. Well, here's to the trip!' He drank more boldly this time, licking his lips again as he set down the glass and lit another cigarette. 'Oh I'm sure glad you turned up here, Magnus. It can get pretty lonely for a guy in a place like this.'

Magnus finished his drink, and Novak poured him another, and Magnus lay back again and wondered at his good luck and thought about Mr George Novak, who was so shy and generous and pleased to see him. Nice shy bird-watcher all alone on holiday in Iceland, God help him. But there were only two things about Mr Novak that mattered. He owned a bottle of Johnnie Walker Black Label in a country that was dry, and he had chartered an aeroplane to Reykjavik.

CHAPTER 3

Novak lit a fresh cigarette from his last, picking up his rucksack and the half-empty bottle of Scotch. Magnus said: 'There was a kind of big blond oaf downstairs when I came in making one hell of a racket on the jukebox. Do you know who he was?'

Novak shook his head: 'I was asleep then — didn't hear a thing. Sleep like a log. Might have been one of the fishermen, though.'

They went downstairs and outside, with still no one in sight. Novak must have already paid his bill. The muddy Volvo was his — hired from a local garage, so he said. He made no enquiry about the fate of the minibus, standing forlorn now in front of the hotel.

Magnus wondered idly how long it would take them to get down from the Haëli to claim it. As he climbed unsteadily into the seat beside Novak, he glanced back up the road to the mountains. He could just make out the snow line, dim with mist. He started to laugh. Thank God for the sugar, he thought. The bastards. He leered sideways at Novak, who had turned into the road, driving along the lake away from the mountains.

'You're a good boy, Novak. You and Johnnie Walker!' He slapped his thigh and chuckled.

'How far is it?' he added thickly.

'Couple of kilometres.'

'Very convenient.' He twisted round and peered back through the rear window. The road was empty. 'Damn convenient!' he said again. 'Oh you're a good boy, George Novak!'

Novak smiled: 'I'm always glad to be of assistance.'

'What do you do back in the States, besides watching birds?' His tone was not consciously aggressive, but the whisky burnt hot in his belly and he had still had no breakfast.

'I'm an engineer.'

'An engineer, and you take a month off in Iceland to watch birds, eh?' He paused broodingly. 'What do you engineer, George?'

Novak was silent.

'It seems a damned odd thing for an engineer to come out here and watch birds for a month,' Magnus said; and Novak tapped out a fresh cigarette and lit it with his free hand, driving cautiously as though in traffic.

'I'm sorry, I'm drunk. I didn't mean to be rude, George.'

'That's O.K., Magnus. You had a hard night. You let off a bit of steam — I don't mind.'

'D'you think we'll be able to take off?' He glanced out across the lake where the birds still wheeled low and fast over the water, through shafts of pale sunlight; but along the horizon he could now see clouds banked up high and heavy above the mountains.

'It depends what the weather's like in Reykjavik,' Novak said.

'And if we can't take off?'

'If we can't take off, then we'll just have to stay in Helfoss till it clears.'

Magnus squinted sideways and nodded. A recluse, he thought — minds his own business, hasn't asked me the first thing about myself, except that I've come over the mountains from the Vatnajökull. Scar-faced and looking like death, with only £17 to my name, and he hasn't asked me why I'm here, or what I'm doing in Iceland, or why I've left my car and haven't got any luggage or even a coat. George Novak was a paragon of discretion.

They had turned off the main track round the lake. About half a mile ahead Magnus saw a windsock fluttering from a pole. Here airfields were obviously as common as railway stations in other countries. Novak was lighting another cigarette. Smoking and boozing before breakfast, thought Magnus: Whatever would John Cane say?

He focused on the hands of his watch: five minutes to eight. There was a hangar no bigger than a cowshed, with three silver planes in front of it, looking like toys. Novak parked outside a hut at the end of the hangar and pulled his rucksack off the back seat. Magnus shouted, 'That's right, mustn't forget old Johnnie Walker!'

Novak had stuffed the bottle back into the rucksack, and now took it out again and handed it to Magnus, smiling: 'I won't join you for the moment, Magnus.'

'You're a good fellow, George!' He took a deep swig from the bottle, and his ears sang and his throat burned; he did not even feel the cold as he stepped out, examining his three scuffed shoes. He looked up grinning, trying to balance on three feet. A car was approaching up the road from Helfoss. It was a black Beetle Volkswagen and there were two men in it. He stared, with a curious stiffening in his legs.

The car drew up almost beside them. From the driving seat a thickset man got out carrying a briefcase, followed by a younger man with a little moustache. They nodded at Novak as they passed him; the thickset man unlocked the door of the hut and led the way in. Novak introduced the younger man: 'This is Mr Olsen, Magnus. He's our pilot.' Olsen shook hands, while the thickset man sat down at a desk and opened his briefcase. Magnus hung back by the door, holding on to the Johnnie Walker.

The thickset man said something to Novak and picked up a telephone. Magnus smiled at the pilot and offered him the whisky. Olsen shook his head and turned away; he did not look pleased. Novak said softly: 'Please don't embarrass him, Magnus. He has to fly.'

The thickset man was talking quietly at the telephone. Magnus opened the door and peered outside. Clouds still on the horizon; but the road back to Helfoss was empty. The man on the telephone hung up, and spoke to Olsen, who nodded and strutted through the door. Novak smiled at Magnus: 'O.K. — we're off!'

Magnus hiccupped and grinned. Novak was counting out money to the thickset man, who began to write him a receipt. 'You can pay me back in Reykjavik,' he said to Magnus, leading him outside.

The plane still looked like a toy. Magnus felt the floor rock as he climbed in, and was at first afraid to move in case he put his elbow through the side. The whole thing seemed as flimsy as silver paper. He looked up wonderingly at Olsen sitting beside him, fitting the earphones over his head, flicking a couple of switches. The control panel looked no more complicated than the dashboard of a family car. Olsen said: 'Fasten your belt.' Novak leant forward in the seat behind and helped him find the straps. It was then that Magnus began to feel that the whole thing was a trick: they could not possibly cross those mountains and glaciers in this frail machine. He crouched forward against the belt, holding the whisky bottle between his legs.

Olsen pulled out the choke; the engine coughed a couple of times, like an animal, then woke up with a shrill roar, and the plane began to shudder and sway, with smoke drifting past the windows. Olsen had removed the earphones, there was a crackle of voices, his hands moved over the controls like a blind man feeling in the dark, and the plane began to taxi forward. The engine howled, the whisky bottle fell over and rolled under Magnus' seat, there was a lurch and they were off the ground in less than eighty yards. The little town of Helfoss tipped on its side and was gone. Through the Perspex Magnus watched the lake slide away into that ashen waste which Cane had beheld with such stricken ecstasy.

He groped under his seat and retrieved the Johnnie Walker, turned and shouted at Novak: 'Like a drink, George?'

Novak put a cigarette in his mouth and smiled. Magnus took the hint and drank. Olsen was intent on the controls: the altimeter creeping round the dial towards 4,000 feet, air speed 95 knots. Fast as a sports car as the crow flies: faster than that poor old minibus. He peered out at the rolling sky, at a range of sugar-loaf mountains, trying to trace the route he had taken during the night, but it was lost in the vastness of the view, as anonymous as a black and white reconnaissance photograph.

The engines droned dully; his head slipped to one side, vibrating against the aluminium door. The bottle nudged his leg and he felt for it again and showed it to Novak: 'You're making me feel lonely, Georgy Porgy! Remember, I rescued you from loneliness.'

The face behind the green lenses said nothing. Magnus turned to Olsen. No drink for him. Olsen had a job to do. Olsen was going to get him across those mountains to a town called Reykjavik. Magnus took another sip and relapsed uncomfortably against the thunder of the door.

He slept for a moment and saw jets landing at London Airport and a big blond Pole urinating at a press conference and heard an awful thud as he brought down the heavy varnished rosewood stick on Skliros' head. A hand was tapping his knee. The man was no longer wearing earphones and the sides of his hair stuck out like straw. His hands were still on the controls, but he was looking at Magnus with a strange frozen expression, trying to nod over his shoulder.

Novak sat behind with the mouthpiece of the radio in one hand, a heavy automatic pistol in the other. 'He's changed course. Nothing to worry about — better go back to sleep.'

Magnus laughed crazily: 'Oh I'm an old timer, don't worry! Where are we going — the Haëli?'

'Sit back and relax.'

'Supposing I don't relax?'

'You just drink some more whisky, Magnus.'

'You will be in serious trouble,' Olsen said. 'This is a criminal act.'

'The responsibility is no longer yours. Providing the weather reports are correct, you have no problems.'

Magnus grinned: 'Some crazy bird-watcher!'

'Why don't you go back to sleep?'

'Why don't you have a drink?'

'You drink it all, Magnus.'

Magnus looked at Olsen, and Olsen was looking straight ahead at the clouds. A professional pilot doing his job. 'George, I'll tell you what. Why don't you blow Mr Olsen's head off and be done with it? Then we'll all be laughing.'

'Mr Olsen will do as I say.'

'Supposing he doesn't? You got a parachute?'

Novak squashed out his cigarette on the floor, but the gun in his hand did not flinch.

'Magnus, for three years I flew with your Royal Air Force during the war. I could fly this plane on my head with one arm tied behind me.' Olsen flushed, but said nothing.

Magnus lifted the bottle carefully in one hand. 'Well that seems to clinch it, Georgy Porgy. There's only one thing — supposing I make trouble?'

Novak shook his head. 'Why don't you have another drink?'

'I've nothing to lose, up in it to my neck already, you know that?'

'I know.'

'Are you going to help me, George?'

'Go to sleep, Magnus.'

'Go to hell! I'm not a bloody child.'

'Of course you're not.'

Magnus looked at Olsen. He had the real solution: dutiful silence in the face of a gun. A serious gun this time, a .45, and Magnus noticed that in contrast to his sickly pallor, Novak's hand was broad and steady, resisting even the vibration of the plane. A real heavy, this time, shades and all. Perhaps even better than Skliros.

'Can I have a drink?' he shouted.

'Finish the bottle,' Novak said, in his smooth Seaboard accent.

They had landed on a hard black beach. The sea was held off behind a barrier of rocks under a bleak sky. Magnus screwed up his eyes and looked at Olsen, then at Novak. Olsen seemed calm. The landing place must have been well selected. Novak was undoing his safety belt with one hand, holding the gun in the other.

'Where are we?' Magnus said wearily: a question it seemed would never be answered.

'We're in the north,' Novak said. 'We get out here.'

All Magnus wanted to do was to go back to sleep. He said, without moving: 'Go ahead and shoot me Mr Novak — you damned bird-watching engineer!'

'If I don't, somebody else will,' Novak said gently: 'And I mean that, Magnus. I only want to ask you some questions.'

'I'm too drunk to answer questions.' But Novak had opened the door and pushed him through. He landed on all fours, and Novak's gun was in his back as he started up. 'If you play the fool, Magnus, I'll kill you — believe me.'

'You damned bird-watcher.' From somewhere close he could hear the sound of the sea, as he began to stumble across the sand, seeing Olsen standing beside the plane. Novak called something to him, and the pilot jumped back in, and a moment later the engine roared. 'Lucky old Olsen,' Magnus muttered.

Novak was smiling as he caught up with him, putting the gun away inside his hunting jacket, producing instead the now almost empty whisky bottle. 'You almost forgot this, Magnus. And don't worry about the plane. You're with us now.'

'Oh Jesus wept!' He began to feel the cold for the first time since leaving Helfoss: he was back to square one, with only Novak to lean on — George Novak with a .45 instead of Peter Skliros with a .22.

'Are you too drunk to listen, Magnus? This is the last act. After this, you can go home.'

'Who are you?'

Still holding the bottle in one hand Novak pulled out a buff card in a celluloid frame. At the top was a black spider, the rest in writing, full of long words made up of y's and z's. Magnus pushed it back and grinned. 'I'm pissed, George. Gassed out of my mind. That old eagle there doesn't mean a thing to me.'

Novak put the folder back in his pocket. 'Don't worry. You'll have a sleep and then we'll talk.' He put his hand on his shoulder, pushing him gently. From behind them the little plane skimmed over their heads banking steeply back towards the hinterland. 'He's got a radio,' Magnus said.

'Not any more,' said Novak, 'I broke the connection.'

Magnus shook his head: 'Naughty, George.' They rounded some high rocks along the shore and he saw a ship about a quarter of a mile out to sea. Below them two men sat in a rowing boat, pulled up at the edge of the surf. Magnus looked at them, then bent down and began to laugh: 'Oh George, you're marvellous. I thought Cane and his boys were pretty smart, but you've got them beat all the way. Where did you whistle up this lot?'

'On the radio. I sent the last message while you were asleep.' He took Magnus' arm and together they clambered down the rocks to the boat. The men wore oilskins and flat leather caps, and Novak spoke to them in the language of Krok and Maya — a memory confused with pain now, as Magnus stumbled to the back of the boat and sat down, hunching his shoulders against the wind.

The two men began to pull away from the beach, with the waves smacking against the sides and an icy spray cutting into their faces, while the shoreline tilted like a seesaw. Magnus cupped his hands and shouted: 'All right, Georgy, I'm game. I've got no family, no next of kin. Just throw me over the side.'

Novak clutched his hunting jacket round him and said nothing. Even in the wind his face was the same paper-white mask. Only once did he move, bending to light a cigarette under the flap of his jacket, and when he brought his head up again, the smoke reached Magnus, sweet and sickly. He put his head between his knees, saw the whisky bottle lying in an inch

235

of bilge water, picked it up and flung it into the waves, then hung over the side, trying to measure the distance between the shore and the ship.

He had no clear idea of how long he sat in that rowing boat; but suddenly the wooden sides were bumping against a black wall; somewhere high above a man was lowering a rope ladder. Novak stood up and grabbed the end of it, and Magnus looked at him and shook his head: 'You're not really expecting me to get up that, are you?' He was no longer frightened, even angry; all he wanted now was to be left alone. His arms felt as weak as string, and Novak said, 'Come on now, you can do it.' One of the seamen hooked his left shoe into the bottom rung, and there were two more men above waiting with arms down to grab him as he came level with the deck.

They pulled him aboard like a sack and laid him down on some slimy planking that smelt of fish and tar. There were cranes and coils of rusted wire, and a red and white flag with the spider-black eagle in the middle, flapping from the stern. The name of the ship was painted in dirty white letters below the windows of the bridge: *Syrena Gdansk*.

After a time they picked him up, and Novak held him under the arm and led him down a steep flight of steps into a gangway that was full of Polish voices shouting above the wind. Novak opened a door, pushed him through into a hot dark cabin full of kerosene fumes. He sat down on a bunk, clasping his shoulders and trying to lock his jaws shut, his mouth sour with whisky vomit. After a time the nausea and shuddering passed. Somewhere in the ship a noise started up like a pneumatic drill. It seemed to go on for a long time, making conversation impossible. Novak was on the bunk opposite, lighting another cigarette.

The noise stopped; Magnus guessed it was the anchor chain. They weren't wasting time. Novak said: 'Feeling better?'

'Crackerjack.'

Novak chuckled: 'I must say, I've never seen anybody hit Johnnie Walker so hard!'

'Don't talk about him,' Magnus said. 'I'm through with Johnnie Walker.'

'I'm having some strong tea sent up, and then you can have a sleep.'

'Cuppa tea and a lie down, eh? What the hell is this, Novak — a luxury Polish cruise?'

'Just a trawler.'

'Carting about a few million roubles' worth of the latest anti-submarine equipment?'

'No, no, it's legitimate.'

'And you call it up, just like that, from a hijacked plane over foreign airspace? You seem to have got it made, Georgy! Except that Olsen will have seen the ship.'

Novak gave a delicate shrug — an almost feminine movement in the oily darkness of the cabin. 'We'll be out of territorial waters in an hour.' He began opening a fresh packet of Salems — his third that morning.

'And then where? Poland?'

'That's right — Gdansk. It takes four days.'

A sailor came in carrying two mugs of black tea. Magnus reached up for one and heard the thump of engines, thinking again, *My God, they're not wasting time.* Four days to go, then Poland. He sat up rocking on the edge of the bunk. 'It was the girl, wasn't it?' he said at last.

'The girl?'

'She put you on to me? Where is she?'

Novak shook his head: 'You're a journalist, Magnus — you don't reveal your sources, do you?'

Magnus looked at his dark reflection in the tea and laughed: 'Oh I've got nothing to hide. No job, no passport — pissed out of my mind, and probably wanted for murder back in London. By the way, where were you really going this morning when I walked in?'

'Reykjavik — like I said.'

'Pulling out?'

'Oh no. Getting ready to move in. Only I didn't expect you to turn up so quickly. That drive over the mountains was quite an achievement!'

'And what were you doing in Helfoss?'

'Watching. We've had our eyes on the house for some time.'

'You? Polish secret agents got up as Yankee bird-watchers? Too many movies, George.'

'I worked for ten years in the States,' Novak said quietly. 'Polish Trade Mission. Drink your tea.'

'That give you the right to kidnap foreigners at gunpoint?'

'I don't have to ask your permission. Not when you're involved with a gang of screwballs who go around knocking off my fellow countrymen.'

Magnus eyed him gloomily: 'So that's it? You're out to avenge Bogdan Krok. Well, I didn't do it.'

'I'm not out to avenge anyone, Magnus. I just want the organisation destroyed.'

'Good luck to you!' He raised his mug in a toast: 'Bunch of arch-poops!'

'Arch-poops?' Novak's cigarette paused in mid-air.

'Soul-buggers! Self-righteous moralists with their private telephone lines up to St. Paul and their retinue of healthy virgin thugs who want to clean up the world — cut out the cancer, the green sickness of Sodom — and build the new Jerusalem! You go ahead and destroy them, Georgy!' He drew in his breath, nauseated by the kerosene fumes. 'Squeeze me for all the information I've got — although I doubt it's worth a hijacked plane and a whole trawler to Poland, I warn you — and then you can put a bullet in my head. I don't suppose you boys are too particular, are you?' He laughed again: 'Georgy Novak — their man in Reykjavik!'

Novak was looking at his cigarette with a slightly pained expression. 'You got me wrong, Magnus. I don't want to harm you. When this is all over, you'll be looked after I promise you.'

'You mean, you'll offer me political asylum?' And he had a chilly vision of finishing his days pensioned off in the company of a few seedy compatriots — drunks and misfits who had stumbled somewhere up the diplomatic ladder and chosen the dark way out, through the Curtain.

Novak watched him through a coil of smoke. 'There'll be no need to offer you asylum, not after the organisation's been smashed. And I can tell you, you're a lot safer at the moment on this ship than you would be in London — let alone Iceland. Now drink your tea.'

Magnus drank his tea, and this time there was no need for drugs. Novak's whisky had seen to that. His head slipped back on to the canvas pillow, and instead of the chiming of clocks in a Kent farmhouse, it was now engines pounding through the Arctic Ocean.

PART 5: LUBIAN

CHAPTER 1

He talked on and on, with the lamp swinging slowly above them to the roll of the ship. Novak sat on the bunk opposite, chain-smoking and writing it all down in pencil, interrupting only to elucidate the odd detail. There were no threats, no tension; and Magnus talked freely, concealing nothing. He had escaped from Cane, only to be overtaken by Novak; he was Novak's creature now, and must do as he was bidden. He had begun at what seemed the beginning — the dinner at the hotel for the Regent's Park Sporting Club — and ended with his arrival at that other hotel in Helfoss.

When it was at last over, Novak folded up the sheets of closely-written notes, put them all away inside his hunting jacket, then got up and shouted something through the door in Polish. Magnus caught only the word 'vodka'. When Novak sat down again he was smiling. 'That was great, Magnus! Very concise. You've filled in a lot of gaps, and confirmed a lot of other stuff we've had on our files for some time. We've had our own sources in Warsaw and London and lately in Iceland — but until now there's been no tangible link, no positive lead. Until we found you.'

'Me?'

'Yes. You.'

'But I've given you everything. I can't help you anymore. Unless you send me back to London, where I can try and have Skliros put away for a life sentence.'

Novak shook his head. 'We're not interested in Skliros. He's a little man — a useful limb of the organisation, functional but not vital. Cut him off, and perhaps we maim the beast, but we don't kill it. To do that we have to go for the head.' The door opened and a sailor appeared carrying a litre bottle of white spirit with no label, two glasses and a plate of brown bread. 'And that's where you come in, Magnus.' He waited while the man uncorked the bottle, then waved him away and poured both glasses to the brim. 'Your health!'

'How do I come in? I've told you — I don't know who the head is.'

Novak sipped his vodka. 'You may not know who he is,' he said slowly, 'but it's still possible you can identify him.'

For a moment the ship seemed to hold in mid-roll; the engines grew muffled; Magnus sat very still. 'Oh don't talk bloody nonsense. How can I identify a man I don't know?'

Novak gave his small white smile. 'You know, without knowing.' Magnus took a long pull at his vodka, remembering a dread fantasy he'd had since childhood: of being tortured for information he did not have. But so far there had been no violence, no drugs: just Novak's soft transatlantic voice and cheap vodka, sousing it down as they thumped through the Arctic waters.

'You've got it all wrong, I can't help you.' He looked across at those square tinted glasses, and they stared back, expressionless against the square white face.

'Oh but you can, Magnus.'

'But how?' He was sitting forward, palms sweating. 'I've told you, I don't know the man!'

Novak nodded with exasperating calm. 'True. But we have reason to believe you may at some time have met him.'

'Is it one of those names I've given you? Hilder? Henry Deepe? Or Cane himself? Who is it?'

'Ah, now that would be jumping the gun. Like tipping off a witness before an identification parade. It would spoil the whole effect.'

Magnus laughed bitterly: 'So that's it? Just line up the gang and have me file past and point out their leader?'

'Oh no. There won't be any parade. Just the one man — and you.'

'So you know who he is already?'

'In one sense, yes.'

Novak went through the unhurried ritual of opening another packet of cigarettes. 'I want you to think very carefully. At any time during your meetings with Cane, or with any of his friends, did you ever hear mention of the name Lubian? Alexander Lubian?'

'No — not that I remember.'

'It's an unusual name. You'd have remembered it if you had heard it?'

'I might. Is this the man you think is head of the organisation?'

Novak leant forward, his elbows on his knees, studying his cigarette. 'Mr Alexander Lubian is only a name — one of many we've had on our files now for years. The records go back to before the war. The name itself is unimportant — it's one of several known aliases. What is important is the man himself.'

'And you think I may have met him under some other name you don't know?'

'Quite possibly.'

Magnus stared up at the lamp swinging from the ceiling. The vodka and lurching floor and muggy fumes of the cabin were beginning to take effect. He wondered if Novak were bluffing — whether the introduction of this mysterious Lubian were merely a distraction, a means of keeping him confused and guessing, to await a more sinister interrogation when they reached Poland. He looked blearily across at him and said: 'Haven't you got a photograph you can show me?'

'We have very few photographs of him. They're mostly pre-war and very bad. But they wouldn't help, anyway. It's not just a simple identification we're after. We want you to confront the man in person.'

'But I don't see —'

Novak smiled: 'You will, Magnus. You will.'

'So you think it's crazy? An international conspiracy of the Left and Right with no apparent political connection?'

Novak leant against the deck rail, watching the waves gleaming dully under distant northern lights. The wind was icy, and they both stood swaying in sou'westers and oilskin capes. 'Magnus, what would you say all tyrannies had in common?'

Magnus was on his guard: the question seemed suspiciously naive. 'Oppression, cruelty, one-party rule — or does that sound too much like a soft-headed bourgeois liberal?'

Novak grinned, breathing smoke into the wind. 'Just a level-headed democrat, Magnus. But you've forgotten another feature common to almost all modern ideological tyrannies. Puritanism.' Magnus hugged his arms together under the oilskin. 'Purity,' he murmured. 'Purity, virtue. Is that what they're after?'

'Something in that line. Shall we say, a moral renaissance, of European civilisation?' He cupped his hands round his cigarette, trying to relight it. 'You said that Cane and his boys had private telephone lines up to St. Paul?' He shook his head. 'Not St. Paul, Magnus. Hitler, Stalin, Chairman Mao — the leaders of almost any ideological dictatorship you care to name.

'You know that under Hitler good German girls weren't supposed to wear lipstick? And that today, in the D.D.R. — what you call East Germany — they have a whole department in the Ministry of Culture to regulate the hemline of their girls' skirts! And while Dr Goebbels was burning the works of every worthwhile writer in Germany — because they were decadent and bourgeois — Comrade Stalin was banning everything from Dostoievski to Prokofiev because they were bourgeois and decadent too. Volkskunst, Social Realism — the Thoughts of Chairman Mao or Colonel Cane. What the hell's the difference?'

He had given up trying to light his cigarette and groped for another. Magnus grinned: 'George, are you a convinced Party Member?'

'I'm not a politician. I have a job to do — to protect my country from subversive foreign elements.' He stepped back into the shelter of the bulwark. 'And that goes for your friend John Cane and his organisation.'

'You're not comparing Cane with Hitler and Stalin?'

Novak shrugged: 'He's in the same line of madness — or would be, if he ever got real power. I'm not saying he'd ban Prokofiev — he's too civilised for that — but he and his boys would have one hell of a time cleaning up your swinging Britain! New laws, decrees, police powers of censorship, committees of vigilantes. And no more mini-skirts and long hair and rude words on television. Instead, you'd get good wholesome culture — middlebrow rubbish for patriotic Britons — with perhaps a few book-burnings in Trafalgar Square to keep up the spirit of the thing.

'But this is all hypothetical. Cane and his friends aren't going to get into my power — now or ever.' He had turned towards the steps down to the cabin. 'Let's talk about the subject in hand,' he called over his shoulder. 'Alexander Lubian.'

'He first came to the notice of the authorities in 1932, when he was jailed for six months for publishing an article attacking the private morals of one of Marshal Pilsudski's ministers.

'Born in 1907 in Cracow, and won a scholarship to Cracow University.' He paused. 'How much do you know about pre-war Poland?'

'I heard that in September 1939 your cavalry went into battle on horseback, wearing kid-gloves and dress-shirts.'

Novak did not smile. 'Not far from the truth. We were sick before the war. A feudal autocracy propped up by the Church and the Army, and under the whole rotten structure was the breeding ground for every kind of half-crazed European fanatic. Alexander Lubian, in his student days, may have been interested in the early Communists; and later he had at least one contact with a Falangist group in Cracow. But Lubian was always an individualist. By the time the authorities began to take any interest in him, he had already dreamt up his own special formula for the salvation of Europe — an ideology based on a moral reawakening of western civilisation.'

'Most religious movements have preached the same thing at one time or another,' said Magnus.

'Certainly. And some of them have been remarkably successful. So — at least, until the last few days — has Lubian's.'

'What happened to him after he graduated?'

'He went into business. He began by dealing in devotional articles — crucifixes, rosaries, even started marketing altar wine.' He gave a little chuckle: 'And do you know what he called the concern? *Virtus. Virtus* Incorporated.'

Magnus remembered that tattooed snake on Tom Meredith's biceps, and he began to understand what Novak meant when he said that Lubian's ideology had been successful.

'In 1932 Lubian started a broadsheet called *Glos*, "The Voice". It only ran into a few issues before the libel case against Pilsudski's minister, when it was closed by the police. After that we have very little record of him until 1938 when a number of firms — several with international connections — were merged into a parent company, which was none other than *Virtus*. Lubian seemed to be doing well. As chief shareholder and controller, he was reckoned to be one of the richest men in Poland. At this time he also started publishing *Glos* again — under the new title, *Vox Virtutis*. It had a circulation of only a few thousand, mostly in the Cracow and Warsaw areas, and at a time when street fighting between Socialists and Fascists was at its height, he didn't attract much attention with his attacks on "decadent pseudo-culture" and immorality among the youth, particularly the students. But with the Nazi menace growing daily, a bit of casual screwing on the Cracow campus didn't upset people too much! Lubian the tycoon was of importance, but as a lay evangelist he counted for nothing.

'Or so it seemed in September 1939. We now know, however, that apart from the *Voice of Virtue* he had also formed a society — he was careful not to call it a party — with the title, *Fraternitas Virtutis*, the "Brotherhood of Virtue". There seems to have been no membership, and we have no record of their activities. In fact, at this time it's quite possible there were no activities. The war came, and during the Nazi occupation the "Brotherhood" probably consisted of only a few dozen members, operating in the main resistance centres. Then, in the summer of 1944, Lubian met Colonel John Austen Cane.'

He paused to get another cigarette alight. 'Lubian was a section commander in the A.K. — the anti-Communist Home Army. We know they met at least three times in the Cracow area between April and August. Cane, as you know, was a liaison officer with British Intelligence. We can only speculate on what exactly passed between them, but it seems reasonable to assume that during these meetings they realised they shared a common ideal — the moral revival of post-war Europe. So far, so good. And then we come to a very odd chapter in Lubian's life. In November 1944 he was arrested by the Soviet authorities.

'We don't know what the precise charges were. Poland was being liberated by the Red Army' — he said it without a trace of irony — 'and after the Warsaw Uprising a great many Poles who had fought in the A.K. found themselves in trouble with the new government. Lubian spent two months in the Mokotow prison in Warsaw, and then was suddenly released. We know that a few hours earlier he had been visited by a high-ranking member of Soviet Security. So we can assume that Lubian did some pretty fast talking, and ended up making a deal with the Soviet authorities. We also know that from the moment of walking out of that prison he vanished into thin air — and with him all trace of his "Brotherhood of Virtue", as well as his pre-war fortune that must have amounted to several million dollars.'

'And you think he used his fortune to bargain with the Russians?'

Novak was swivelling his cigarette between his lips like a pistol. 'Oh no! Lubian had something far bigger to bargain with.'

He poured what was left of the litre of vodka, grinning as he went on: 'He knew that a hard ideology is worth a lot more than hard currency — as your American allies are beginning to learn to their cost. And Lubian was clever enough not to mix his ideology with politics — that was his great secret and his great strength, and Soviet Security were shrewd enough to take advantage of it. So by the end of the war Lubian had vanished, and with him a sizeable fortune, as well as his organisation.

'For the next eleven years we had no record of him, but we concluded he must have moved West. A fanatic dedicated to the destruction of those forces which he sincerely believed would otherwise destroy European civilisation.'

'And what happened after eleven years?'

'October 1956. The only bloodless revolution in our history — led by Polish Communists against the Stalinist rulers who suddenly found themselves out in the cold. And they didn't like it. You've heard of General Roman Morowski?' he added.

Magnus nodded, recalling that his mention of General Morowski only a few days ago had nearly involved him in a nasty incident with Bogdan Krok.

'He's a hard man,' said Novak. 'One of the Old Guard. He has no time for the students and the intelligentsia — the people who really brought Gomulka to power in 1956. You see the damned irony of it now? Left-wing, Right-wing — they're reversed. It's now the Stalinists who are the reactionaries, while crazy fools like Bogdan Krok are seen in Poland today as the progressives, the radicals.'

This time his laugh was savage: 'Look at your students in the West! All anger and protest — ban-the-bomb, legalise drugs, up the Reds! But what's on the other side of the coin? Diehards like General Morowski and crusaders like John Austen Cane and tycoons like Sir Lionel Hilder — and behind them all, Alexander Lubian. These people hate youth, they hate change, they'll do anything to protect their position and power, and nothing serves them so well as a good dose of old-fashioned Puritanism!'

'Krok was framed and murdered in Britain. Why?'

'Primarily, because the "Brotherhood" operates out of Britain. Secondly, because people like Krok and Duzinska — and there have been others, too — would hit the international headlines.' He drained his vodka and gave himself another. 'Britain and Poland. Two European nations divided into opposing halves of Europe. You've got to realise that not only is Lubian a fanatic — he's also a supernational romantic. For him what you call the Iron Curtain is not so much a barrier as an advantage. He sees that while Europe may be divided politically and economically, it can be united morally.'

'And where does Iceland come in?'

'A convenient hideaway. Warsaw and London are pretty public — but who'd think of looking in a grand hotel on the edge of a glacier?'

'You say the "Brotherhood" operates out of Britain. So why am I to be taken to Poland? Is Lubian in Poland?'

'He will be by the time we get there.'

'Why?'

'He has some unfinished business to attend to. You, Magnus.'

'Christ.' He reached for his drink. 'Why me?'

'Because his organisation allowed you to get away — and you know too much. He's the boss, and his friends in Poland are going to want an explanation. They'll know by now that we've been watching Iceland, and that the Haëli's no longer safe as a meeting place. That's one of the reasons I let Olsen get away, so he'd raise the alarm. But Morowski knows he's still safe in Poland. And Lubian will go to Poland to meet him.'

'How does he travel there?'

'On a Polish passport — issued in his own name.' He smiled. 'You must remember that with the kind of money and friends he has, details like passports are no problems. The Stalinists may not be on top in Poland any more, but their power's been growing rapidly. And Lubian and his Brotherhood have been helping them — helping them by discrediting Polish liberal figures abroad. In fact Lubian's grand plan for the moral purging of Europe happens to fit in very neatly with the more naked political ambitions of General Roman Morowski and his friends.'

'Isn't there anything you can do to stop them?'

'Me?' He gave a soft laugh. 'What can I prove against Lubian? The Soviet government cleared him once, more than twenty years ago, and now he's just another Polish ex-patriate. That's not a crime in Poland. And there's no evidence — nothing to connect him with Cane or the "Brotherhood". Nothing, that is, except you.' Magnus sat examining his empty glass. 'So I seem to be in a privileged position,' he murmured joylessly, as Novak went on:

'We don't expect you to identify Lubian the Pole — but Lubian the Western conspirator, enemy of the Polish people.'

'And if I can't identify him?'

'Then our journey will have been wasted.'

'Why don't you just try and kill him? Telescopic rifle, cyanide bullets — you must know a few tricks?'

Novak shook his head. 'Too crude. Our way will be much cleaner and more effective. Besides' — and he spread his hands out, palms upward — 'we try to be civilised.'

'Like kidnapping me at gunpoint over Iceland? Come on, George, let's get really civilised. Let's have another bottle.'

Novak opened the door and shouted for the sailor.

CHAPTER 2

The coast of Poland appeared in the late afternoon of the fourth day. A darkening blur between steel-grey sea and sky. Magnus was on deck, freshly shaved, his oilskin fastened to the throat against the bone-freezing Baltic wind. Novak had lent him a grey shirt, together with a safety razor, cake of soap and toothbrush — all the luggage he possessed, now stuffed in the pockets of his rumpled worsted suit. His hair was wild, and he wore no tie, and he felt like a true Comrade.

The only sound above the beat of the engines, was the cry of gulls gliding over the oily water. The smokestack above him gave an ear-cracking groan. When it stopped Novak was beside him, slight and spruce in his polo-necked sweater which was as white as a surplice.

'Sopot!' he said, gesturing to starboard. 'One of our most popular seaside resorts.' The words had a bogus reverence, like a guide showing tourists round a dull cathedral; then, as though sensing that Magnus was unimpressed, he added: 'It's beautiful in the sun. Not flashy like the Riviera. But gay — full of young people — beautiful girls in bikinis — even the daughters of the Party officials who borrow their fathers' villas for the weekend and play American jazz records and drink scotch whisky.'

'Swinging Sopot,' Magnus murmured, looking out at the strip of bleak empty beach. Could this be one of the dens of iniquity that so inflamed Lubian and Cane and the whole mad gang of them? The last of Novak's tea-time vodka was beginning to die in his belly; and Sopot was past them now, giving way to a fringe of gloomy buildings growing out of the dusk — their last port of call, Gdansk.

There were no red stars, no slogans or banners. A port, like any port. Cranes, funnels, green-black smell of oil and seaweed. The beat of the engines dropped, the bows began to swing.

Magnus felt nothing as he watched — neither fear nor excitement, not even curiosity. He was filled with a strange vacant calm. There were no police on the quayside. A group of sailors stood waiting with ropes. More sailors scuttled about on deck. Novak took his arm: 'I think it would be better if you stayed down in the cabin while we tie up.' The words were casual, but definite, as though addressing an unwanted guest.

Magnus nodded, and was just in time to see a long black saloon car swing round the corner of a warehouse and come to a halt on the quay, about fifty yards from where more sailors were rolling up a gangway. He watched the rear door open, and a man in black hat and overcoat climb out. The ship bumped against the quay, and Novak tugged gently at his arm, leading him towards the bulkhead.

Down in the cabin he peeled off his oilskin and sat listening to the grinding of cables. The engines were silent now; he could hear footsteps above, then a long muttered conversation at the top of the steps down to the gangway.

It was twenty minutes before Novak reappeared. He seemed in a hurry, thrusting something into Magnus' hand and saying, 'Right, let's go!' Magnus opened a passport and stared at his photograph; it was like coming face to face with an almost forgotten friend. He began to turn the pages — the frontier stamps like landmarks in his life. He looked at Novak: 'I've got a visa, I suppose?'

Novak nodded: 'Twenty-eight days.' It sounded like a prison sentence. Magnus found it near the end of the passport, covering a whole page under the black spider emblem, issued in London four days earlier.

'We haven't much time,' Novak said, picking up his rucksack. 'And leave your oilskin here — I'm afraid it's the property of the Polish Merchant Marine.'

The deck was deserted. There was no sign of the man in hat and overcoat; but the car was still there, fifty yards down the quay.

No one took any notice of them as they walked down the gangway, Magnus shuddering with the cold. Novak stepped up beside him, leading the way towards the car. No Customs or Immigration — Iceland, Poland — it was like bloody Royalty! He caught a glimpse of a crowd of sailors inside a shed waiting to have their papers stamped, and suddenly he wanted to be among them, submitting to the routine bureaucracy. For walking outside with Novak made him feel estranged, detached from reality. 'Your frontier police are just wonderful, George! Is it always like this?'

'Your papers are in order,' Novak said quietly.

'Do I get the same treatment when I leave?'

No answer. They had reached the car — an ugly luxurious Zim with shaded rear windows. The driver, sitting in front of a glass partition, did not even look at them as they passed him — a big man in black leather cap and gloves. Novak opened the rear door. It was growing dark and Magnus did not see the second passenger until he was half inside: a shadowy figure in an overcoat, sitting back in the corner behind a fog of black tobacco smoke.

At first he thought it was the man he had seen from the deck; then he saw the hair, bronze-red even in the dim light of the windows, and heard her voice as he slumped down beside her: 'How was the trip?'

'Oh it was a great trip.' He felt their thighs pressed together through her overcoat, as Novak sat down on his other side and closed the door.

'You look tired,' she said, and touched his hand, her fingers like cool knives in the dark. He began to laugh:

'Yes, I'm tired. Tired and dirty and far from home.' He remembered he had not bathed, even taken his clothes off, for nearly five days now, and was grateful for the stench of her cigarette. She passed the packet across to Novak, whose supply of Salems was now exhausted, then said something in Polish, to which he just nodded.

'Thanks for the passport,' Magnus said, as the engine purred to life. 'I must get you a spare key when we get back to London.' The car did a leisurely U-turn and began to hum back up the cobbled quay. 'Did you take it that night?' he added, 'or break in later?'

'Next morning — when I heard that Bogdan had been killed.'

He nodded: 'It didn't occur to you that I might need it myself?'

'You'd already left. We knew that.'

'Of course.' 'Course' was the operative word: every move planned, bearing plotted. What was to follow would be a trial of strength and organisation between Lubian's Brotherhood and Novak's Intelligence Service. Magnus was to be a vital agent in that struggle, but one stripped of all free will. Yet he was not frightened. Finding himself in their total power brought a perverse sense of freedom, a release from all responsibility. No luggage, no currency, not the least idea where he was going — just his passport, which he felt now inside his pocket, giving him the illusion of security, in the company of people for whom the word 'security' had a somewhat ambivalent worth.

Outside, lamps began to flare on through the twilight. They turned down a broad street, under solemn Prussian architecture that still bore the pockmarks of the war. There were a few people about, and almost no traffic. A row of dim shops; queue in heavy clothes waiting for a tram; man in goggles and crash helmet astride a motorcycle by the kerb. He looked up as they passed and kicked viciously at the starter pedal, no doubt conscious that the only people who rode about in Zims were the Party bosses.

Magnus could feel the pressure of Maya's thigh again, her fingertips still touching his hand, and his blood quickened, remembering that first time he had seen her — belted raincoat and white luggage on the Red Dragon express, settling down to read *Encounter*. The image now was less elegant — bulky overcoat, jeans and flat shoes.

'Am I allowed to know where we're going?' Magnus said at last.

'Warsaw.' It was Novak who answered.

'Tonight?'

'Tomorrow. We're stopping tonight in the country where you'll be receiving more instructions.'

He turned back to Maya. 'How did they get you out of London?'

'I got myself out. B.E.A. to Paris, then Air France to Warsaw.'

He nodded: girl in jeans, British passport, ticket to Warsaw. Her profile was blurred for a moment through cigarette smoke. She was quite unreal; she had never been real. Appearing from nowhere, picking him up drunk and vanishing after tea, to reappear several weeks later on the floor of his Battersea flat listening to Beethoven sonatas. And now riding with him in a swank Soviet limousine through grim Polish suburbs into the night.

It was all part of their technique, of course: keep him intrigued, baffled, tell him nothing. He tried again though: 'All right, George, just tell me this. You're a mixed-up Marxist patriot who doesn't like Stalinism or the Brotherhood. That explains why you're doing all this. But how did you get Maya to co-operate?'

'Better ask her.'

He turned to her: 'Well?' But she said nothing, her face turned to the window.

'Maya has her loyalties,' said Novak, 'and that's all that concerns us.'

'Loyal enough to get herself trusted by the Brotherhood to do a few dirty jobs for them?'

'They trusted you,' he said; 'and we have not enquired too closely why.'

Magnus began to cough; the fug of smoke in the car was becoming unbearable. 'Can you open a window?' he said. Novak rolled his down an inch.

'Because you're not really interested why they trust me,' he went on. 'You want me for a specific job. When that's over, you'll wash your hands of me. All right, I've got myself into this mess, and I'll have to see it through. But I want to know first how you got Maya into it.'

'That doesn't concern you.'

'The hell it doesn't! She's a British citizen and she's either working for a hostile government, or for an organisation engaged in criminal activities in Britain.' As he spoke, he felt her fingers slip away from his hand. Novak's voice reached him low and tense above the slipstream from the window:

'I should be careful what you say.'

He sat back, resigned. 'Don't worry, I'm not going to turn her in. So you get your Mata Haris cheap and easy, and good luck to you!' Beside him, Maya sat very still, the cigarette in her hand burning away into a curled finger of ash. She spoke without moving her head from the window:

'I do it because I hate them. I want to destroy them.'

'Who? Bogdan Krok?' he said maliciously, and she swung round in her seat, almost falling into his lap:

'That's not true. It was all a mistake, you know that — you were there! I didn't know they were going to kill him.'

'Not kill him — just bugger him up on a drunken driving charge, in the hope that he might not get his work permit from the Home Office. And no doubt if that hadn't worked, they'd have tried something else — perhaps the old queer charge next?' He laughed spitefully: 'Although they'd have hardly asked you to help there.'

For a moment he thought she was going to strike him. Her hand jerked forward and the ash dropped messily on to his trousers. Novak interrupted: 'You're hardly the one to talk, Magnus. You believed in them. You believed in John Cane. You didn't come forward when they framed those boys in Cardiff, did you?'

'I didn't have any proof.'

'Oh sure, sure. Except that on your own admission Cane immediately afterwards took you into his confidence. Now I'll tell you something. Maya's clean as far as the Brotherhood's concerned. She's never had any fancy ideas of cracking down on long-haired pop singers and cranky avant-garde liberals. She's broadminded — she believes in live-and-let-live.'

Magnus looked at her again. 'Why do you hate them so much, Maya?'

She was sitting back again in her corner, her eyes huge and hollow in the dark. 'Because of what they did to my father. They disgraced him, destroyed him.'

Outside, pine trees swept past like giant moths in the headlamps. The road was straight and empty, with no traffic except for a single prick of light through the shaded rear window.

'What happened?' he said at last.

'They had him framed on a rape charge — a disgusting case with a girl in a Warsaw hotel. A cheap little whore they'd bribed to pick him up and get him to buy her some drinks, then take him back to the hotel he used when he was up on visits. It wasn't very discreet, I know — but he was a colonel in the Army stationed down in Cracow. But my mother was dead — killed in the Uprising — and anyway why shouldn't he have had an evening out!' she cried, accusingly. 'They must have paid that bitch a few thousand zlotys. She ran out into the corridor screaming, with nothing on, and the police were called, and she told them she'd been raped. There were witnesses, and she was very convincing in court. They sent my father to prison for two years.'

She spoke with a strained, hushed anger, not looking at Magnus. 'And in Poland there's no reduction of sentence for good behaviour. He served his two years, and when he came out he was disgraced, his career in the Army finished — even after he'd fought the Germans right through the war, including the Uprising!'

'Why did they do it?'

'He knew too much. About General Morowski, and his interest in this crazy *Fraternitas Virtutis*. He'd always hated the Stalinists. When they took over complete power in 1947, they had him arrested, along with hundreds of others, because he'd fought with the Home Army.'

'But you got out?'

'I was only a baby. My mother was dead, and in 1946 my father was sent to the American Zone of Germany as part of the Polish Mission, and he took me with him. Then, when the Communists started taking over, he was recalled, and he went — he wasn't afraid of them! But he left me with some Polish friends in Germany, and just before he was arrested he managed to get a message out, and the family adopted me. A year later they moved to England, and after five years I got my passport — all nice and legal, don't worry! Except, as you said, I'm now working for a hostile government.' She fell silent, the corner of her eye flashing suddenly in the single light that still peered at them through the rear window.

'What happened to your father then?' he asked.

'He was amnestied after Stalin's death. And in 1956, when Gomulka came to power, they gave him back his old job in the Army — as a full colonel in the Cracow area. He was a very respected soldier.'

'But he supported the regime?'

'Father was never a Party member,' she said staunchly. 'He was a Polish patriot doing his duty, not running away. And I'll tell you something to prove it.' She was sitting on the edge of her seat now, facing him, with the light from behind still flashing in her eyes.

'Only four days before he was reinstated, the Hungarian revolution began. And on the third day of his command, Warsaw tried to send a hospital train with medical supplies to Budapest. The train went through Cracow on its way to the Czechoslovak border. But the Czechs stopped it. They said they wouldn't allow any supplies to go through to help the Hungarian counter-revolutionary Fascists. Can you believe it? Students and workers and schoolchildren fighting tanks in the streets, and those Czech pigs sent back our bandages and penicillin!' She laughed: 'But when the train got back to Cracow, and my father heard what had happened, he put it in a siding and called up a battalion of his crack paratroops who were doing ski-training in the Tatra Mountains. He put a man on every footplate armed with a sub-machine gun, and ordered them to ride down to the Czech frontier. The Czechs didn't stop it a second time. It went straight through to Hungary, delivered the supplies in Budapest, and returned to Poland without a shot fired.'

Magnus noticed that Novak had remained very quiet through all this. 'So how did you get involved with the Brotherhood, Maya?'

'I came over to Poland last year to see my father just after he'd been let out of prison. And he told me everything — how this *Fraternitas* was discrediting anyone associated with the new liberal movements. He'd collected a lot of evidence about their activities in the Army and their connection with General Morowski, but before he could act against them, they got at him first — they broke him.

'They're very clever, you see. They knew that some trumped-up political charge would get him an audience. People would have listened to him in court, and the rumours would have spread. They couldn't risk that, so they decided to disgrace him morally. Who'd listen to an officer accusing his superiors after he'd been found guilty of rape?'

'So you agreed to help by acting as an agent provocateur for the Brotherhood inside Britain? How did you manage to contact them?'

Novak snapped something in Polish and she fell silent. Magnus sighed: 'All right, I can guess. You used the East-West Cultural Association. Old-style Communist front organisation pretending to further coexistence. Steiner was your contact? It was he, I suppose, who arranged the stunt in Cardiff against the B.B.C. — and later against Krok?'

'It wasn't difficult to join,' she murmured, 'if you knew the right slogans.'

'Like preferring the Red Army choir to the Rolling Stones?' He detected a tiny smile beside him in the darkness, as he added: 'How did you get on to me?'

'Through *The Paper*,' and Novak sprang forward in his seat, shouting at her in Polish.

'Oh to hell with you, George!' Magnus said, 'I'm not going to shop her to Scotland Yard or this General Morowski. You've been playing the old Secret Service spook for four days now. Why don't you give me a break? Maya's not going to tell me anything that's going to damage you.'

Novak relaxed a little and muttered, 'So you know now — it was someone who works for *The Paper*.'

'Hugh Rissell, eh? So my sardonic old News Editor turns out to be a double agent for a foreign power?' He shook his head and began to laugh: 'Hugh Rissell and Maya! It's too damn ridiculous.'

'You're wrong,' Novak said. 'And since there's nothing to be gained by making false accusations, I'll tell you. It was a man called Poole.'

'Poole?' For a moment he was at a loss; then he remembered that wall eye glaring at him among the alleys of filing cabinets, imagined the computer-like memory clicking up the names he'd asked for: Cane, Hilder, Pym. 'So the old fox suspected I was spying on them?'

'He reported to us that you were interested.'

'Why?'

'He used to be a Party member. Not anymore, but he's still got some idealism left. He doesn't care much for the Stalinists, or the *Fraternitas Virtutis*.'

'But what made him suspect that someone on *The Paper* had anything to do with it?'

But the question was never answered. Novak had looked back through the rear window. The prick of light was still there, far down the road. He slid back the panel in the glass partition and was shouting something at the driver, whose head jerked up under his leather cap as he glanced in his mirror. At the same time the car gave a gentle lurch and began to accelerate rapidly.

The light behind drew back into a pinprick, but did not disappear. The road still ran on straight as a runway, the pines now thinning into flat fields.

'We're being followed,' Maya said. 'There's a motorcycle behind.'

'Sit well back in your seat,' said Novak, 'and do exactly as I tell you.'

Magnus sat back and felt the road thundering under them, the slipstream from the window rising to a howl. Novak closed it suddenly.

'Are you sure?' Magnus asked.

'If he keeps on at this speed we will,' said Maya. 'You don't get ton-up boys going for joyrides at night in this country.'

'There's a village in five kilometres,' Novak said. 'If he's still with us after the village —' His words were lost in the roar of the wheels.

Magnus looked round and the light was still there, tiny but clearly visible. Beside him Maya sat rigid, her mouth set hard, her eyes watching the road racing towards them.

They reached the village a couple of minutes later. A glimpse of low houses crouching against the fields; a muddy square and the wall of a church swinging round in the headlamps, as the car turned out again into the countryside.

'Brace yourself,' Novak said; and the next moment Magnus felt an arm flung across his chest and he was almost catapulted through the glass partition, as the huge car shrieked and bounced, swerved round and slid to a sudden halt. The engine stopped, the lights went out.

No one moved. Magnus could see nothing but the dial of his watch; even Novak had put out his eternal cigarette. The only sound was their breathing. Then Maya muttered something and Magnus cried. 'For God's sake speak English!' Those strange Slav syllables had an eerie quality now that he could no longer see her.

'We'll wait for him to pass,' Novak said, 'then see if he pulls back.'

He rolled his window down a couple of inches. Ten seconds passed. Then, very faintly, the purr of an engine. It grew quickly into a roar through the stillness, a beam of light swinging on to some trees opposite, flattening across the road — which Magnus now saw was at right angles — then flashed past with a high-pitched howl and was gone. The darkness closed back at once, the sound droning into the night.

Quietly Novak opened his door and got out. Magnus could hear him talking to the driver, but could still see nothing. Maya did not move. He said, for no definite reason: 'Novak's got a gun.'

'He wouldn't use it here,' she whispered. 'They'd hear it in the village.'

The driver had got out now, closing his door carefully; then a flashlight came on and moved round to the back of the car. Magnus heard the boot being opened, something being taken out and carried round to the side of the road. The flashlight moved quickly now, crossing the road, flickering across the bark of some trees.

He tried to take Maya's hand and clutched at her knee by mistake. He could hear his heart thumping in the silence, which seemed to trap them together with an uneasy intimacy. He found her hand at last, squeezed it slowly, and she squeezed back, and for what seemed a long time they sat like this, holding hands and waiting.

The flashlight returned across the road, then went out. A minute passed. Two minutes. Maya's hand was cold, their breathing growing louder. Then they heard the motorcycle again.

The pencil beam came flickering back down the road. The squat shape of rider and machine flashed into view, jerking, jumping, then seemed to slide sideways in a great white glare of tree trunks, as something flew off the top of the driver's head and the front wheel rose, almost gently, and began to ride up one of the trees, the beam rising vertically now, cutting through the branches far above. The engine gave another howl and the black-clad rider was climbing the tree alone: hesitating, swinging over like a monkey to reach the next trunk, then flopped down and rolled into the road.

The machine went on whining and kicking among the branches for a couple more seconds, then crashed back into darkness. The Zim's headlamps had come on full, and Novak and the driver were already out again, running across the road. Magnus started after Maya, stumbling into a wire somewhere in the dark, and heard Maya suddenly laugh — a quick cruel sound, followed by excited talking in Polish. He joined the three of them and looked down.

The man lay on his back as though caught in the act of stretching — legs splayed out, one elbow crooked at his side. But the face was odd, incomplete — it finished at the bridge of the nose. The top of his head had been sliced off like a boiled egg. The mouth was small and prim, lips closed. It would have happened before he'd had time to scream. There was blood and pulp on the road, and the helmet lay a few feet away, with the goggles trailing beside it, covering something that looked like a golf ball.

Novak was brutally unzipping the leather jacket, pulling out the man's papers. He flicked through them, nodded and looked up at Magnus: 'You recognise him?'

'Hardly — just the mouth...'

'He's the one who killed Bogdan, isn't he?' Maya said. She was pale, but showed no obvious emotion.

Magnus nodded and turned away. The silvery-blond hair would be under the helmet. He'd been crossed three times now, but this time he would never get even.

Novak stared at the body for a moment, then knelt down, replaced the papers inside the jacket and zipped the torso back up as though it were a parcel. 'He had Polish papers,' he murmured. 'That means they're worried, or they'd have used one of the local boys.' He glanced at Magnus: 'Officially you've seen nothing. He was going too fast, left the road and hit a tree.'

The driver was already untying the thin wire that had been drawn across the road between two trees, at roughly four feet above the ground. No one spoke as they climbed back into the car. Magnus sat in the corner this time, away from Maya, with the window rolled right down.

The Zim pulled into the road and drove fast through the cold clean night.

CHAPTER 3

It was a big room built of pine logs that oozed sap like golden syrup. A wooden balcony ran round the four walls and a stove of glazed tiles roared gently in the corner. The air was sweet and heavy with pine and Balkan tobacco.

Magnus sat in a rocking chair, drowsy after a long bath and meal of borsch and stewed mutton prepared by Maya. On a stool beside him was a mug of tea-and-lemon and a tumbler of Zubrowski herbal vodka. It might all have been the setting for some Slavonic commercial: Maya, in dressing gown and slippers, curled up on a sofa by the stove hugging another mug of tea, while her father sat opposite them both in a carved wooden chair, sipping cherry brandy. Only the murmur of Novak's urgent telephoning from the next room confused the image of domestic bliss.

Ex-Colonel Stanislav Czernovski put down his glass and patted his lips. 'You would do well to have a good sleep, Mr Owen. It has been a day of drama for you? And that accident with the motorcyclist —' He gave a faint gesture of his hand, which was long and slender, and oddly at variance with the rest of his appearance.

He was an enormous man, pink-cheeked with thinning hair and a reddish grey beard which he tugged and stroked as he talked. His mouth was Maya's, though slightly loose and pouchy at the corners, and his eyes were blue and unexpectedly mild; they did not belong to a ruthless or embittered man. In other circumstances, Magnus might have put him down as an eccentric inventor or failed progressive poet. He did not look in the least like a hardened soldier, except for the brown leather jacket that bulged over his great shoulders, showing no trace of padding.

'Novak said he was an English policeman — the one who killed Krok?' He stroked his beard thoughtfully. 'Holy God, they must be getting desperate!'

Magnus did not want to think about Skliros.

'An old Polish trick,' the Colonel went on, 'one we learnt against the Germans — flick!' He brought his finger down across his eyes, just at the point where Skliros' face had ceased.

Magnus glanced at Maya, but she seemed to be asleep. Her father added: 'You have no further problems, Mr Owen? Nothing that specially bothers you?' His English had a deep lilting accent that reminded Magnus of Welsh.

He gave a tired smile. 'Everything bothers me, Colonel. But I'm signed on with you now — I'm committed. If you lose out, I lose out too. Isn't there an old Russian proverb: that when a man has been swallowed by the Devil, there's only one way out?'

The Colonel seemed overjoyed by the remark; he leant forward and shook with laughter till his eyes were wet: 'Oh, it's a long time since I heard that one!' He dabbed at his eyes and was suddenly serious again. 'You were committed, of course, from the moment you had your first contact with the Brotherhood — with John Austen Cane. You can hardly complain now.'

'It should be an honour to be committed,' Maya called sleepily from the sofa. 'Especially when we're just about to destroy them for good!'

Magnus nodded from his rocking chair. 'Oh I'm honoured all right,' he lied: 'I'm not complaining. I'm a journalist — I'll do anything for a good story.'

'And what a story, Mr Owen! You'll be the hero of the Polish people, sir!'

'If we win,' Magnus replied. 'Remember that policeman we killed this evening.'

'Ah, but that just proves what I have been saying!' His eyes were bright, his hands swaying delicately as though conducting a piece of music. 'Lubian is scared, he is in a panic. Why else would he do such an idiot thing as to risk importing an Englishman here? I'll tell you why! It is because he does not dare commit his forces in Poland — that is, the forces of General Roman Morowski.' He took a gulp of cherry brandy, dribbling some in his beard as he went on:

'Because Lubian's supporters here are beginning to smell a rat! What do they see? Bogdan Krok is murdered in a London hotel! The story is on the front page of every Polish newspaper, even *Tribunya Ludn*. And Morowski is no fool, believe me. He will work with Lubian as long as there is no scandal. These old Stalinists are realists — not mad moralists like Lubian and his friends. They make deals like businessmen, but when there is the first smell of scandal they will drop Lubian and his *Fraternitas* — so! — finished!' He rubbed his hands as though disposing of something highly disagreeable; then poured himself another cherry brandy.

'But you say Lubian's already in Warsaw,' said Magnus. 'So they haven't dropped him yet?'

'Lubian is in Warsaw for one reason, Mr Owen. He has come to explain himself to General Morowski. He has talked himself out of worse corners than this, and he will try to do it again. Only this time' — he winked slyly over his glass — 'this time we're going to have a little surprise for Mr Alexander Lubian.'

270

The door opened and Novak came in. He crossed to the stove, pausing to light a cigarette. 'I've just been informed,' he said in English, 'that this afternoon our Consular Division in Copenhagen issued a twenty-eight-day visa to John Austen Cane. He is booked on a direct flight to Warsaw tomorrow morning, due at Okieci Airport at 1.40 a.m.'

The Colonel brought his hands together with a loud smack. 'The beautiful idiots! They play right into our hands — are they crazy?'

'Crazy?' Novak gave his taut little smile. 'Our agent Wytchek also reports that Lubian has set up his headquarters on the thirty-second floor of the Palace of Culture.'

The Colonel's mouth dropped open: 'Palac Kultury?' He leapt to his feet. 'Palac Kultury!' he bawled.

Novak shrugged: 'It's a pretty strategic place. The whole tower's sealed off, but the lower part's open to the public, with at least eight separate entrances. It won't be easy to cover.'

Colonel Stanislav Czernovski was wiping his eyes with laughter. 'But Holy God, what a choice! A poetic choice! The Palace of Culture — the sterile culture that Lubian has dreamed of all his life!'

'The sightseeing platform has been closed off for repairs since the end of last week,' Novak said, tapping his cigarette against the stove. 'Wytchek also reports that the arrangements were made through the Palace Works' Committee, and Lubian set up shop there three days ago. So we haven't got a lot of time. My own theory is that he and Morowski will get in touch tonight, and that a further meeting, probably with Cane, will take place in the next twenty-four hours.'

'Morowski will have to be there.' Czernovski had stopped laughing, suddenly quite serious again: 'Or they may plan to slip out and hold the meeting somewhere quite different. They are clever devils.'

'We're keeping a close check on Morowski's movements through a young aide. And Cane, of course, will be under surveillance from the moment he arrives at Okieci. The real problem will be the Palace itself. Exhibition halls, swimming baths, sports centre, People's Theatre, Congressova nightclub — they'll all have to be watched. But it's my guess Lubian will stay put. He'll think it's a safe perch for him.'

He turned and explained to Magnus: 'It's the tallest building in Europe. A gift from our Soviet comrades after the war. From the top you get the finest view of the whole of Warsaw — the only place in the city where you can't see the damn thing!'

Czernovski chuckled gaily: 'Thirty-two floors and our friend Lubian must choose the top! It has a kind of mad splendour about it,' he added, giving himself another cherry brandy.

'It's known as "Stalin's Prick".' Maya said sleepily. 'Somebody ought to blow it up. They will one day.' She yawned and unfolded her legs from the sofa. 'If we've got to be up at three-thirty, I think I'll go to bed.' She stood up and embraced her father warmly, on tiptoe. Although she was a tall girl, beside him she looked almost frail.

Magnus kissed her hand, Polish-style, and watched her greedily as she walked to the stairs, her slippers smacking softly on the pine floor. Novak excused himself a moment later; and Czernovski and Magnus were alone.

Magnus was exhausted, longing for sleep, but desperate for some last word of reassurance. The Colonel looked at him: 'Another drink, Mr Owen?' He came across with the Zubrowski bottle, chuckling happily: 'I like a man who drinks!

I can certainly see you're not one of those mad idiots in the *Fraternitas.*'

They drank each other's health, drank the health of Poland, and to the death of the Brotherhood. There was a pause. Magnus heard a door close upstairs. 'Novak seems to have done a remarkable job?' he said at last.

'Ah, Novak is splendid!'

'What about the other side?'

'Oh, they are good too. But they lack the finesse of Novak. He is a real artist. And besides, in this operation we not only have Novak — we have you, Mr Owen!'

He drained his glass and stood up, smiling beatifically. 'But now you are tired and must sleep. We leave early for Warsaw.'

Magnus saw it was almost midnight. He climbed out of his rocking chair and the Colonel laid a hand on his shoulder, walking him to the door. 'My daughter, Mr Owen, she is a beautiful girl, don't you think?'

'She is very beautiful,' Magnus said, and Czernovski laughed: 'A miracle when you look at my ugly face.'

They began to plod up the stairs. 'She had a hard beginning. Born just before the Uprising, and then her mother was killed — you know that?' He sighed: 'It means nothing to tell you English, but in those two months in Warsaw we lost a quarter of a million people. Two summer months when you could not see the sun through the smoke — while our Russian comrades waited across the Vistula, because Stalin told them they were not to get their boots wet!' His fingers dug painfully into Magnus' shoulder. 'Not easy for a baby to grow up. And I was not much good to her — a stupid old soldier. But the people who looked after her in England, they were good people, I think.' He paused at the top of the stairs to turn out the lights. 'I am rather drunk now, Mr Owen. But I think it is perhaps better she makes her life in a good country like England? Don't you think?' He clamped both hands on his shoulders and kissed him on the cheek. 'I like you, Mr Owen — I think you would be very good for my daughter. She is a fine girl.'

Magnus felt vaguely abashed. 'Colonel, I know nothing about your daughter. It's been hide-and-seek all the way. And we're not finished yet. But just tell me one last thing. Supposing I hadn't cooperated — or that Novak hadn't trusted me?'

The Colonel shook his head. 'Then I expect we would have had to kill you. Sleep well, Mr Owen. Tomorrow will be a long day.'

CHAPTER 4

The sky was blue above the pastel shades of the Stare Miasto, the Old Town of Warsaw. Steep baroque houses, each painstakingly reconstructed after 1945 from the drawings of Canaletto. The Kawiarnia at the corner of the square had a discreet but dignified shabbiness: balding carpets, rows of pastry cakes and a grand piano on a dais under a moulded ceiling. The waitress was slender and middle-aged, dressed like an English parlourmaid; the coffee she brought was pale brown and tasted of acorns, the boiled egg came beaten up in a hot tumbler.

Magnus sat alone at a corner table. It was more than an hour now since he had been dropped in a side street like lost luggage and told to wait. Novak had been worried that the Zim might attract too much attention.

He waited. He had nothing to read, spoke no Polish, and the only money he had — besides his £17 in cash — was a 100-zloty note which Maya had pressed into his hand as he left the car. He had no further orders, no proper idea where he was. The menu was in Polish and French — the egg nicely described as *oeuf anglais* — so he had little trouble ordering.

He waited listlessly, unshaven, his eyes aching with lack of sleep. He had passed a bad night, alone, listening to the silence of the pine forest, waking several times to think he heard Maya breathing somewhere very close.

Then came the drive to Warsaw, beginning in the dark, through the grey of the morning and the bleak mud plains of Poland which the Germans had called panzer country.

His first glimpse of the capital had been a sprawl of blotched concrete and streets of unfaced brick like raw meat; shambling, shapeless crowds, trams of incredible antiquity sparking across great vacant squares, past acres of rubble. The pinnacle of the Palace of Culture had loomed from far off, soon visible at every corner. A wedding cake of white tile, rising above fluted Grecian columns, the walls of its skyscraper tower punctured by mean little windows. Magnus had looked up at the top floor, just under the sightseeing parapet and the television masts — reflecting that it was really no more absurd than their choice of that neo-Gothic folly, the Haëli, in the middle of a lava desert.

At eleven o'clock a white-haired man entered the Kawiarnia, shook hands with the waitresses, who helped him off with his muffler and overcoat, then stepped on to the dais in a dinner jacket and white tie and began playing Chopin sonatas.

Half an hour later a tall blonde girl arrived, carrying a copy of *Le Monde*. Magnus watched her choose a table in the farthest corner from him. She wore a red tartan dress with matching peaked cap, long tartan gloves and white cotton knee socks. Magnus was no expert on women's fashions, but it did occur to him that long tartan gloves were rather overdoing it.

The man in the dinner jacket went on playing Chopin without a break, varying the sonatas with nocturnes and mazurkas. After about an hour the tartan girl left, passing Magnus' table without even a glance at him. He began to feel as though he did not really exist. He got up and went through to the toilet, hesitating between the two doors, *Dla Panow, Dla Pan*. The decision was made for him by a grubby little man who came lurching out of one of them and bumped into him with a snarl of Polish.

Magnus slipped past him and locked himself into a cubicle which was splashed and stinking, with torn sheets of *Trybuna Ludn* spiked on a nail. As he got up he felt a rush of fear: the little drunk had been the only person to speak to him since leaving the Zim that morning. The man had gone when he returned to the Kawiarnia. Instead he saw Maya, a handbag slung over her shoulder like a schoolgirl's satchel, talking excitedly to one of the waitresses. Her face lit up as she saw him: 'Ah, thank God! I thought something had happened.'

'What did you think had happened?'

She had turned, calling again to the waitress. 'I thought you might have left,' she said, giving the waitress some money.

'Left for where?'

She smiled brightly: 'It doesn't matter — you're here now. I'm sorry you've had to wait so long. Like some lunch?'

'I'd like something to drink.' The Kawiarnia sold no alcohol.

She nodded: 'We'll have both.' As they walked out, Magnus realised that the music had stopped; the pianist had gone. He wondered if he was being unreasonably suspicious. 'So what kept you so long?' he asked her.

'I was making a deposition to the police.' She saw his expression and smiled: 'Don't worry — they're Novak's friends.'

'Deposition about what?'

She shrugged, swinging her handbag over her shoulder: 'Jan Steiner mostly — we can certainly break him, if none of the others. I didn't mention Skliros though.'

'And me?'

'No. We want to keep you right out of it until the last moment.'

They had reached the restaurant, down a stone stairway, into a hall like a monastery refectory. It was packed and dense with cigarette smoke. They had to queue, shouting to make themselves heard above the din. No one seemed to notice that they were speaking English.

'I can't give you any other news,' she cried, 'but I know that father and Novak have been busy on the plans all morning. We're due to meet them tonight at eight o'clock in the Congressova nightclub under the Palace of Culture. It's the most frightful place!' She caught a waiter's eye and smiled, just as she had done that first time in the Park Hotel in Cardiff. Here the waiter was either overworked or spoilt; he ignored her. She shrugged: 'The restaurants are really the worst things in Poland! Always full, and no service.'

'How bloody,' said Magnus, feeling he must be losing his sense of humour. Here she was, cheerful, prattling, as though discussing plans for her coming-out party in the Congressova nightclub. Daddy and Uncle George arranging everything, and instead of having her hair done, she'd been making a few depositions to the Polish Security Police, while Magnus Owen was left stranded for four hours in a coffee-house listening to Chopin. He wondered why they hadn't put him in a flat somewhere. Maya, he noticed, had changed from her jeans and sweater into a dress; so she and the others must have somewhere to go.

They were shown at last to a table, sharing it with a middle-aged couple in a corner alcove where the cigarette smoke hung like a bonfire.

Magnus said casually, as they sat down: 'There was a girl in the café with a copy of *Le Monde*. I didn't think you'd be able to get Western newspapers here.'

'Oh yes. *Le Monde, The Herald Tribune* — even *The Paper*. It's very chic here to walk around with foreign newspapers — even if you can't read them.' She picked up the menu. 'We'd better order Hungarian — paprika and goulash, and a bottle of Bull's Blood. Polish food's awful.'

The couple beside them ate in silence, and seemed to take no interest in them. Maya at last caught the waiter's attention and ordered. When he was out of earshot, Magnus leant forward and asked quietly, 'Is there going to be any violence tonight?'

'I don't think so.' Her voice was curiously untroubled. 'Novak is very well organised.'

'I've no doubt. But so are the others.'

'I know. But tonight we don't expect trouble. The guards on the Palace are only the normal security units. They're not dangerous.'

He nodded: 'Just a few old nightwatchmen against Novak and your father? Supposing Lubian has his own guards?'

'They wouldn't try anything. Not if Morowski's there — the very last thing he wants is violence. But we must leave the security side to Novak.'

'Of course. Novak's in charge. Even my toothbrush and razor belong to Novak. By the way, where can I change some money? I owe you a hundred zlotys.'

She reached out and clasped his hand. 'You're depressed? Please, don't be. Everything'll be all right after tonight, you see! You'll go back to London and have a marvellous story. Absolutely exclusive!'

'And who do I write it for?'

'Anybody you like — you name your price! I expect you'll be on television too. You'd look rather terrific on television — wild lone wolf!' She leant over and ruffled his hair, then nodded up at the waiter who was holding a bottle of Bull's Blood. There was no ceremony about tasting it; both glasses were filled and Magnus drank half of his in a gulp. He looked across the table. 'Maya. Do you know who Lubian is?'

'Me?' She sounded almost shocked. 'Of course I don't!'

'But I do?'

She shrugged: 'Well, Novak and father say so. So I suppose you must know.'

He laughed dismally and took another drink. 'You're a nice uncomplicated girl, aren't you? And I don't understand the first damn thing about you. I suppose it's a bit late to try and find out?'

'Well, I haven't given you much chance. Perhaps when we're back in London?'

'Will you be going back to London?' The suggestion caused him a pang of excitement.

'Oh yes. I couldn't come back and live in Poland now.'

'That's what your father said last night. He got very sentimental about you — I think he was trying to marry you off.'

She laughed: 'He's a terrible romantic! He's also a snob. He thinks the English are the most marvellous people in the world — after the Poles, of course — and that you're a nation of gentlemen!'

'You haven't told him I'm Welsh and married already, with a two hundred pound overdraft and no job?' He refilled their glasses, as the goulash arrived.

'So you think it's going to be all right after tonight? You think I'm going to be able to go back to London and write a marvellous story, and that'll be the end of it?' He shook his head. 'I'm not a hero, Maya, I'm just stuck with it — too idle, or too bloody-minded to try to escape. I suppose you wonder why I didn't use that hundred zlotys to take a taxi to the Embassy this morning? I've got my passport — all I had to do was tell them who I was and get myself on a plane back to London. No trouble at all.'

She sat munching her goulash. 'I'm glad you didn't,' she said at last. 'Novak's had two men watching the Embassy all morning.'

'So that's why I was stuck in the café all morning? Because Novak still doesn't trust me?'

'Novak has to be sure.'

'Supposing I'd gone to the Embassy? Would Novak's boys have picked me up and dumped me in the Vistula?'

'Novak is very serious. You must have confidence in him.'

'Oh I do! Don't worry, I have every confidence in George Novak!' After the second glass of Bull's Blood he began to feel better. When they had drunk the bottle, he suggested another. 'You mustn't get drunk,' she warned.

'Of course not. Lubian and Cane and General Morowski would be horrified. Does General Morowski drink, by the way?'

'I have no idea,' she said, ordering more wine, and they drank it while the restaurant began to empty, touching hands across the table when it was finished. Still only 4.15 — and eight o'clock seemed a long way off — but the waiters were gathering in a corner, staring at them deliberately. She passed him the money under the table. 'We can risk walking down to the river,' she said, standing up. 'If we meet John Cane in the street, it'll be just too bad.'

There was a sharp chill outside, exhilarating after the heat of the restaurant, although he still had no coat. 'We'll walk fast,' she said. 'That wine was good, wasn't it?' They were under a row of reconstructed eighteenth-century houses; tall windows and frail balconies; an apothecary's shop with stained-glass door and gilded serpent above the lintel. She slipped her arm through his, hurrying them both down a twisting cobbled slope. The street ended in a wasteland of broken bricks and scrubland, the backs of the houses dirty-grey like the backs of a film set. He looked up at the Old Town huddled on the hill: an eighteenth-century print by Canaletto dominated by the spike of the Palace of Culture.

Below them the edge of the river was slimy, pitted with rubbish. A man in leggings trudged through the mud, carrying a bucket. But the river was real: a broad fast-flowing torrent at which the Red Army had halted for two months in 1944, while in the city you could not see the sun. He found it hard to imagine that Maya had been up here, somewhere in the inferno, as a tiny child.

She held his hand tightly and said: 'Don't worry, after tonight there'll be lots of other times.'

He stood for a moment listening to the trams grinding across Poniatowski Bridge. 'Other times?' he murmured.

'When we're back in London.' She nodded vigorously.

Across the river black clouds were rising above the suburb of Praga.

CHAPTER 5

'The alarms are worked by electronic eyes set at knee level at the head of each flight of stairs.' Novak glanced at Magnus: 'A routine precaution when the building was finished, in case some citizen with a sense of history tried to commit an act of sabotage.' Fifty yards away, across a deserted marble floor, the orchestra was playing a mongrel tune from *My Fair Lady*.

'The alarms communicate only with the security guards' offices, which are just above here.' He nodded up at the domed ceiling. 'But that's all been taken care of, the guards have been warned and won't make any trouble. As far as we know, the alarms are not connected with Lubian's floor. Anybody who goes up would use one of the two lifts, and these probably do have alarms. So we'll be walking.'

Around the circular hall waiters stood like sentinels. Most of the tables, set back behind the marble columns, were empty. From the middle of the floor a fountain splashed distantly through a green glow.

Novak continued: 'It will take approximately twenty minutes to reach the thirty-second floor. We will have six men with us — three of them going on ahead.' He glanced again at his watch, then lifted the bottle of Georgian champagne out of the bucket and poured three glasses. Magnus was calculating whether his leg would take him up one floor in less than one minute.

'Excellent champagne,' Novak murmured, 'from the homeland of Stalin himself!' They raised their glasses meaninglessly.

'What weapons are you taking?' said Magnus.

'Machine-pistols and a couple of tear-gas grenades. They won't be needed.' Novak was still in his tinted glasses; but instead of the polo-necked white sweater he wore a black suit, black shirt and white tie. Through the bilious gloom of the nightclub his face appeared like a skull cut out of paper on the end of a white stick. 'If there is any shooting at all,' he said, 'you and Maya will retreat at once and take cover.' She said something in Polish, but he cut her short: 'I want no amateur heroics. The men we are taking are professionals.'

Magnus watched a waiter leading three men round the far wall beyond the fountain. Novak turned to him: 'The initial moment will be the critical one. But you will be protected. They are all crack shots to a man.'

'Thank you,' he murmured, with a sip of champagne.

A young man stopped in front of their table, bowed and said something to Maya, who glanced at Novak. The young man spoke again, his body held stiffly forward from the waist. She smiled and shook her head. The young man jerked his head at each of them and withdrew. It all happened very swiftly. A moment later Novak rose and was gone, in the opposite direction. Maya and Magnus were alone. 'What happened?' he said.

'He asked me to dance.'

'You refused.' He said it as a statement of fact, knowing suddenly that he was scared.

She nodded: 'He had a good look at both of us. But Novak will deal with him.'

'Perhaps he wanted to dance with you,' he said, pouring more champagne. Once again he had her all to himself, but now that Novak was gone he felt very alone. She broke in with a laugh: 'You expect me to dance in that morgue!' — then looked up with a delighted cry.

Above them stood her father, his massive frame buttoned up in a chalk-striped suit, a handkerchief sprouting from the top pocket, his hair and beard glistening with moisture. He kissed Maya on the cheek and sat down, his leg colliding noisily with a tape recorder under the table. 'It has begun to rain,' he said. 'A really dirty night. How are you, Mr Owen?'

'Waiting. Where's Novak?'

Colonel Czernovski lifted the champagne from the bucket, frowned and let it drop back with a splash. 'Your choice, or Novak's?' He shook his head: 'The French are the only people who know how to make that stuff. The Russians should stick to vodka.' He craned his neck out, looking down the rows of pillars in both directions, muttering, 'Holy God, what a melancholy place!' He leant across the table. 'I have just seen Novak outside. He is talking to a young man who claimed to be a student from the Polytechnic.'

'He asked Maya to dance,' Magnus said.

The Colonel snapped his fingers for a waiter. 'Whoever he was he was too late,' he said, turning back. 'General Morowski arrived here just over an hour ago.' He looked up as the waiter appeared, giving an order in Polish. 'Don't worry, Mr Owen, the General will take his time up there. Let them all settle in. They have a lot to discuss. There is no need to hurry our friend Mr Alexander Lubian.'

Maya poured more champagne. She seemed disconcertedly relaxed — whether as a result of the afternoon's wine, Magnus could not decide. He found himself wondering whether Colonel Czernovski was armed.

'You have everything, Mr Owen? All your documents? Passport — your identification as a journalist?' It was the first time anyone had mentioned his Press card since leaving London.

The waiter returned with a tray and two thimble glasses, one full of clear liquid, the other ruby-red. The Colonel lifted the clear glass, turning first to Maya, then to Magnus: 'To the end of this damnable *Fraternitas*!' He took the glass between his lips, throwing his head back with both hands free, swallowed the drink, disgorged the glass and sat back, patting his mouth. 'Ah, I shall enjoy seeing the General's face tonight. It will be a moment!'

Novak slipped round the pillar. He said something in Polish, and the Colonel disposed of his second drink and stood up. 'It is time, Mr Owen. *En avant*!' Magnus finished what was left of the champagne and squeezed round the table after Maya, while her father counted out several 100-zloty notes. Novak had pulled out the tape recorder from under the table and they started off.

Magnus followed last, round the edge of the hall, to a pair of metal doors with a bar across them, like a cinema exit. The clank as they opened was lost in the music: Cole Porter ravaged by fifty State violinists.

A soldier stood on the other side in battle-dress and rubber boots, machine-pistol slung behind his shoulder. He saluted and fell in beside the Colonel, who led the way down a corridor with dim globes of light along the ceiling. They came to a corner where two identical corridors intersected. Here a second soldier stepped out and saluted. Besides a machine-pistol, he also carried a pair of canisters the size of beer cans clipped on each side of his belt. The Colonel turned right, into a catacomb of blank walls, with no doors, no signs of ventilation, although the air was surprisingly fresh.

'These are what are called communicating galleries,' Novak explained. 'It seems that poor Ivan's architects miscalculated, and they found they had a lot of space left to fill up.'

They reached a pair of doors with brass handles. Czernovski put his shoulder to them and they swung open. Beyond lay another circular hall, about half the size of the nightclub, surrounded by the same marble pillars, under a dome whose rim gave off a mauve light. Three more soldiers, all with machine-pistols, came to attention and saluted. It was otherwise deserted, except for two giant figures standing guard over the door opposite — a concrete labourer in flat cap, wielding a sledge hammer, and a girl in headscarf clutching a sheaf of wheat to a bosom the size of a burial mound.

Apart from the padding of boots and clip of Maya's heels, the only sound was the faint sucking of air conditioners. Below the giant labourer and his mate was another pair of doors. These led into a narrow corridor with a cement floor and wainscoting of chipped gilt paint. This ended at a red curtain from which came a burble of voices like a cocktail party.

They halted. Czernovski gave an order and three of the soldiers ducked through the curtain.

'People's Theatre,' Novak said. 'It's the interval — nothing to worry about. We'll give the soldiers two minutes. The other three come with us. You and Maya stay at the back with Corporal Marek.'

Corporal Marek and his two companions stood to attention, with no expression.

Suddenly Maya belched. She muttered something in Polish, and said to Magnus, 'That damned champagne!' The soldiers did not flinch, eyes front. Magnus said to Novak: 'What happened to the man who asked Maya to dance?'

'He's being held for questioning.'

Colonel Czernovski snapped an order to the soldiers and parted the curtains.

The theatre crowd was round a corner out of sight. They hurried through a small door into another gallery — acres of liverish marble under more concealed lighting. The stairs began after about fifty feet. They were wide and shallow, with a turn between each floor where there was a window of opaque glass against which they heard the drumming of rain. Magnus noticed the beady electronic eyes at the corner of each turn.

The first five floors stretched along corridors of closed doors. At the sixth floor the lighting stopped and Czernovski produced a pocket torch. Novak stumbled once, changing the tape recorder from one hand to the other. Magnus began to pant; his leg ached and he had already lost count of the floors. He wondered if twenty minutes had not been an optimistic estimate for the climb.

Once, when they had all stopped together for breath, they could hear the pad of the soldiers' boots, several floors above.

Corporal Marek climbed patiently, in step with Magnus' limp. No one spoke; then Novak whispered: '*Dwadziescia pięc*! Twenty five!' He had rested the tape recorder on the landing. The rest of them stood in the dark catching their breath, listening to a new sound — a steady booming against the walls like the sea. It was the wind. The only light now was the circle of Colonel Czernovski's torch. The air had the dead flavour of an attic. Czernovski's torch began to climb again.

Magnus had lost track of the floors, when the footsteps stopped. Ahead, level with the stairs, was a strip of light from under a door. The Colonel's torch went out. The door was flung open; there was a shout, the landing was ablaze with light, the door full of men.

It was a brightly-lit room with a pair of chandeliers reflected in a mahogany table. The six soldiers stood round the near side of the table, pointing their guns at a man seated in front of a bowl of fruit.

But Magnus was not looking at him. In a chair in a corner sat John Austen Cane. His shoulders sagged, his face oddly shrunken, the eyes fixed and lifeless. It was as though, in less than a week, he had become an old man.

Novak was kneeling over the tape recorder, pressed a switch and the spools began to turn. There was a hush, broken only by the wind beyond the shutters; then Novak stood up, holding out the hand-microphone, and spoke in Polish. The man at the table shrugged and picked an apple from the bowl in front of him.

He was about sixty, blunt-faced, with a tiny button nose, iron-grey hair combed back from a widow's peak, thick neck pitted with acne scars. A calm brutal face, made sinister by the childish nose. Two discreet red decorations adorned his lapel and one sleeve was empty, tucked up under his shoulder. He spoke in English — perhaps for the benefit of Cane — his voice slow and harsh:

'So you have come for Alexander Lubian?' His eyes flickered across the faces in front of him. 'I regret, gentlemen, you arrive too late. Lubian is finished.' With the apple still in his hand he took a clasp knife from his pocket, snapped it open and jabbed it in the direction of Cane. 'Who do you want, Pan Novak? Me? Or this *Fraternitas Virtutis*?' He added something in Polish, and Novak turned the tape recorder off with his foot.

The man looked at Magnus. 'So you are this famous London journalist? The friend of Mr Cane?' He nodded and began to peel the apple with his one hand.

Magnus turned to Novak: 'Who is this?' he whispered.

The voice grated back across the table: 'I am General Roman Morowski. In my official capacity I now warn you all — Pan Novak, Pan Czernovski —'

'Colonel Czernovski!' Maya shouted. The General said something in Polish that made her go pale. 'Warning you formally,' he continued, 'that I shall deny all accusations. In the case of these two spies' — he nodded at Magnus, then Maya — 'there will be counter-accusations in accordance with Polish law.' His eyes were back on Magnus: 'You understand your position, Englishman?'

It was Novak who replied, in English for Magnus' benefit.

'He understands perfectly, General. It is you who don't seem to understand your position. On my authority as an officer of the Committee for Public Security, I now arrest you on charges of conspiring with foreign agents to commit crimes against citizens of the Polish State.' He said it all in his quiet deadpan accent, like a Harvard lawyer reciting his brief; then went back and translated it into Polish, while the soldiers' hands tightened perceptibly round their weapons.

General Roman Morowski listened without expression. When it was over he took a bite out of his skinned apple and sat back, grinning like a dog. '*Dobrze*! So, Pan Novak, you oblige me to fight. And I warn you, I fight hard.' He glanced at Cane. 'I only regret,' he went on, speaking now as though to Cane alone, 'that it should be on the side of these weak fools, these dreamers who want to save the world with morals!' The grin had become a rictus full of half-chewed apple.

'I ask you again, Pan Novak, what do you want? To force me to fight with these idiots? Or do you want to eat this *Fraternitas* alive? Because if so, I give them to you' — he waved his hand at Cane — 'all of them! It is not a bad bargain, and I advise you to accept it. You will not have a second opportunity.'

At that moment Cane came to life. It was not so much a physical movement, as the expression in his eyes. As he spoke the whole room turned to him — all but Morowski, who was busy scalping a second apple.

'You are right, General. I have now seen what I should have seen long ago. You are a corrupt, dishonourable opportunist. A disgrace to the rank you hold, the uniform you wear, the country you still pretend to serve. The Englishman here —' his eyes did not move from Morowski — 'he and the girl are both traitors, moral pygmies. But you, General, are even lower — the lowest of all men. You're a coward. A moral coward.'

There was silence, except for the wind. General Morowski went on working at his apple, wincing for a moment as the knife slipped through the peel prematurely. Apart from this, the only trace of emotion was a tiny muscle that jumped a couple of times in his jaw. They all stood watching him, waiting. Cane had slumped back again in his chair, his eyes closed.

When Morowski finally spoke, it was in Polish, and for a long time. The others listened without interrupting. At the end he added in English, with a nod at Magnus and Maya: 'Get rid of these two — send them back to England. They are useless to you now. The *Fraternitas* is finished. But you cannot afford to fight me as well, Pan Novak.'

Novak shook his head. 'First I must see Lubian.'

Morowski nodded at a door next to Cane's chair. Novak gave an order and two of the soldiers crossed the room, their machine-pistols at the ready. Novak gestured to Magnus, then picked up the tape recorder and walked towards the door. Magnus followed, with Maya and her father just behind. The other four soldiers remained in front of the table where General Morowski sat licking his fingers.

Novak opened the door. The soldiers stood back, covering him. There was no sound from inside. Novak went first, flanked by the soldiers, then Magnus, treading almost on tiptoe. The room was dark except for a bedside lamp. There was a desk with two telephones and a stack of newspapers — Polish, English, French, German. Magnus caught a glimpse of *The Paper* folded on the top. The windows were heavily curtained, groaning with the wind.

On the bed a man lay, his head propped on a heap of pillows, the blankets clutched up round his neck and coming undone at the side of the bed, where a naked foot stuck out at a curious angle, as though belonging to someone else.

Novak put down the tape recorder and turned it on, as Magnus moved towards the bed. The face on the pillow watched him with half-closed eyes.

'Owen? You're Owen, aren't you? You shouldn't be here, you know that? You left your desk. You disobeyed orders. You have no right to be here. Absolutely no right at all. You will consider yourself no longer in my employment and collect your cards. The News Editor's secretary will arrange for you to be paid your notice money. That is all. You may go.'

It was said in a clear, flat tone, without any movement from the bed. Under the lamp his face had a shiny surface like greaseproof paper. Magnus stared down at him, as the lips began again: 'I told you to go, Owen. You are unworthy of the post and responsibility with which I entrusted you.'

Novak had moved up beside him and whispered, 'You know him?'

Magnus looked at the naked foot sticking out of the bed. 'Is he sick?'

'Tell us who he is,' Novak said; but the voice from the bed cut him short:

'General Morowski has left his place in the line. So has Owen. They are both dismissed. I shall institute a full enquiry when I return. It has been a deplorable episode. The moral fibre of my closest and most trusted is rotted through. Only Austen has stayed till the last. I hope to make some amends for his humiliating treatment. There will be a full enquiry, the whole business brought into the open — a Royal Commission, if necessary. Nor will your behaviour, Owen, escape exposure. I shall make certain that you never again hold any appointment in British journalism. You will leave now.' His voice was still clear, but beginning to weaken.

'Who is he?' Novak said again.

'Broom. Sir James Broom. He owns *The Paper*. I only met him once.' He looked up as General Morowski came in.

He stepped up to the bed, taking out a packet of long cigarettes with hollow stems, tapped one out and twisted the end into a filter. 'He is dying,' he said, looking down at the face on the pillow. 'I have seen men in his condition many times. He is burnt out, broken by the fatigue of battle. He is old. He will not survive.' He got out a match and lit the cigarette with a single gesture, put back his head and inhaled.

'If you still accuse me, Pan Novak, I plead guilty to only one charge. There was a time when I had respect for this man. I respected him because he himself respected the only true things that matter in life. Work, social order, the purity of the masses.'

'He was a Capitalist,' said Novak.

Morowski shrugged: 'He was a dreamer.' He took a last look at Sir James Broom, whose eyes were closing until there was only a shining slit under each lid; then turned and marched out of the room.

Maya had moved up beside Magnus, and stood looking down at the face on the pillow with a mixture of fascination and disgust. 'What happened?' she said at last.

'You heard Morowski,' said Novak. 'He's suffered some kind of stroke — perhaps a brain haemorrhage. The General must have laid it on the line for old Lubian!'

'So I needn't have come after all?' said Magnus.

'You clinched it,' said Novak: 'Morowski won't dare act now. Not unless he tries to gun us all down — and things have gone too far for that. He'll cut his losses.'

'He is a realist,' Colonel Czernovski said gravely. 'The main thing is that the *Fraternitas* is smashed!'

They had heard nothing above the wind, and yet as though warned by some magnetic impulse, they turned together. In the doorway behind them stood Cane.

He came forward slowly, and they drew back to let him up to the bed. 'Excuse me,' he murmured.

Novak motioned Magnus towards the door. Cane was to be allowed to bid his master a last farewell in peace. But just as Novak was bending down to turn off the tape recorder, Maya laughed — the same cruel laugh she had given over Skliros' body. 'Just look at him!' she cried, 'lying with his foot out of the bed, and he doesn't know.'

Cane behaved as though he had not heard. Novak said something in Polish and they all filed out of the room, leaving Cane and Sir James Broom alone.

Next door General Morowski was seated again at the table, smoking. He nodded up at Magnus and Maya: 'I would strongly advise, Pan Novak, that those two leave Warsaw as soon as possible.'

'They might embarrass you, General?'

Morowski dropped his cigarette and trod it into the carpet. 'I am not easily embarrassed, Pan Novak. Officially, I came here tonight to arrest both Lubian and Cane on charges which you yourself made against me earlier. Now that you have agreed to withdraw these charges, I shall leave the matter of the *Fraternitas* to you.' He looked up at Colonel Czernovski and began speaking in Polish, while Maya listened excitedly.

When he had finished Morowski rose and offered his hand across the table. Czernovski strode forward and took it, and for a moment the two of them stood there hand in hand, expressionless, closed off in their private world of military lore.

When they finally let go, Morowski bowed round the room, Colonel Czernovski saluted him, the door was opened by one of Novak's soldiers, and General Roman Morowski was gone.

Maya had run forward and had her arms round the Colonel's neck, kissing him all over his face, shouting in Polish. Magnus looked at Novak: 'What the hell's happening?'

Novak shrugged: 'The Colonel has been reinstated in the Army on Morowski's personal authority.'

'And you believe Morowski?'

'You heard what the Colonel said — the man's a realist. He also claims that he came here tonight to arrest Cane and Lubian himself. It's probably a lie, but we can't prove it. Besides, if we try to move against him we sacrifice the Colonel's career. That was the price Morowski has agreed to pay. Reinstate the Colonel and we forget the whole deal. Power politics.'

As he spoke there was a muffled crash from the next room. Novak shouted an order, and the two soldiers at the end of the room threw the door open. They were met by a blast of icy air, followed by a barrage of newspapers. They all ran forward. Magnus found himself trampling on that morning's edition of

The Paper, carried off the desk by the wind. The bedroom curtains billowed in and the shutters slammed with another crash. Cane had gone.

One of the soldiers closed the door and the newspapers subsided on to the floor. Magnus pushed his way up to the window and looked out.

The city lay in patterns of tiny lights under the roaring wind. Far below he could just see the outline of a ledge, jagged with pinnacles and statues representing the glories of Social Realism. There were more ledges farther down, more statues; but it was too dark to see anything in detail. They'd probably need more than one stretcher to collect him.

He stepped back, his hair blown in his eyes. Cane would have been happier to have gone on the Eiger.

Behind them, Sir James Broom lay as they had left him, his naked foot jutting out, eyes still open. They had not seen Cane jump.

Colonel Stanislav Czernovski stood at the bar and paid for his two drinks, a vodka and a cherry brandy, with an English pound note. Magnus had given it to him just before they said goodbye, since the bar only accepted Western currency.

Outside, the airliner was manoeuvring its way round the tarmac. The Colonel watched it steady itself, looking down the row of windows and wondering which seats they had. The next stop was Paris. He had paid for both tickets himself, although the Englishman had offered to pay — had offered him a cheque on an English bank!

He listened to the scream of the jets, then turned back to the bar. He had just enough English change left to stand himself another pair of drinks.

Up in the warm insulated cabin they released their safety belts and leant over to watch the last lights of Warsaw. Far in the distance the Palace of Culture was marked by a red glow from the television mast. It was soon gone, and then there was darkness.

The stewardess smiled and asked what they would like to drink. 'Champagne,' Maya said, 'French champagne.' She turned to Magnus: 'Not that awful Russian stuff. It made me belch.' She slid her hand into his, her hair heavy against his cheek. They would be in Orly in two hours, fifty-five minutes.

A NOTE TO THE READER

Dear Reader,

If you have enjoyed the novel enough to leave a review on **Amazon** and **Goodreads**, then we would be truly grateful.

Sapere Books is an exciting new publisher of brilliant fiction and popular history.

To find out more about our latest releases and our monthly bargain books visit our website:
saperebooks.com

Printed in Great Britain
by Amazon

27528530R00165